THE WINTER COURT

The Elite Guards

AMELIA HUTCHINS

THE WINTER COURT

Copyright ©March28, 2019 Amelia Hutchins

ISBN: 978-0-9977201-4-3

Authored By: Amelia Hutchins
Cover Art Design: Tenaya Jayne
Copy edited by: E & F Indie Services
Edited by: E & F Indie Services
Published by: Amelia Hutchins
Published in (United States of America)
10 9 8 7 6 5 4 3 2 1

Also by Amelia Hutchins

The Fae Chronicles
Fighting Destiny
Taunting Destiny
Escaping Destiny
Seducing Destiny
Unraveling Destiny
Embracing Destiny - *Coming Soon (Final Book)*

The Elite Guards
(Part of the Fae Chronicles)
A Demon's Dark Embrace
Claiming the Dragon King
A Demon's Plaything
A Winter Court

A Guardian's Diary
Stands alone
Darkest Before Dawn
Death before Dawn
Midnight Rising - *Coming Soon (Final Book)*

Playing with Monsters series
(Part of the Fae Chronicles)
Playing with Monsters
Sleeping with Monsters
Becoming his Monster
Last Monster Book *TBA*

Upcoming Series

<u>Wicked Knights</u>
Oh, Holy Knight
If She's Wicked 2019

<u>A Crown of Ashes</u>
Coming Soon

If you're following the series for the Fae Chronicles, Elite Guards, and Monsters, reading order is as follows:

Fighting Destiny
Taunting Destiny
Escaping Destiny
Seducing Destiny
A Demon's Dark Embrace
Playing with Monsters
Unraveling Destiny
Sleeping with Monsters
Claiming the Dragon King
Oh, Holy Knight
Becoming his Monster
A Demon's Plaything
A Winter Court
If She's Wicked 2019 (Full story from Oh, Holy Knight)

WARNING!

Warning! (Cont'd)

story than can be found in standard dictionaries. They are intentional and not mistakes.

About the hero: chances are you may **not** fall instantly in **love** with him, that's because **I don't write men you instantly love**; you grow to love them. I don't believe in **instant-love**. I write flawed, raw, caveman-like **assholes** that eventually let you see their redeeming qualities. They are **aggressive**, **assholes**, one step above a caveman when we meet them. You may *not* even like him by the time you finish this book, but I promise you will **love** him by the end of this **series**.

About the heroine: There is a chance, that you might think she's a bit naïve or weak, but then again who starts out as a badass? Badasses are a product of growth and I am going to put her through **hell**, and you get to watch **her** come up **swinging** every time I knock her on her ass. That's just how I do things. How she reacts to the set of circumstances she is put through, may not be how you as the reader, or I as the author would react to that same situation. Everyone reacts differently to circumstances and how Ciara responds to her challenges, is how I see her as a character and as a person.

I don't write love stories: I write fast paced, knock you on your ass, make you sit on the edge of your seat wondering what happens in the next kind of books. If you're looking for cookie cutter romance, this isn't for you. If you can't handle the ride, ***un-buckle your seatbelt and get out of the roller-coaster car now***. **If not, you've been warned.** If nothing outlined above bothers you, carry on and **enjoy the ride!**

DEDICATION

This one is for you, the forgotten one.
To the ones who dance to their own drumbeat. You are your own kind of beautiful. Don't ever let them dim your sparkle to fit in. To the broken ones trying put their puzzle back together. Sometimes, being broken is beautiful, and that chaos makes you shine ever so brightly among the dull, perfectness of everyone else. Dust yourself off, stand proud, and show the world that sometimes, broken things shine brighter than anything else.

THE WINTER COURT

The Elite Guards

THE WINTER COURT

The Elite Guards

CHAPTER ONE

Sinjinn gazed up at the never-ending snow that fell from the skies. They'd settled deep within the valley that lay within the Winter Court. It was a defendable position from every side as they started to set up their camp for the night. The snow in this region of Faery was relentless, never-ending as it continued to snow day after day. The biting chill of the wind sent the others into an endless march since the moment they'd reached the border. Silence had fallen on the sober entourage that continued their search for the new location of the Winter Court. He rubbed his hands together, igniting his power as flames leapt from his palms. One after the next, he ignited the oak logs that had been piled into the makeshift campfires to stave off the endless cold.

He'd considered calling off the search countless times since setting foot into this blasted land of ice and misery, and yet failure sat like a boulder in his belly. He'd made a vow, and once he'd given his word, come that had trespassed over the Horde kingdom's border, and she'd been the cost of their crimes. His father had kept her, undeterred by the fire in her eyes or the heat of her touch. They were creatures of legends, known for burning down entire worlds to any who tried to capture them, and yet not even they could withstand the power of the formidable Horde. Sinjinn turned away from the fire, taking in the frozen tundra around him with fresh eyes. The court had to be close, because reporting back to his king with his failure wasn't an option.

The ice clung to the trees, making them look enchanted in their frozen beauty. The whitish-blue snow that blanketed as far as the eye could see, pure and enticing. A gentle breeze brought the erotic scent of winterberries, mixed with bloomed winter aconite flowers that splashed cherry red into the stoic white. Poisonous and as deadly as they were beautiful, the aconite flowers still smelled exotic in the land he stood upon.

"I'm heading out to patrol, see if I can find who it was that followed us all day," he announced to no one in particular as he moved away from camp. "I'll be back in a few hours; if not, Lachlan will take the lead."

He mounted his horse, turning it west as he headed deeper into the woods. He stopped beside a frozen lake, staring at the beauty as the moon's image glinted off the icy surface. After a few moments, he turned back, listening to the silence of the night as it stretched into the woods. He could make out critters in the distance. Some of them were larger, predators of the night. Not that he feared those predators, not when his lineage demanded he fear nothing. He was High Fae, and it would be a cold day in hell before anything in these parts got the jump on him.

Sinjinn stared into the night, tilting his head as he listened to the disturbance that sent the animals rushing away from the protection of their nest. Something else was here, something they feared was caught on the breeze as the wind gusted, knocking snow from the tree branches.

He heard it before he saw it, and by the time he saw it, it was too late. His magic sizzled and then evaporated as the buzzing of something fast moving cut through the silent night. Pain burned in his chest, muscle and flesh tore apart as the arrow ripped through him.

He tumbled from his horse, landing in the snow as his vision swam and blurred. Sinjinn tried to get up, but his strength was waning, flowing out with the blood that painted the snow crimson. A thick copper tang slid over his tongue as he stared up at the silent moon that bathed him in its light. Something moved to the right of his vision, and he turned his head, staring as it approached. No, not something, someone.

Ice-blue eyes stared at him through thick black lashes, and hair the color of moon drops escaped the cloak as she bent down, staring at him. She was beautiful, as if the moon had mated the land and birthed this rare beauty who stared down at him through the most beautiful eyes he'd ever had the pleasure of staring into.

"It's him," she said, her voice husky as if she was high on the kill. "It's the prince."

"You're so fucking dead," he snapped, or tried to. His voice came out as weak as he felt.

You're a good friend to worry, but you fret for nothing. He'll never make it to the Winter Court, and that means he will never see me again or know who did this."

"I hope you're right, but I don't think this is going to work out how you think it is. They're notorious trackers and deadly creatures. I will pray to the Goddess that they never find you or that you become one of their victims. Now move, we're wasting time," he snapped as he and Lars lifted the creature into the sled.

Lars held his tongue, staring at the woman he'd asked to marry and been turned down by the king multiple times. His ice-blue eyes held hers with something unspoken as she nodded. He'd agreed to help her because he thought with the Horde out of the way, he'd be free to ask her again. Unfortunately, he came from a poor home with parents who could barely afford to pay hers for their place in the kingdom or the protection it offered.

Unbeknown to him, she paid for them to remain with her. Her own jewels were being slowly sold to keep him and his sickly parents close to her. His dark blue hair was heavy with the snowflakes that fell upon them as they moved the man into the sled and then mounted their horses. Lars hesitated as he watched her mount the horse that would pull the sled. He opened his mouth and closed it as she offered him a reassuring smile.

"I'll be fine, Lars. Go, before anyone notices you are gone," she instructed, and he nodded with something heavy in his gaze.

"If he dies…"

"He won't, he is immortal."

"I have this feeling that if I look away, I will never

see you again," he admitted sadly.

"Don't think like that," she offered and stared back at her prisoner, who groaned as if he was fighting to wake up from the blood loss. "I have to go before he awakes."

"I love you," Lars uttered. "I always have and I always will."

"Lars, this isn't the time," she said, worrying her bottom lip as she stared at him.

Once upon a time, in another world, she'd loved him. He was unlike Bale, who hungered for power, for a place in the world. He would have been her choice for her marriage, but he had a soft spot for anyone willing to lie in the hay in his barn as well. It had opened her eyes to see the brutal truth. He may be madly in love with her, but he'd never be satisfied with just her. Bale, on the other hand, was always trying to increase his stature, to rise to power, and it drove him. He also only wanted her because of the power she could bring him. She nudged her horse forward and swallowed hard as she peered over her shoulder to find him glaring at her back as she started away, towards the unforgiving ice caverns.

It took a few hours to pass through the edge of the Winter Court's lands and into the cave that bordered between her court and autumn's. The cave was bathed in ice, and once they'd entered it, she sealed it behind them, barring any unwanted fiends or creatures from entering it.

The male groaned as she moved him to the chains, using her body weight to hoist him onto his feet as she stared at him. He seemed almost normal, other than his freakish height and bulging muscles. She used her glamour to remove his shirt and then winced as she took in the damage from the arrow, and the flesh it had torn around it. She swallowed past the nausea that pushed to the back of her throat at the mangled mess.

She moved around, fixing and grabbing things to heal his wound as she set a knife in the fire, burning the tip to a glowing orange to seal the wound. Once she'd prepared everything, she moved closer to the unconscious male and flinched when bright sea-green eyes held hers prisoner.

"Release me before I rip you apart, bitch."

She swallowed hard, audibly. Her heartbeat shot into an erratic cadence that physically hurt against her chest. She stepped back, wishing she hadn't discarded her cloak as she'd prepared to tend to his injury. Those eyes slowly took her in, settling on her exposed cleavage before coming back up to lock on her mouth.

"Are you deaf? Or do you just have a death wish, wench?" he demanded, even as he struggled against the chains, opening his wound further.

"If you continue to struggle, you will bleed out. Be a nice monster and hold still so that I may tend to your wounds, hmm?" she offered, surprised by how clear and even her tone came out.

He chuckled coldly, his eyes mere slits as he watched her trembling hand move closer to his flesh. The moment she was in front of him, he kicked out, removing her legs from beneath her and knocking her to the floor. She rolled as his heavy foot came down hard where she'd been. Icelyn growled angrily as she flicked her finger, watching as chains wrapped around and secured his legs.

"I should let you bleed out," she snapped as she moved closer, loosening the chains until he was on his knees and lowered enough for her to work on his injury.

She yanked the arrow out violently, enjoying the hiss of pain that escaped his lips. Lowering herself to his level, she sat on her haunches, staring into eyes that promised violence. Her hands trembled as she brought fresh snow to his wound and held it there to ease the pain. Not that she wished to relieve it, but it would also clean the wound in the process.

"You're shaking, are you afraid of me?" he asked icily, his voice clear and unfettered from the pain he had to be suffering from. When she ignored his question, he continued. "You should be. I'm going to rip you apart."

She peered up at him through her thick lashes, her hands shaking harder as she stared into his glowing eyes. She stood, moving across the room to bring a torch closer, needing it to be able to see the wound as she tended to it. She placed it into the wall of the cave and took her seat again, watching him as he stared at her, taking in her features.

Sinjinn stared at his captor. A slip of a girl who'd stuck an arrow right through his fucking lungs. He'd used what little power he'd had left to heal the wound to his lungs inside, but he'd been drained too much to even attempt the mess that was outside. He was as weak as a babe and at this wisp of a traitorous bitch's mercy. Blue eyes the color of a glacier stared back at him. His heat ignited the moment her fingers touched him, and she pulled back as if he'd burned her.

He smirked, watching as she stared at the white flesh

that now covered the seared pads of her fingers. She used magic to encase her fingers in ice before she trailed them over the wound, pulling a moan of something foreign from his stomach as she worked on his flesh.

She'd used ice, which meant she wasn't a peasant Fae. If she was out here unescorted, she wasn't a princess. It left a few other options. She was either a Lady of the Winter Court or one of their warriors. Her use and knowledge of arrows had been enough to take him down, which made him lean towards the warrior option more.

"You have no idea what you have done, do you?" he asked as he stared at her open blouse, which exposed a decent amount of cleavage that made his belly roar with the need to be filled.

"I took out a Prince of the Horde, and I don't regret it one little bit," she announced as she shot ice into his chest. The pain was blinding and violent as he passed out before he could retaliate.

CHAPTER THREE

He awoke chained to a bed, his body bare minus the blanket that hid his cock from her heavy stare. She sat in the corner, her gaze landing on him as if he would pounce on and devour her. The chances of it happening were high since he was starving, and she was female. She had the brightest blue eyes he'd ever seen in his entire life, as well as white hair that had an alluring blue tint to it. Her pink tongue slipped out, dragging over her cherry-colored lips as she continued her slow perusal of his body, unaware that he'd awaken and was doing the same.

Her creamy breasts were barely contained by the corset she'd worn. Gone was the blouse that wasn't fit for a peasant and the corset pushed her breasts up, revealing more than she'd probably intended for it to do. Those eyes, though, the way they caressed his flesh had his hunger rearing its head, making his needs known.

Slowly, her eyes rose and held his before rounding in surprise. He healed faster than most, but then his Ifrit blood helped with that. Djinns healed at an accelerated rate, and his Fae blood helped speed the process, but what they couldn't do was recharge without feeding.

"You shouldn't be awake yet," she said as she stood, moving closer with the glass of liquid held in her tiny hand. "It is only ice water from the glacier," she explained as she helped him lift up enough to drink. He smashed his head against her hand, spilling the water everywhere on the bed and floor.

"I don't need water," he snarled, hating how weak he was because of what she'd done.

"Then what do you need? You're ashen, which means you're not healing. You are not dying here, that was never my intention."

"No? You shot me in the chest with an iron-tipped arrow. You dragged me to a cave, where you strip me naked and then try to tell me you didn't try to kill me? Are you fucking thick in the head?"

"You're as uncouth as they claimed you were," she hissed as she splashed what little water remained in the cup in his face and then watched as it sizzled on his flesh, as if he was so hot he set it to a boil.

"I need you to come here and ride me," he said huskily as his eyes smiled, moments before her bodice became too hot to wear. She fidgeted for a moment, and then pulled on the leather as it continued to heat against her flesh. It took him moments of staring at her before her clothing was burning her flesh and she was discarding them until she stood in nothing more than a pair of crimson panties. Her skin was red where her clothes had touched her flesh. Her eyes looked from her swollen breasts to his greedy gaze. "Fuck me, snow bunny. I may keep you around as a pet before I break your pretty little fucking neck."

"You think I'll be here when I free you? I can remove those chains miles from here, and you will never know where I am when I leave this cave. If you agree to leave and go back to your part of Faery and never return, this ends now. No one has to be hurt any more than they already have been."

"And why the fuck would I do that? Because you think you have me in a delicate position? I promise you this, there's nothing fucking delicate about me, sweetheart."

"You're dying," she said as she watched him wince as he moved. "Why aren't you healing fully?"

"Because I have not eaten," he growled hoarsely as he watched her boobs bouncing with every move she made. She flicked her wrist, and they were covered by a lacy shift that silhouetted her curves. "So bring your ass over here, and fucking feed me."

"As if I would," she laughed softly. "You're Fae, High Fae, which means you can go weeks, if not longer without feeding."

"We've been searching for the Winter Court for weeks," he said as he let his hungry gaze dip to where her thighs curved to her hips. "There are no women in this court that reside outside it, nor were there any we could find to feed off of."

"You mean pillage and rape, and no, there wouldn't be. Not since the visit from Alazander and his insatiable appetite, which left thousands of women broken shells, have they been allowed outside of the court gates. If you think I care that you're starving, think again, beast."

"You said you don't plan to let me die?"

"I don't," she agreed.

"Yet I don't see any other female here willing to feed me."

"There isn't."

"So you will kill me?"

She stomped her foot and glared at him. Her hands fisted at her sides and her eyes glowed as anger hummed through her. The scent of winterberries and lilacs pulsed through the cave and his eyes flared, drawn by the hunger he felt coming from her.

"I said, I wouldn't kill you, bastard."

"I'm not a bastard, I'm a prince," he taunted, his eyes enjoying the way her flesh flushed in her anger. Her nipples responded, hardening as she stared him down.

"I know who you are and why you are here, Horde bastard. That is why you are now in the ice caverns that no one dares enter, ever. I won't let you succeeded in what you came for, and when I'm sure you've failed, and you've endured enough to know that your kind isn't welcome here, you can go on your way."

"That sounds like you plan to kill me," he shrugged, but the motion forced a wince as he moved.

"Nothing of which I just stated said anything about killing you," she huffed as she placed her hands on her hips and watched his eyes close.

"On the contrary, you don't plan to fuck me, which I assure you, will kill me."

"You're immortal!"

"So what if I am? Even immortals have an Achilles heel. I have to feed, or my body begins to slowly consume what little nutrients it contains. After that, it saps the magic from us, slowly wasting it to try to feed our organs. You can figure out what happens when it has nothing left to use."

"But...but that's not part of this plan!" she snapped as she began pacing, her finger tapping her chin. "How long before you need to feed?" she asked, and his eyes dripped hatred as he watched her.

"Yesterday," he announced as he struggled against the chains. "The iron isn't helping, remove them."

"That's not happening," she said as she began pacing again.

She hadn't planned on having him here long enough to even worry about feeding him. She couldn't place anyone else's life in peril because of her choices, nor would she. She turned and stared at him, deciding to wait a little longer to see if it was a ploy to get her closer to him.

"Either fuck me or free me. You do realize this is an act of war, right? You have a crowned prince sitting in an ice cavern with a wound you inflicted on him. The Horde is already gathered; one word from the king and they will descend on this place and destroy everything and everyone."

"Like you did to the Court of Shadows? How merciful of you to march in and slaughter thousands who couldn't fight back while the sun beat down on the court that morning. You'll never reach the ice palace," she hissed. "You and your kind only have once before, and you will never reach it again. You'll have to do as your father did and wait for us to lower our guard. Do you know what he did to the heir of the Winter Court? Two of them, to be exact," she asked coldly.

"Your lips would better serve me around my cock," he yawned, closing his eyes. "You do know how to suck cock, right? I mean, it won't feed me, but it is such a better use for that infuriating movement they are doing."

"He took the crown prince of the Winter Court out and burned him alive," she growled thickly with emotion. "He waited here, waiting for the heir brands to transfer to the next child, and when they did, he ripped her apart and cooked her too. He fed them their children as the entire court watched. Once they'd eaten every last piece of their daughter and son, he brought forth the next in line and raped her until she was nothing, until she lay there, unseeing, unfeeling. Then he slit her throat and drank her blood. So you tell me, why would anyone welcome you or your kind into the Winter Court again? There are three remaining children left of the king and queen, and that is unheard of itself. But that's the tragedy, isn't it? He raped the queen in front of the king, and when he did, the king couldn't stomach to touch his queen again, so he hasn't. The heirs to this realm are sacred, as every other one has over fifty children, and yet we have three. So you coming in here to take one? It isn't happening!"

"You think anyone could have changed that outcome?" he asked, his eyes dull as he stared at her. His skin was worsening, the color leeching out as she stared down at him. "Alazander was a monster, and everyone is going to have a horror story of what he did to them. He was mad, sick with power. We killed him."

"So what? So what if you killed him? You can't change what happened, nor would you. The only way to change it would be to vacate the throne."

"That isn't happening," he mumbled as his head dropped.

"Hey," she said as she stepped closer, staring down at him. "Get up!" she shouted, but he didn't budge. She moved closer, shaking him, and yet nothing happened. "Don't die," she begged as she lifted the hem of her nightgown and pulled it over her head.

CHAPTER FOUR

Jcelyn slowly stripped down to her panties as she removed the blanket from her prisoner. Her eyes bulged as his thick organ sprang up the moment it was no longer confined beneath the heavy blanket. She closed her eyes against the appendage, pretending there wasn't a six-foot-plus Horde male with an impressive erection sprawled out before her very eyes. Her nails bit into her hands, where they were tightly fisted at her sides. Do this, or go to war. What had she done? What had she expected to achieve in doing this? Avoid marriage to a Neanderthal who would abuse her, she reminded herself. What was the worst that would happen if she let him die? The Wild Hunt would show up at the palace, and no one would be spared. It was the one way they could find the palace, which was precisely how Alazander had found it before.

She sucked in her breath, gathered her courage, and straddled him, stiffening as his hardness met her softness. She slowly leaned over, using magic to produce the key to the cuffs. The scent of freshly fallen snow filled the cave with her whisper of magic. Once she'd freed one hand, she stared down again, sensing if he'd awoken or stirred by her subtle movements. Nothing. Not so much as a whisper from the sleeping male.

Sitting back, she stared down at him. He was bronzed, his skin the color of the sand that ebbed and flowed when the ocean sent waves careening towards the beach. Only right now, it had an ashen paleness to it that worried her. Her heartbeat intensified, growing rapid until she feared it would explode from her chest. Icelyn bent over, inhaling his musky scent. Burnt oak and citrus tickled at her nose, dancing through her senses as if it was an aphrodisiac, created to lower her inhibition. She ran her nose over the flesh of his collarbone before lifting a smidge, finding glowing emerald green eyes. They weren't emerald, though; they were sea-green, like the glass from the bottles after the ocean had beaten them and placed them back upon the beach, to shine. A thinner layer of brown framed them, announcing his heritage of Royal Fae.

"Tell me what to do to keep you alive," she uttered thickly, noting the sheer terror that her voice emitted even though she tried to hide it. Her body clenched as his eyes slowly moved to her full breasts, naked and exposed. She glamoured a tank top over her nakedness, only for his hand to come up and rip the thin shirt from her being.

"You still have your panties on," he growled huskily, green eyes burning her flesh as he dragged his eyes to her aching pussy. His hand moved slowly, cupping the weight of her breast before releasing it to lift those fiery eyes to hers.

It took everything she had not to fling herself away from the man who devoured her with his gaze alone. Her body wept, soaking the place where his cock throbbed between her legs, pushing against her sex. She tried to form words, but the dryness of her throat prevented anything from escaping as she swallowed, forcing her thickening tongue to speak.

"They're staying on."

"Sweetheart, you want to help me? Lose them and slide down that cock so I can fucking destroy that sweet flesh. I feel it weeping with need, and hiding it from me won't save it."

"I said," she snapped as her hand landed on his throat, threatening him with meaning. "It isn't happening. There are other ways to feed you, so tell me what to do so that I can keep your heathen ass alive. If you don't want to help me help you, I can just leave you here for the snow leopards to find and feed upon. I'm sure you'd satisfy their hunger."

"It all ends with those things coming off and you beneath me." His voice had thickened, escaping his dry throat huskily. The room filled with the heady scent of citrus and masculinity. As if his scent unleashed something, her body grew supple as more fluid rushed to her core.

One minute he'd been beneath her, lacking control, and the next, she was being trapped to the mattress by his massive weight. She bucked her hips, trying to dislodge him as he stared down at her, hunger burning in his depths. The scent intensified, her body reacting with a worrisome need that shot through her, coiling in her stomach.

Sinjinn stared down into her silver-ish blue eyes, which were wide with panic. Her lips parted as a scream of fear bubbled up from deep in her chest as the situation registered. He pushed his throbbing cock against the thin, wet panties that were in danger of being ripped off so he could feast on that seductive scent her body was sending off. Fear and lust burned from within her, and he wanted to taste both.

He searched her face before he brushed his lips against hers. Sinjinn tasted the fear that exuded from her, her ruby red lips trembling as he tasted her arousal, something she didn't hide, or was unable to. She was younger than he was, but there was a naiveté that shone from her eyes that beckoned to the wolf inside of him. But that fear, fuck, that fear had his beast pacing, prowling, wanting to draw her blood and taste to see if it was as pure as she appeared to be. Her body trembled, and he smirked coldly; good, she should be afraid. She should be fucking terrified of what she had done.

It pissed him off knowing that this little wisp of a woman had brought him down. That she'd hunted him like he was fucking prey and she was some warrior blessed by Artemis herself, skilled enough to bring him to his knees. He was a High Fae prince, and she, she had to be either a fucking high-born lady or warrior to the Winter Court. If his brothers knew she'd brought him down, he'd never hear the end of it.

His tongue pushed past her full lips, delving deeper into the unknown. Fuck, she tasted like winterberries; her little tongue struggled to keep away from his, even as he chased it with his own. He'd slipped into the welcoming heat of her mouth, showing her with his tongue what he planned to do with her tight little body. Sinjinn devoured it, enjoying the noises she made as she struggled to ignore what it did to her aching cunt. He wouldn't rape her; that much he knew. He had never forced a woman, even under worse circumstances. But he sure as fuck intended to scare her for what she'd done to him.

His thick cock rubbed against the lace panties she wore, scratching the rough material of the lace that covered the front. He worked her body, knowing by her wetness that she wasn't immune to his body. He didn't need to invade her supple flesh to feed, only force an orgasm or two from her. He needed her wanton, unhinged by what he was doing so that she let go. Her emotions alone wouldn't be enough to gain enough magic to release himself from the iron chains, but her orgasms promised to add just enough so that he healed and could eventually escape.

"You bastard," she seethed, bucking her thin hips as if she had a chance in hell of escaping the cage his body created over hers. He brought his fingertips up to her face, holding her chin as he stared down into those wide silver eyes. No, not silver. They were the color of ice over a frozen lake, a mixture of blue and grey that reminded him of the skies before they released a violent storm.

Warmth spread from his hands, magic igniting as urgency to take what he could by entering her body. It would be such a simple thing, to push those thin panties aside and plunder her welcoming heat. Her gasp was enough to slip his mouth against hers, claiming it in a slow, erotic mix of dominance and possession. Her unskilled tongue pushed against his slowly; methodically it ran against his as she joined the kiss. Her body writhed under his, as if something had ignited inside of her, and she burned to figure it out.

He could feel her sex clenching against his with every move he made. The slick folds weeping with arousal that flooded her panties, soothing the ache in his balls as it slid over them. If he wasn't mistaken, his captor was both unskilled and had suppressed her need to fuck. He didn't stop kissing her, grinding his cock against her petal-soft flesh as she mewled and moaned hoarsely as her body turned against her, purring in readiness for him.

Sinjinn's hand slid down her lean belly and pushed aside her wet panties to discover her wet curls that welcomed his fingers to her swollen flesh. She was sopping wet, her body moving methodically in an ancient dance, as old as time. He pushed them through her slick sex, groaning at finding her body so ready, so fucking willing to take him. Why wasn't he fucking her? She deserved it for what she'd done to him.

Her moans grew louder, needier as he slowly worked apart her flesh. She was swollen with need, her body demanding he fill her aching cunt and give her what she craved. He swallowed her noises and considered drawing it out, torturing her until she was wild with need and willing to give him whatever he demanded just to end the ache he knew she felt. If he wasn't starving, he would, because her body welcomed him. It craved him and responded to him with an intensity that he wanted to devour.

He added another finger to his slow exploration, and she arched into his touch, moaning louder as if his heat was too much to bear. Sinjinn pulled his mouth from hers, biting the soft, plump lip that trembled as he explored her wet, naked pussy that ached to be fucked.

"Are you always this wet for your victims?" he asked huskily, his voice dripping sex at the way she responded to his touch. He needed to rip the thin material from her body and plunge deep into her flesh, bury himself to the hilt, and punish her for harming him. She was writhing, beyond hearing him as her body took control. Like a nymph who had given in to her baser needs, wild with the loss of her inability to control it.

"Just do it," she whimpered breathlessly.

His finger pushed past the barrier, plunging into her body as a soft scream ripped from her lips. She clenched against the intrusion, feeling him stretching her as he slowly pulled it out and then pushed in, hard. A violent cuss tore from her parted lips as the white-hot ball in her stomach unfurled, needed something more. As if something greater than she could have imagined was just beyond her reach, waiting.

Icelyn wasn't sure what she wanted more at the moment, to die from embarrassment or to figure out how he'd made her body betray her. It was as if it no longer belonged to her, and he had claimed it. His finger pushed deeper into her sex and her legs spread, as if giving him further access to places that were forbidden. She rode his fingers, her body moving on a collision course with disaster. He slowed his finger, pushing in and out, his thumb tracing her pleasure zone which attached to every nerve in her body.

"You want this," he acknowledged as he watched her coming undone for him. He withdrew his fingers, pushing his thick cock through the wetness her body awarded him with for his attention to detail. He pulled on his other arm, shaking the bed as the chain caught, preventing him from moving down far enough to lick that sweet pussy clean. "Release my hand, female," he growled, needing to taste her. She was beyond hearing, her mind lost to the pleasure he pulled from her, slowly. His head lowered, capturing one pink-tipped nipple between his teeth, letting them scrape her flesh as a hiss escaped her lips.

When she didn't release him, he continued sucking her heated peak between his teeth as his fingers pushed into her tight sheath, two this time. Her body clenched as his teeth nipped, mimicking her body as it sucked against his digits greedily. Fuck, she was tight; her body clamped down, as if it could push him from it, protecting the innocence of her core from the monster that ravaged it. Finding it was like a splash of ice water over his head. He continued to push deeper, stretching her untried body to its limits as he lifted his head, watching her white-blonde hair drenching with sweat as she fought against the orgasm.

Her rose-colored nipples hardened, signaling how close she was to her release. Her pussy soaked his fingers, her body's natural reaction to allow deeper access. Her eyes closed tightly as she inhaled his earthy scent, her mouth opening to his kiss, which was hard, unforgiving as he claimed it. The growl built from deep in his lungs, bubbling up until light exploded behind her eyes, and her body released a violent shiver.

He fucked her flesh hard with his fingers, holding her in the orgasm that had her shaking and screaming into his kiss. He fed, he fucking took everything until he felt the barrier of her mind, and still, he took until she quieted against him.

Icelyn had never felt anything like it. Her entire body clenched and bucked against him, uncaring that he was stretching her flesh until it ached. The white-hot ball insider her belly had grown until it dropped to where he coaxed it out of her. Lights of every color exploded behind her eyes, and she'd soared higher than she'd ever managed to before.

Then everything changed. She'd felt the pull; the black abyss of his kiss was sucking everything from her. She pushed against him, pinned on his fingers as he continued to hold her body prisoner as he fed from her. Too much was being stolen, too much was leaving her mind until she was trembling for another reason altogether.

She grabbed his neck, tightening her hold as her mind slipped away. Tears slipped from her eyes as he lowered his mouth to hers and chuckled against it, sending a wave of unbearable heat sliding over her flesh. His fingers continued, uncaring that she didn't respond, or couldn't. As if he'd forgotten them in his quest to feed from her.

"You're so fucked right now, little snow bunny. I'm about to show you why we're on the top of the food chain, and you're beneath us on it. I hope you do like chains."

CHAPTER FIVE

Icelyn stared at the male, unable to move or make noises other than to gurgle. She was trapped in her own mind. She could feel him still touching her swollen folds, playing with her needy flesh. He was slowly milking her body for every drop it had to feed him. Only it no longer responded, unable to react and unfeeling. She felt absolutely no pleasure from his touch, just emptiness. As if he'd trapped her or made her prisoner in her mind and body. Had he turned her into a fucking zombie? They could do it, locking an unwilling victim into a sense of nothingness that eventually led to death. Their victim neither hungered, nor fed, never waking from the state they'd left them in.

It was taking what little mind she had left to hold her glamour to her. What happened if he continued feeding as he was, leaving her depleted with no magic to spare? What if he fed until her identity was revealed, and her court was rendered to ruins? Tears rolled down her cheeks as she considered what this meant for her court.

Her little sister, her innocent laughter and inability to hate anyone or anything? Frostine wasn't ready to be the heir; she was too sweet, weak and unwilling to rip lands or titles from people. Her parents were often forced to do such things, but Frostine would never be that type of leader, and the court would fall. It wasn't just a simple matter of stripping lands; if one transgressed against the crown, she'd be forced to take their life, and that was something she couldn't do.

She felt a spark growing, her body unmoving as he coaxed another orgasm from her flesh. His mouth touched against her lips, slowly capturing them and pulling on her bottom one. He smiled coldly as he watched her eyes followed his every move. Once more, his finger trailed through her sex, pushing into her body as a shiver raced down her spine, proving he hadn't taken everything from her. He withdrew his fingers and brought them to his lips, sucking them clean loudly as he moaned, knowing she watched him.

"You taste good," he moaned as once more he did the sensual action, tasting what he couldn't reach with his mouth. "You're my prisoner now, sweetheart," he chuckled as he bent down, kissing her mouth with her arousal coating his lips. Something shattered in the cave, but it sounded distant. Before she guessed what had happened, men came pouring in with weapons drawn, ready for battle. One by one, they lowered them as they took in the scene before them.

"Gods, Sinjinn," Cailean groaned as he pushed his blade into the sheath and then took in the full situation on the bed. "I thought you'd been hurt, fucker. We found your horse and blood. Ryder is going crazy. He felt you fall, took control of the horse, and said you were dead. He couldn't locate or feel you anymore. He also claimed some female warrior had taken your corpse as a fucking trophy."

"I was attacked, but I have it under control, as you can see," he muttered as he stared down into her eyes. "I was shot with an iron arrow from this little she-cat, who is now my prisoner," he murmured before lifting his arm, showing off the iron cuff that still held him chained to the bed. "A little help would be nice."

"You seem rather fine to me. Maybe we should just come back later?" Lachlan asked from where he rested his lean frame against the cave's entrance. "Hate to be a bother or anything."

"Get your ass over and free me," Sinjinn drawled, his body still hard against her soft curves.

"You look to be in pretty good shape for someone who was shot and lost half of your blood in the snow. She must have been an amazing feast," Cailean said as he leaned over, grabbing a strand of her white-blonde hair and testing it between his fingers.

"She was fucking delicious," he announced as he pushed his cock against her naked flesh once more.

"Does she have a name, or shall we just refer to her as *Delicious*?" he snorted as he released the strand of soft hair. He stared down into her eyes and frowned. "She's FIZ, isn't she?"

"She deserved it, and more. She's mine now, my prisoner until I decide her fate." His growl was harsh, angry as he licked her bottom lip before sucking it between his teeth to nip on it. "And she'll remain mine since she weakened me. I'll keep her around to be sure I heal and I'm able to feed. Then when I am fully healed, I'll show her the same kindness she showed me."

"Do you think it is still wise to head towards the Winter Court? Ryder said that we should turn around and head back to the stronghold. He will send out scouts to scour the court for the location of the palace."

"We're done here for now. We will return home, and let the scouts report back with the location of the ice palace."

Lachlan released his hand after only a moment of jimmying the lock. It didn't bother him one bit that they were heading home or leaving this cold, lifeless land. It also didn't bother him that his brothers watched him climb his naked ass off the female, staring at his ass the entire time. His endless state of arousal, though, that bothered him that they knew he hadn't claimed her. Their eyes seemed to take in her naked flesh, her large breasts and trim hips. Cailean whistled as his eyes settled on the white-blonde curls at her apex and Sinjinn growled.

He glamoured a thin dress over her nakedness, to shield her from their prying eyes. The dress would offer her little comfort against the cold. His eyes seemed to note how it hugged her lithe frame and ripe breasts without hiding everything from his prying eyes, but enough that the others couldn't fully make out her features. He wanted her to suffer, and knowing she would gave him pleasure. His chest still burned, aching from where she'd shot him.

He prayed his beast hadn't strayed far from where he'd gone down. He hated the idea of walking out of this place. Whatever magic was being used, it affected even High Fae. They couldn't' sift, nor could they easily close the distance from which they'd come with the endless snowdrifts or icy trails.

"Tell me you brought my horse," he groaned as he glamoured his own armor on, touching his chest where it continued to ache.

"We brought him," Lachlan confirmed. "He wasn't far from where you went down. He was what alerted us to the blood and had us searching for you. Him and the acrid scent of your blood burning in the snow," he said as he narrowed his eyes on the girl, who had yet to move. "That's going to make it rather difficult to move her, brother."

"Grab those chains and help me secure her. My chest isn't healed completely, and without fully draining her dry, it won't work. I want her alive to suffer for what she has done," he admitted.

Icelyn peered around the room full of High Fae with no emotion other than a sinking feeling in the pit of her stomach that was relentless. She was lifted by the blonde one, unable to stop her head or body from being flopped around as if it no longer had bones. A moan escaped her lips as heat pushed behind her eyes, tears threatening to escape as she mentally berated herself for her stupidity.

Sinjinn took a seat on the bed, accepting the slight burden onto his lap. He held her hands together, against her stomach as her head rolled forward. He pulled her head back against his chest, uttering into her ear.

"In a few moments, I'm going to bring you back. If you fight me, I will either fuck you, or drain you dry, or put you back into this state of utter nothingness. You will have no will, no voice, or anything else. You will be nothing more than something I use to feed from, merely alive until you cease to be so. You're my prisoner now, snow bunny. I did warn you that you would regret this, didn't I?" he chuckled against her ear.

Tears rolled from her eyes as his words registered. She was utterly at his mercy and heading towards the Horde stronghold, which meant she had to escape him. His hands cupped her breasts as the others watched with hunger glowing in their rainbow-hued gazes. She'd messed up, and if she didn't escape, they'd destroy her home. Why had she thought she could do this and get away with it? She'd taken a Prince of the Horde down with an iron-tipped arrow, and now, he'd ruin her for it. She'd never been this rash, or quick to be foolish, but the idea of marrying him had sent her mind whirling with the atrocities that would be brought upon her in his hands.

"I need the room," he growled and waited for the others to slowly exit before he pushed her onto the bed and stared down into her eyes. "I fear this may hurt, and I am going to enjoy it a lot more than you will."

His mouth brushed against hers, sending a wealth of butterflies dancing in her lower region. His fingers lifted the thin shift she wore, dancing over her swollen flesh and slid through her heat, burning her flesh until pain ignited, soothed only by his fingers when he lifted them and then repeated the action. Her body began to buzz with his movements; his tongue pushed past her lips, and all at once, pain ripped through her.

Icelyn's body jerked as pain ripped through it, her mind seared with heat so intense she thought her brain would melt. He continued kissing her, her mind aching as her emotions came whirling back until her hand lifted and pushed him away. She fought his touch, even as his green gaze consumed hers until her body jerked and the orgasm released. It was violent, soul-crushing, and stolen.

"Mmm, you're delicious," he uttered thickly as he lifted from the bed, and stared down at her flushed cheeks and crumpled form. "Get up."

She shook her head, refusing to be a willing hostage.

"Oh, sweetheart, I wasn't asking." He grabbed the chains, forcing her to stand up or be dragged. Once she was up, he pushed her forward, watching as she fell to her hands and knees. "Don't worry, snow bunny. I'll show you the same mercy you showed me."

Awesome, because she'd shown him nothing more than a sliver of mercy, which had ended up with him taking a lot more than she'd wanted to. How had his men found him so quickly? She was picked up again and shoved forward, her eyes landing on the men and the horses that surrounded the mouth of the ice caverns. Icelyn stared at the golden eyes of the horse, the one she'd spared. There were over thirty men with them, all staring at her as if she was some murderous bitch who would be treated as such.

It moved up closer to her, pushing her aside as it nuzzled Sinjinn and then bucked it's head, sending the horse's mane flying in the crisp cold wind.

"I'm fine, but fuck the Winter Court, brother. Send out your scouts, and let them know I claim whoever she is as my prisoner."

The horse tilted its head, staring at Icelyn as the

fine hair on her neck rose with awareness. There *was* something ancient in those eyes, something predatory about the way it watched her. Something that wanted to rip her apart, or worse.

"No, either a warrior or a high lady of the court, she uses ice magic. Either way, she's mine."

Icelyn turned her head, studying Sinjinn, who spoke to the horse as if it understood him. As if there was someone else on the other end, peeking through…

CHAPTER SIX

Snowdrifts blanketed the world in a whiteout. The men continued for hours, never tiring as they forced their way further away from her home. They trekked over the snow caves and down through the ice-covered valleys with an ease that bothered her. It was as if they'd done it many times before. With every step they took, they put her at a further distance from her home and closer to her enemies who lay in the Autumn Court.

It was widely known that the Autumn Court loathed the Winter, and often sent raiding parties in to discover the location of the ice palace. Yet try as they may, they never did. However, they could tell Sinjinn who she was, since she was the one who was forced to endure the summits every spring that adjoined all courts as one. Icelyn's palms sweat with the fear of discovery. She moved her back from his chest, trying to put as much distance between her flesh and his. Her bound hands slipped, and she almost tumbled forward, off of the horse.

His arm wrapped around her, pulling her back against his massive frame. His heat enveloped her, which both comforted and irritated her. Usually she welcomed the cold; however, he'd drained her, and she had to somehow keep enough magic to hold the glamour to her. He had drained her until what little magic she had left was teetering out, which meant she couldn't stave off the chill. She was doing her best to conserve it, to somehow hold the glamour to her with her remaining strength. Between freezing to death or him knowing who had shot him, she preferred freezing.

"You're shivering," he murmured into her hair, tightening his hold on the horse's reins. "I thought the people of the Winter Court were immune to the bitter cold. And you of all people, I figured you'd welcome it after burning so hot for me."

"You misjudged the situation," she said through teeth that chattered so violently, they threatened to crack. It wasn't just cold; it was as if the land was holding its breath, preparing to let something fierce and wild loose upon them.

"Lean against me, and stop trying to pull away," he warned, pulling her even closer, if it was at all possible. His heat soothed her, pushing through the ice that clung to her dress and flesh from the endless snow. She was turning blue, the same shade of her hair. To his men, he shouted for them to hold as he eyed the area around them. "Lachlan, take a few men and see if there's a valley we can easily defend up ahead. We'll break here for a few to warm up."

"On it," Lachlan offered as he watched Sinjinn

settle the female onto her feet, only for her to crumple to the ground. "She's lesser Fae, meaning that iron may end her before you can get your revenge." He searched through his saddle bag and tossed another set of chains at her, pegging her shoulder, which made her cry out in pain.

"She's at least part High Fae, she can wield glamour," Sinjinn pointed out as he dismounted and pushed the hair from her shoulder, exposing a rapidly growing bruise. "Maybe you're right. What other creatures can wield glamour out here?" he asked.

"Have you tried asking her what she is?" Lachlan chuckled before he dismounted and knelt beside her, pushing her bluish-white hair away from her face.

"She wouldn't tell us, not with the chance of the Horde coming down on them. She's smart. She brought me down, which means she was out there following us. She tracked me, and the moment I was alone, she made her move."

"You know when you said someone was going to knock me over the head?" Cailean laughed. "Karma done got you, bro."

Icelyn watched them, noting the familiarity in which they spoke to one another. There was a closeness that pulled at her chest, reminding her of her siblings. They pushed against her skin, opened her mouth to check the bluntness of her teeth, and she did the only thing she could, she bit one, kicked Sinjinn backwards, and head-butted the blond before she was on her feet and running towards the cliff they'd just come up. She leapt into the air to jump, but someone plucked her from midair and threw her into the deep snow.

"I don't think so, sweetheart," he warned as he stared down at her. "It won't be that easy."

"Go to the Horde, heathen!" she screamed, and he smiled.

"Oh, honey, I *am* the Horde."

He bent down, pulling her up by the chains that drained her strength, and stepped backwards, eyeing her. He smiled as her glare intensified and the other men came closer. Sinjinn shook his dark head, watching her with a cockiness that ate her soul. Before she knew what she was doing, she kicked him between the legs and swung her leg out, taking his feet out from beneath him before she came back up and tried to land another blow. Something knocked her down, and she screamed in frustration as she tried to get back up, glaring at Sinjinn, who threw daggers at her—well, with his eyes as he held his crotch.

"Then, this was fun," Cailean chuckled.

"Lachlan, change her chains before you leave, and find something solid to tie her to. She can freeze for a while to think about what she's done."

"I am not a child who needs a time-out!"

"No? Then tell me who you are, and which house you are from. You're obviously Winter Court, or you wouldn't have the ability to use ice. It's widely known only high-born of the race can wield ice magic, and you used it, several times so far. You're well-trained, but you're not trained enough for war, which means you're not from the Winter Court's guards, which means you are a lady, even if you don't act like it."

She snorted, and he raised a brow. "Suck my dick," she hissed.

"You don't have one," he uttered huskily. "Remember, I tasted your delicious pussy, and you screamed for me. Tell me you haven't forgotten what we did together already?"

Icelyn's cheeks turned redder than the berries that grew wild in this unforgiving land as the other men laughed and tried to smother their responses with their hands. She eyed the ground as she thought of whom she should become to him, but with his heated stare, and the intensity of the other's, she was coming up blank.

"Here's an easier question, what's your name?"

She lifted her eyes as she chewed her kiss-swollen bottom lip, and once again her mind went blank.

"So, you have no name, and you're just alone without a court? So if I were to break your pretty little neck, no one would notice you gone?" he mused.

"I have people," she blurted.

"Who?"

"As if I'd tell you! You're as bad as your father! You and your murderous people marched into the Winter Court and killed heir after heir. Your father fed the crown princess and prince to their parents! You're monsters! You want to kill me, go for it. I fucking dare you. Prove to me how much you are like that monster."

"Were you there when it happened?" he asked, and she blanched. "You were."

"I'm done talking to you."

"He killed for fun, but that..." He paused as the others nodded and her eyes glowed with emotion.

"Her eyes glow," Cailean pointed out.

"No brands, though, no royal markings," Sinjinn mumbled as he watched her closely. "No house signa either. Maybe she's a cast-off or a bastard? One who didn't remain in the court? It would explain her wildness and lack of guard."

"So what do we call her?" Lachlan asked.

"Snow, because she seems to spend most of her time on her arse in it," Cailean said as he pointed to where she'd fallen.

Blood dripped from her nose as she watched the men multiply before her eyes. Her hand came up, wiping away the blood as she shook her head. Iron poisoning. Unlike them, she was weaker, she was lesser; she was nothing. She was beneath them, nothing but lesser Fae, and not anything they'd keep.

Icelyn tried to get to her feet, several times, without success. Eventually, she just lay in the snow, praying death was swift and merciful. It wasn't that she necessarily wanted to die, but she deserved it. If she was discovered, an entire court of innocent lives could pay for her deeds. It was hopelessness that washed over her, enveloping her as her mind latched on to the last of her strength to hide her identity. One last attempt had her upright, but the world spun around her, cold nipping at her flesh as the frost settled into her bones. She watched as a dark shadow came closer as her body gave out, falling back into the welcoming arms of the cold which she had once thrived on. All that welcomed her were icy fingers, as if the land itself had felt her betrayal and sensed the pending doom she'd brought to it with her actions.

CHAPTER SEVEN

The sound of crackling forced her eyes open. It broke through her heavy, sleep-filled mind, the comforting sound reminding her of her room inside the palace. She almost thought she was locked in a dream. The scent of freshly picked citrus fruits made her belly rumble with hunger. Someone touched her, and she pushed them away, needing a few more moments of sleep before waking. Her hair was pushed away from her face and she groaned, making her argument known. She felt her body being lifted and something warm wrapping around her, sheathing her in heat. Her skin itched horribly, as if she'd been outside too long playing and her mother had pulled her inside and sat her in front of the massive fireplace inside the throne room. She swallowed a whimper as it worsened how slick with sweat her body was and becoming more aware by the moment of the burnt citrus scent of Sinjinn close by.

Icelyn tried to sit up, but the blanket he'd wrapped her in was too tight and inescapable. She wiggled, struggling to fully open her eyes and awaken from the stupor which held her locked in the between of wakefulness and sleep. Had she whispered in her sleep? Had he uncovered something he could use against her?

She blinked away the slumber that made her eyes heavy, languid. Sinjinn was knelt down in the middle of the tent, stroking the fire in a brazier, his hands outstretched as orange flames danced from the tips of his fingers. The fire leapt towards them, as if seduced by his touch, dancing erotically for him in a mesmerizing hue of green and blue as he beckoned them higher. She struggled against the bedding once more, winning the fight to lift to her knees in the middle of the thick, coarse blankets.

"And so she lives," he mused without bothering to look at her.

She peered down at her nakedness and swayed as she struggled to lift her arms to shield herself. She moaned as she struggled to make words, her hunger pangs growing as she looked around for food. Everything ached; her body was a mass of soreness that throbbed as it told her she needed to heal, and yet she couldn't. He still hadn't looked in her direction, and she didn't dare stand up and show him her birthday suit.

"You're less likely to try to run from me naked," he shrugged, uncaring that she glowed red from embarrassment as her mouth opened and closed. They were alone, in a tent. It wasn't just highly improper, it wasn't happening.

"You expect me to sleep in a tent with you, naked and alone?" she scoffed indignantly.

"I expect you to do whatever I tell you to do," he

said, finally turning his burning green gaze away from the fire to scorch her with it. He stood, exposing his lack of shirt and rippling muscles to her angry gaze.

The jeans hung low on his hips, exposing brands that slipped up his waist to his shoulders and then back down them. She averted her gaze as he got closer, unable to pull the blankets up around her as she sat on them.

"The iron drained you, so you'll need to feed. Since you're at least part High Fae, you feed from fucking. Curious thing, aren't you? Most of the High Fae tend to be around the Higher Courts, not hiding inside the lower ones."

"I'm not sleeping with you."

"No, you're not. If I wanted you to ride my cock, Snow, I'd tell you to ride my cock. I didn't offer you my cock, now did I? No, this will be a simple feeding. I wouldn't lower myself to taking you."

"Because I'm beneath you? Or is it because I'm lesser, weaker, and so unworthy of your high standards? I'm nothing to you and your people," she growled venomously, unsure why it would sting so bad that he thought this, and it was too close to what she'd been taught so brutally since a child. Her anger grew, and she tried placing her hands on her hips, yet the chains made it impossible, which ended with an awkward struggle to manage it before she gave up. "You and your kind are so full of yourselves."

"What I meant was, I won't rape you, Snow."

Her eyes turned to mere slits as she glared up at him. "My name isn't Snow or Snow Bunny," she argued. She felt like a caged animal, pacing in the small confines as it searched for a way to escape the predator hunting it.

As if she was in a snare and the predator was circling in for the easy kill.

"No? Then what is it?" he asked as he stopped mere inches away from her. His heady stare dropped to her heaving chest and then even lower to the ice-blonde curls of her sex, and she realized her mistake too late. She was taunting him naked, nothing between his heavy stare and her naked flesh.

"I...I should go," she said as she hiked her bound hands up and pointed over her shoulder with her thumb.

He smirked as he watched her, his smile all teeth and lethal as he slowly pursued her until she yipped as the ice-cold side of the tent came in contact with her back. He grabbed her waist, pulling her against his body, which sent heat pulsing against her flesh.

"Your name, now," he demanded.

"Elyn," she murmured as she placed her hands against his chest.

"Elyn," he repeated, letting it roll off his tongue before he threw her towards the bed, which was surprisingly soft. The chains hadn't allowed her to catch herself from falling, so she exhaled a sigh of relief at finding the bed so. "I don't believe you. You can keep your name and your secrets, but you will feed. We have a lot of ground to cover, and I'd rather throw you into the glaciers than have to deal with one weak little woman who refused what was offered."

"I don't feed from sex," she mumbled as she stared up at him. Her eyes feasted on the abs that seemed to ripple with strength as he knelt on the bed, staring at her glowing eyes.

"You do, you just never have attempted it yet," he

said roughly.

Before she knew what he'd planned, he lifted her bound arms over his neck, trapping her against him with the chain secured there. His clothes melted away and his thick cock sat nestled between her folds. His eyes glowed as his hands lifted, exploring her achy breasts as he rocked his hips. She was unable to look away from him, locked in his hypnotizing stare.

Sinjinn palmed her breast, holding back the growl that built from deep in his chest as her pussy cradled his aching cock. He wanted to lift her sweet hips and drive his pounding erection into her sweet heat, but he wouldn't be the bastard his father had been. Her full breasts begged to be kissed, and yet he didn't touch or do as he wanted to. Instead, he rubbed her body against his, dropping his hands to her hips as he let the friction build between them.

Her mouth opened and he crushed his against it savagely as he dominated her will. Her tongue pushed against his, her breathing ragged as her body betrayed her and took what his offered in return. Substance, he told himself. It was for substance, a mutual effort to not starve from the iron that ravaged through them both.

The female's muffled cries escaped past her lips as she bucked against him, taking control to get her body to the point of no return. He cupped her ass, rubbing her against his cock as he assured that she hit that pleasure zone with every thrust, every twist of her hips as her eyes grew heavy with lust, glowing silver-ish blue with hunger.

Icelyn was coming undone, her body buzzing with energy as she rubbed against his silken length. It was as if someone else was controlling her, forcing her body to replenish what it had lost by any means necessary. A coil inside of her was unwinding, unfolding, and she worked towards it. His growl only made her need it more; the way his hands bit into her flesh was amazing.

Fire burned her flesh and she recoiled, or tried to. He smirked, letting his fingers drift over her sides in the softest touch that sent heat smoldering through her. It singed, and yet it didn't hurt, as if he was using wax and letting it drip over her flesh, only it was his touch.

"Please," she whimpered, unsure of what she needed. She felt something aching deep in her core, an emptiness that begged to be filled.

"Please what?" he growled as he lifted her body until he was posed at her entrance, ready to plunge into it and stake claim.

"Please get the fuck off me," she uttered thickly.

"What?" he asked as if he hadn't heard her right.

"You make me ache," she admitted.

He smirked as he lowered her back down to the bed and followed her down. She was delicate, and yet sturdy. The fire that burned in her eyes called to his Djinn, begging him to claim her. He turned his eyes from them, lifting her leg to expose her flesh.

His fingers pushed inside her heat, two to fill her sweet pussy that gripped him hungrily. She smelled of wild berries and freshly fallen snow. Her mewling was loud enough that the others would hear it outside the tent, and he couldn't bring himself to care. Instead, he moved them with a purpose as his own release tightened in his balls, begging to fill her. He ached, he fucking ached to be inside of her, and he'd never ached to be buried in a woman's warmth before.

She uttered a prayer to the Goddess as if she could be saved. As if he'd let anyone save her from him now. Not until he'd had his fill of her. He pulled away, removing the chain from over his neck, and stared down at her.

"You've never been fucked, have you?" he asked, his gaze flitting over her swollen pussy and the sheen of sweat that covered her body.

"I...no," she admitted.

"I think that's the first thing you told me that wasn't a lie."

"Just fix it," she growled.

"Fix your virginity?" he asked as he pushed her legs apart, reveling at the pink flesh and white-blonde curls that did little to hide her arousal.

"*No!* I need that," she cried as she tried to cover her sex with her bound hands.

He responded with a laugh as he lowered his mouth and let his heat fan her naked pussy. She cried out, her body jerking with awareness as he brought his hands up to claim hers. He held them against her stomach as his mouth descended on her slick folds, lapping at them as she cried out and lifted her head to stare in horror at him.

Her hips rocked as her eyes watched, her ruby red lips opened into a perfect 'O' as he pushed his tongue deep into her slit, letting his teeth graze her delicate flesh as she watched him use his mouth to bring her pleasure.

Icelyn was losing it. It was that simple. His mouth was heaven; the feel of his tongue on her flesh had her silently begging for more. His glowing gaze consumed her mind as she was helpless to do anything other than watch as pleasure so hot and so violent threatened to consume her. He released her with one hand, pushing his fingers into her core where that tongue had just been, and she cried out. The fullness drew an ache of need into her soul, begging to be filled.

Sinjinn's mouth sucked her clitoris and then she was screaming as she fell over the edge. Her body shook violently as a sob exploded from her lungs. It was intense, earth-shattering, and cataclysmic, and she wanted it to never end.

He watched her coming undone as his balls ached painfully. A bastard would take advantage of the pleasure, of the way she'd come undone, and claim ownership of that sweet pussy, but he'd watched enough women be abused at his father's hands to know where to stop. Instead, he climbed to his knees and slid his cock through her arousal. He pumped it with his hand as he reached up, grabbing her hair to bring her up far enough to see that she fed. Her body still trembled as the waves of pleasure flowed and ebbed.

Icelyn mumbled incoherently as she fought to escape the pleasure he'd given her. Her eyes dropped to his cock that he gripped, pumping it with frustration. She pushed his hand away, and he growled.

"The only way you feed is if I finish too," he snapped.

She stared at him as she worried her lip with her teeth. Her tiny hand wrapped around his cock and she watched it with wonder as she slowly began following what he'd been doing. He growled, which caused her eyes to lift to his, afraid she was doing it wrong. His were closed, his face was tight with tension, and she frowned.

She bent down, ignoring the chains that bit into her wrists as she licked the smooth tip. He gasped, and she peered up at him with uncertainty. When he didn't say anything, she lowered her mouth again, flicking her tongue out to caress the rigid edge, and then she licked it to the tip before wrapping her lips around it and tasting the saltiness of his arousal. Her hands slipped from beneath her, and she took all of him into her mouth without meaning to. She swallowed around him and then withdrew, using her hands to wipe away the drool that had escaped.

"Gods damn," he bellowed as he stared at her.

"I suck at that," she said as she dropped her gaze.

"I really wish you would," he snorted as he pushed her down and closed his eyes, remembering how her mouth had felt as she'd swallowed his cock. Her clumsy exploration had been enough to blow his cork, and yet he'd held back, afraid she'd have tasted his need. He placed his hand on her flesh, opening it enough to gain sweet, slick friction as he started moving in earnest. Her tiny hands went palm-down on his chest and his brands began to pulse beneath them. Her eyes glowed with need as she watched him using her body to find his release.

He really wished he wasn't the asshole to respect a woman's choice right now. He wanted to be in her warmth, buried to his fucking balls in her wet flesh. He exploded, dripping his cum on her belly and she screamed as it burned her. Oops, guess his Ifrit wanted her to know that it meant business this go 'round.

She didn't even try to feed. As if she had no idea how to manage the simple task. He pushed his power into her, forcing her to take from him as he'd taken from her. Her body buzzed and then trembled as his power entered her, pushing the substance into her soul. Those sweet red lips opened on a sigh that pulled a smile to his lips.

So, his little warrior had never fucking fed. That was two truths he'd learned about her tonight. He pushed her to the side and lay beside her, pulling the blankets up around them as he secured her chain to his hand and slept blissfully.

CHAPTER EIGHT

Icelyn felt like she'd eaten those berries that Lars often had brought back from the human realm. She couldn't stop moving from one foot to the other, or get her eyes to stop bulging. As if he'd pushed all of his energy into her and now she had nothing to do with it. She eyed him as he watched her, his eyes mere slits as he dressed, uncaring that she watched him.

"It will wear off soon," he grumbled as he turned, muscles bunching as he walked towards her. His sea-green eyes studied her before he grabbed her arm and reconnected the cuffs in front of her.

"How many more days before we reach your home?" she asked offhandedly.

"Enough for you and me to spend a few more nights together," he growled darkly as his glowing eyes lifted to lock with hers. "Enough days to discover who you really are, Snow."

"Can't I just be me?" she asked, her words rushed as the energy bounced through her.

"But you're more. You're from a house of the Winter Court, which means you're a lady. The fact that you're a virgin confirms it. Last night you said you needed it, not that you didn't want it. That tells me you're saving it for a beneficial marriage and we all know that's only something they do in the lesser courts. That it is something solely done to better the royals of that court when outside alliances need to be made."

She swallowed, realizing her mistake. It was hard to think around him, much less make coherent thoughts when he was using that devilish mouth of his. He produced a cloak from thin air and handed it to her. Carefully, she tried to put it over her shoulders and failed.

"Here," he said, taking it from her bound hands and placing it over her shoulders. His fingers grazed her neck as he lifted her hair to place the hood over her head.

"It shimmers?" she said when it seemed to go iridescent with the slightest movement.

"It's what we wear when we travel, to alert others that we're Horde and passing through their lands with permission."

"But I'm not Horde," she pointed out harshly.

"No, but you're a prisoner of the Horde. You are mine now, until I decide otherwise."

Icelyn frowned as she followed him as the tent began to collapse with them still inside. It took three steps to every one of his to keep up. Once outside, she wished for the protection of the tent as the men wore knowing smiles as they nodded or patted Sinjinn on the back.

"Well done, taming the little one, makes her more...

amicable to her situation?" Lachlan asked, and Sinjinn snorted as he turned to peer at her over his shoulder.

Her face was red; heat infused and burned her cheeks as he stared at her with an impish grin that held no remorse. He didn't waste time as he lifted her onto the horse, following her easily as he mounted it in a swift, fluid motion. His arm pulled her body back against his, encircling her waist just below her breasts.

"We will meet you at the next camp," he informed the men who were taking down the tents. Once they'd acknowledged his orders, they started forward with his brothers and a handful of other guards.

The ride through the rough terrain with her body connecting against his was maddening. Every connection sent sparks spiraling through her and made her painfully aware of the ache between her legs. She felt incomplete, like he'd started something that had awakened something within her. Every once in a while his hold would tighten, and she'd go stiff in his embrace.

"Which house are you from?" he asked once they'd had a hefty lead on the other riders.

"Does it really matter?" she asked softly, her lips heavy with the weaning of his magic as it slowly left her.

"Not in the larger picture, but when we enter the Winter Court, it would be nice to know who will be punished for your crimes."

"Punish me," she offered over her shoulder, catching an alluring whiff of his unique scent. She'd never before associated burnt citrus with a male, not until him. There was also a hint of something woodsy, something raw and wild in his genetic makeup that was uniquely him.

"I plan to," he chuckled heatedly against her ear as his breath sent heat rushing to her spine. His hand lifted, removing the hood to reveal her ice-blonde hair, slowly pulling a thick strand of it to curl around his finger. He yanked it back, and she hissed, even as he uttered against her ear. "I'm just getting started with you."

"Is that supposed to scare me?" she asked. She hoped he wouldn't notice the curve of her spine where it had arched against his action, or the pulse that seemed to be located between her thighs. She pushed them tightly against the horse that bucked his head, as if it bothered him.

"It should," he offered as he let her hair drop to her shoulder.

Icelyn expelled a shuddered sigh but then stiffened when his hand rested on her thigh, lifting the thin dress he'd fashioned for her with glamour. He pulled it up, exposing her inner thigh against the cold air. His fingers drifted over it several times, torturing her.

"Do you mind?" she asked, but his snort was answer enough.

Those fingers pushed against her pussy and she swallowed down the urge to throw herself from the horse. He didn't care; in fact, he slowly pushed his fingers casually through her achy sex as if he owned it. A moan entered her throat as the horse trotted, sending his fingers harder against her delicate flesh. It didn't deter him; instead, he continued to whisper against her ear as if she could focus enough to hear what he said.

Sinjinn wanted to turn her around, bare her pretty white curls to his heated gaze, and fuck her right here, right now. He wanted his name to escape those ruby red lips, to hear her beg him for more. He should free his aching cock and just lift that sweet ass of hers onto his throbbing need. But...he wouldn't. Instead, he just stroked her sweet flesh, enjoying the discomfort it caused her, knowing the others were close by and her current state of need could be discovered at any moment.

She didn't shy away from it or argue at what he was doing, which was curious. Instead, she leaned her head back and closed her eyes, giving him full reign of that sweetness he craved. She was an enigma, one he wanted to unravel. There was no questioning that she was innocent, he'd tasted it as he'd licked that pink flesh until she'd been a writhing, quivering mess. When he asked her where she was from, she offered herself up to the Horde, which not many would willingly do.

She wasn't a martyr; she wasn't even the fucking type to be in that category. She was skilled with weapons, and yet she had little life experience. Elyn—if that even was her name—could sense the danger she was in and yet she'd only allowed a few tears to drop at her expense. He released her flesh and covered her with the cloak, knowing she ached. Her body was strewn tightly, her nipples hard enough to cut glass with from his touch.

"You're wet," he said huskily against her ear as he pulled her closer.

"There's a storm coming," she said, ignoring his words as panic pulsed through her.

"There's always a storm coming."

"No, there's a massive storm coming. We need to take shelter, now!" she urged as her wide eyes turned to his.

Icelyn felt the temperature shift. The sky had darkened, and rain had begun to fall. The wind kicked up, whipping her hair around as she broke eye contact to stare up at the angry sky. The layer of rain that was falling through the clouds was frozen with magic, meaning by the time it reached them, it wouldn't be flakes. It would be rain that instantly froze to whatever it landed on.

With storms like the one preparing to assault them, even those who enjoyed the cold didn't venture out of the Court. She wouldn't freeze to death, not like the others she was with, but the world around them would become dangerous, deadly.

"You're not listening! It's going to start at any moment, and it will freeze anything it touches, including you! Animals cannot withstand the cold, which is why there aren't many in the region. Trees will grow heavy from the ice that accumulates, making them unable to remain upright. The snow will become packed, and they will be unable to pass through it without being harmed."

"If you want to be alone with me, sweetheart, all you have to do is ask."

"We'll *die* out here," she uttered with fear clutching her words.

Sinjinn lifted his head, staring up at the rain that seemed harmless enough. As he watched, it started to intensify, and he frowned as he stared back at his brothers, who were also watching the sky. Hail began to pelt them, and he frowned deeper, his forehead creasing as he smelled the air and only caught the whiff of the woman and her winterberry and fresh snow scent.

The men galloped until they were in line with him,

and nodded as he sent a message through the mental link they shared. *Find shelter, now.* He, however, held his prisoner and pretended he wasn't doing as she'd instructed. It took less than an hour to find a cave large enough to fit them all in.

Horses were pushed inside as well, towards the front of it as they restlessly danced over the shell-like rock material that bathed the floor of the cave. It was a lot like the one she'd taken him to, but this one didn't have a bed. Sinjinn moved her to a boulder and left her, staring out through the opening as ice pounded relentlessly. If it wasn't so violent, it might have been beautiful.

"I hope the others took cover," Cailean uttered hoarsely.

"If not, they're dead," she whispered eerily from the rock as a frown marred her mouth. "The King of the Winter Court is unhappy, and now the world knows it."

Icelyn prayed her father got over his fit, or that he hadn't discovered her friends who had helped her. She prayed to the Goddess that they were safe, unharmed by the wrath he held tightly reined except for when his mask slipped, and the horridness he hid was revealed.

CHAPTER NINE

The fires were lit, and the men chose to lay beside them, uncaring that the others were trapped outside, in what was one of the worst storms Icelyn had seen in a long time. The last time her father had done this to the land, it had been when Alazander had raped her mother. Since that day, the storms came and went, but they never reached this intensity.

If she had to guess, it was that she was missing or he'd discovered her transgression against the Horde, knowing he'd be the one to put her to death if she survived them. It was law; no one could lift a finger against the Horde even if they took everything, or killed an entire village. Her father had set it in motion after they'd come to court to deal with those who had assaulted one of his sons. Sure, the son hadn't been hurt, but he could have been maimed by the arrow they'd shot at him as a warning to leave their land. They had so much history with them, so much pain that gnawed at her and her people, that it was an endless wound that seeped still.

Sinjinn pulled her against him and covered her mouth, forcing her eyes to widen in alarm. She started to fight against his hold, but he chuckled in her ear. She relaxed, albeit only slightly as his fingers pinched her nipple through the thin dress.

"I'm hungry," he purred as he rocked his stiffened cock against her ass. "If I didn't know any better, I'd blame our current predicament on you. But only royals can change the weather, and only those from the lineage which rules. That lets you off the hook," he murmured as his tongue flicked her earlobe, sending a shiver racing up her spine.

"You'll wake the others," she uttered hoarsely through his hand as she turned to stare up into his glowing eyes. He smirked, as if the idea excited him. "It's not letting up outside," she said, swiftly changing the conversation and steering it away from the dangerous glint shining in his gaze.

"No, it's not. How often does the king get upset enough to do this?" he asked, but there was a hidden dagger in his question.

"It may not be the king, it could be one of the others," she pointed out as he watched her. "It depends on what is happening at court."

"Why did you really shoot me and then drag me to a cave, woman?" he asked, and she blinked at his fluid change of subject.

"You're Horde, what other reason could I possibly need?" she retorted as she sat up and looked down at him.

"It's been decades since the Horde has asked for the

tithe. You hate us, but to me, it seems more personal. You wanted to hurt me, to torture me. You wanted me to feel that arrow as it tore through my flesh. That's why you used iron instead of iron-coated. There's also the mystery of how you knew I was coming, or that I'd entered the Winter Court's lands. Only a few were privy to the fact we were coming, and most of them belong to the royal family."

"What you did, it's inconceivable."

"What my *father* did," he corrected. "He was a monster."

"But you're not?" she scoffed as she lay back down, dismissing him.

He pulled her closer, pushing the bodice of her dress aside to run his finger over her budded, rose-colored nipple. Sinjinn knew what his father had done to the Winter Court; he'd had nightmares of it for centuries after it had occurred. What the people didn't know, or any who hadn't been of the inner Horde, was that these were the same atrocities he'd promised his own children if they strayed or challenged his orders.

Alazander had gone mad, and with it, the entire world had become his hunting ground. If anyone so much as looked at him wrong, an entire bloodline would be wiped out. They'd followed his laws, his rules, and his orders in order to survive. It wasn't a choice to disobey him; it wouldn't end in their death. He went after everyone you loved, took everything from you, and left you alive to feel it. He'd put you at the head of the table and torture them as you begged for it to be your death, for him to use you.

Ryder had ended that, he'd killed him and then had

endured what came next: The transfer of the beast. As the heir of the Horde, it hadn't been a promised thing, but had been expected, and honestly, they'd been relieved when it had chosen him as worthy to wield it and rule the Horde. Legends stated that with the housing of the monster, it could drive the wielder crazy and mad. Not one of them had wished to hold it, not even Ryder.

As the oldest child, it was he who had taken it, but only to keep the rest of his brothers safe from what could happen. Once it was finished, they'd hidden it from the courts, hidden it from everyone, and held the stronghold by brute force against the Horde and other creatures who'd tried to take it from them, never releasing the monster from his cage where it had rattled.

Sinjinn pulled her closer, his own memories marring his mind as he felt the others listening close by. He felt their tug, their minds melding to let him know he wasn't alone in those horrid memories. He pushed his father away from his mind and kissed her shoulder before his teeth sank gently against the flesh.

She let loose a surprised yelp that tightened his groin and coiled in his belly. He imagined her wide eyes, shocked by what he'd done. The beast he held snickered, knowing the mark would allow it to track her through any world, any place. Her mouth would be open, and those fuckable lips would beg to be filled.

"You bit me? Like...like a dog? Tell me, you uncouth heathen, is that a tail growing between my legs as well?" she seethed, and his brothers choked as they tried to smother it before it caught air.

"Yes, I bit you," he chuckled against her neck. "If you don't go to sleep, I'll do a lot more to you with that *tail* between your legs."

"It's tough to even attempt to sleep with that thing there. Can I cut it off and throw it out of the cave? It would be so much easier to sleep then."

"You know how you can fix it? You can use that tight throat like you did last night and it will go down all on its own."

"I hate you," she hissed.

"I hate you too, Snow."

"That's not my name."

"Neither is Elyn," he snapped. "O, *Thee* of So Many Secrets," he hissed.

She smiled into the dark and then turned, staring at the endless storm that seemed to grow stronger with every passing moment. Maybe if she were lucky, it would swallow them all up and leave nothing behind. It would leave her court safe from the Horde, her sister and brother wouldn't be stained or murdered by what she'd done, and in the end, that was all that mattered. It had always been all that mattered to her.

CHAPTER TEN

Five days passed before the ice storm changed to snow. The entire court was coated in ice, making travel near impossible. The men took the horses out, staying clear of the leaning trees and deadly icicles that threatened to fall from their precarious perches high up in the ancient oaks. The ice blanketing the top layer of snow made walking dangerous, which she learned as she took her first step out of the cave and slid ass-first into Sinjinn, bringing him down with her.

"Gods, woman, are you trying to kill me?" he snapped angrily.

"I slipped!" she hissed, her temper short and unleashed.

"Be careful!"

"Fine!"

"Fine," he snarled as he stood up, leaving her on the ground.

She struggled to get up, but with the slick ice beneath her and her hands bound, it was an impossible feat. She started to crawl back towards the cave, only for her hands to slip and her face to go down hard on the ice. Tears burned in her eyes as she lifted her face from the unforgiving cold and stared down at the pool of blood. Sitting back, she searched her face and found a small cut on her lip and an endless flow of blood that dripped from her nose.

It took her longer to get back into the cave than out of it, since she crawled, uncaring that it left a trail of blood behind her. Once inside, she pushed up onto her feet and moved towards the boulder to examine her face. She could easily heal it, but with the world outside a solid sheet of ice, and unable to feed, she didn't dare use an ounce of magic that she needed to shield her identity.

Everyone was on edge, and she didn't blame them. Nor did she like the fact that she was the only woman here, and they were complaining about being fed. She'd listened as they'd whispered as they thought she'd slept. The others were out there, and there was no sign of them yet. The king had called them, telling them to come back immediately, and yet she wasn't sure how or why they thought such an insane thing. No one could have gotten word through that storm, and she'd not seen hide nor hair of anyone approaching the cave.

Ripping a piece off of her dress, Icelyn brought it up to apply pressure to her nose. Pain throbbed from where she'd hit her face into the ice, magical ice which would make it impossible to escape the Winter Court. Her father was out looking for her, and his storm had been a deterrent from them escaping. That meant that the chance of them leaving here had diminished, which wasn't a bad thing for her.

"No, you will go and find them so we can get the fuck out of this frosted fucking wonderland!" one of the men shouted. "We cannot continue like this, period. We have to move soon. There's no food, no tents, and if I have to listen to her moan one more fucking time I'm going to lose my shit. I'm starving, and she's looking like a delicacy about now."

"You won't touch her," Sinjinn's warning was thick, as if something had taken control of his mouth. "I'm changing; I'll find them and bring them back. My beast can manage the ice a lot faster. Don't you fucking touch her, I don't care if her hair is on fire and she can't put it out, you let it burn!"

"Bro, if her hair is on fire, we're putting it out. That shit stinks," Cailean argued.

"You know what I fucking mean."

She listened, and when no one else commented, she thought he'd left. He hadn't, though, a volley of curses came from the front of the cave and then he was there, towering at the mouth of it as he trailed the blood with his eyes to where she sat.

"Gods, Snow. What did you do?"

"I fell," she said through the piece of dress she held to her nose.

He was there faster than she could track him, pushing the cloth away to inspect the damage. His touch was hot but gentle. His green, penetrating stare made her swallow and flinch as he examined her carefully. For the briefest moment, panic gripped her as she wondered if he found her lacking. He was High Fae, he was used to perfect women, and she was less, she was nothing compared to them.

That lesson had been taught to her after her mother, in her state of shock, had begged Alazander to take her with him. She'd wanted to die, not become his mistress. She'd tried it several times afterwards, trying to get death to welcome her. Icelyn's own father had beaten her, screaming at her and his daughters that they were less, nothing, ugliness that the High Fae would never want or love.

"Where do you go?" Sinjinn asked her as he dropped his hands. When she just stared at him, he continued. "Where do you go when you disappear? You're here, but your mind is elsewhere. Where do you go?"

"To hell, I go to hell," she whispered as she pushed him away and stood, shaking off the memories and how her father's hands had felt as he'd pummeled them until they repeated the words, memorizing them. She could still feel the welts. The sting of his fist and then the nothingness that had taken her into the emptiness, freeing her from his clutches. Icelyn had welcomed the blackness that had threatened her, and no one had been able to stop it. No one could question the king, or what he did. Her father had changed into a monster, just like the one who had rained down hell on his people.

"You're lying to me about what you are."

"I didn't tell you what I was, or who I was, so how am I lying?" she countered.

"You can use glamour, magic, and you wield ice. You also sensed the storm approaching, which we didn't feel. We're more in-tune with the lands, but then there are a few who would be more alert to the change of their own court."

"What are you saying?" she snorted, her heart

hammering wildly against her chest until it became painful. Her mouth dried up as her hands turned clammy, staring him dead in the eye as his mind worked to unravel who she really was.

"Keep your secrets," he growled.

"I intend to," she uttered softly.

"I'm leaving," he announced as he watched her move away and allowed it.

"I understand," she replied as she stared at him.

"You won't escape, so don't even try to. It's dangerous outside."

"For you, yes," she whispered before her teeth began to worry her lip.

"But not you?" he asked as he placed his hands on his tapered hips. "Then why is your face pouring blood?"

"Because my hands are bound, you idiot," she growled.

"And they will stay that way, at least until we reach the stronghold. Then I may just tie you to something else."

"Such as?" she demanded as pictures of cages or worse played out in her head.

"There are a lot of things I'd like to tie you up to, including my bed," he said softly through a smile, but it was feral. His eyes flashed green, but there were flecks of gold in them, as if he wasn't alone in there. She swallowed hard as he dropped his hands and moved from the cave without another word.

She yelped as a thick dress covered her body, and then a heavy cloak fit for a queen surrounded it. Icelyn chose a spot at the back of the cave, far from the fires where the men would gather when they entered, and waited for him to return.

If he ever did.

CHAPTER ELEVEN

Sinjinn tracked the men, searching through the endless snowdrifts that had intensified the deeper he got into the Winter Court. He knew whatever had happened at the court, this was a way of ensuring no one could escape the wrath of the king. In hound form, he covered twice as much distance, using little to no magic that would leave a trail, allowing whoever was out here to track him.

He'd never understood snow blindness until now. The Winter Court had once been described to them as a place of endless horror. It was a place Fae came to find eternal sleep when they tired of living. The only place cold enough to put them into a deep sleep that would shut down their mind. He now understood how it was possible and would never question another High Fae who did it.

The rivers had frozen over; water that splashed into the air had frozen in place. Magnificent waterfalls had created beautiful ornaments that decorated the mountaintops. Trees had fallen, their heavy burden too much to carry and roots had given out. Ancient oaks that were well over a thousand feet tall had shattered upon the ground, making the trail more difficult to find and follow.

Half a day's run from their cave, he smelled the copper of blood and paused. His hackles rose as he tasted it, noting it was Horde. He walked further into the clearing and howled as he came upon his men, slaughtered. Someone had murdered them all. Icicles protruded from their chests or other parts of their body, as if something had taken joy in these killings.

Sinjinn backed away from the grisly scene, and from the shadows, he watched and waited. Within the hour, men came to retrieve the ones that didn't belong to him. His men had fought, and hard.

"Get them up, and remove the ice from the others. It needs to look like an animal left this carnage," a man said as he shook his white-blonde hair, hair like hers.

"He's lost it, you know that, right? These are warriors of the Horde. How long before they come, in force, to right this wrong?" the other man cried, his eyes wild as he stared around.

"Problem?" a taller man asked, his uniform that of a high-ranking warrior.

"What if the Horde comes?" the first one asked.

"What if they do? These men were caught out in a massive unpredictable storm. It's regrettable that the animals got to the remains before we did." The man looked around, as if he could sense he was being watched. "Get it done; the hunt for the others has begun. None are allowed to leave here alive. They've been here for too long. That is going to work for an advantage. The magic will keep them from sifting, while also making it impossible to escape this realm. His orders are to kill on sight, and she is to be left to the elements."

"But it's…"

"It doesn't matter who she is, or who she was. She betrayed the kingdom, and this is the cost. She made her choice. These men paid for it with their lives, for the choice of a spoiled little bitch. If we find her unsoiled by those heathen pigs, we can do what we want with her, but know this, I get that little whore first. Dismissed," he said as he rubbed his crotch, as if he was imagining what she'd feel like.

Sinjinn backed into the brush as he considered ripping the guy's throat out. The moment he began to inch forward, more soldiers came into the clearing, staring at the horrifying sight with unease. He marked every face, every man. He inhaled deeply, memorizing their scents, their weaknesses, and then sank into the thick, icy underbrush stealthily before he turned and ran full-force to his brothers.

Once he reached the cave, he didn't stop running until he was fully inside. He shifted at the last moment into his Fae form inches away from her, fully naked and dripping hatred. He growled with the change, staring right at the female that sat buried in the cloak he'd glamoured for her. She was pressed against the wall, her nose brushing against his as she tried to get away from the anger he fed the entire cave after the discovery of the men's grisly remains.

"The guys?" Cailean asked.

"Dead, all of them," he snarled.

"They didn't get to cover in time?" Lachlan asked as he brushed his fingers through his blonde hair and swore.

"Oh they did, but the Winter Court King decreed war against the Horde, even though he intends to let it be known that they froze in the storm. He thinks he can say animals got to the corpses before they reached them." He stared at her. Sinjinn's anger bubbled up, causing flames to leap from the tips of his fingers. "And you, they plan to leave you to the elements. Tell me, how would the king know of your action so quickly?"

"How would I know? I'm here with you," she whispered hesitantly.

"Why do his guards relish the idea of raping you?" he snapped harshly, his eyes turning red with fire from within at the idea of her being harmed.

"I don't know!" she screamed as she stood up, trembling.

"We're leaving, now. There's a hunting party less than three miles from us who intend to make us into corpses. We will not stop until we pass the border into the Autumn Court."

"But the ice is impassable," she uttered through her quivering lips.

"For the horses, yes," he growled. "Not for one lone female and us."

CHAPTER TWELVE

They ran through the snow, each wolfhound on one side of her keeping her from slipping as they rushed towards the border. Her heart beat wildly, achingly against her chest as fear skimmed her mind. She could feel her father searching for her, using the snow leopards to track her location. She couldn't run and focus enough to call them off. Not and be able to dodge the fallen trees or the obstacle course her father had created.

She stumbled and was righted by a wolf, and then her feet gave out and she fell to the snow. Her air puffed from her lips, cold blue lips that expelled thick clouds of warm air into the freezing cold. The hounds surrounded her as she shook her head as she struggled to stop the pain at her side and the burning in her lungs.

"I can't go any further," she coughed, and the green-eyed hound snarled. "I can't! I have two legs, my lungs are burning, and we've been running for hours. I can't, I have no more energy."

Sinjinn shifted effortlessly, his eyes on her as he knelt before her, naked as the day he was born. A snarl escaped his lips as he pulled her up, against him. He sniffed the air around them and then searched the side of the mountain.

"We climb," he informed, shifting back into his wolf without another word.

Icelyn turned and peered up the sheer mountainside with trepidation. "If we climb Ice Horror Mountain, they will see us. There's no trees," she announced as she stood, gazing around them for the location in which she stood. "There's a river up ahead, with a waterfall, that even when frozen, offers shelter. If they're looking for us, though, that's where I'd expect us to be." She thought out loud, letting him listen as her heart raced and her mind whirled. "There's a cliff a few miles up. It's a sheer drop, about a hundred feet or so. It is cushioned at the bottom by snow. We can slide, but we'll need to be careful.

"There are jagged edges that can tear flesh apart. They won't follow us down."

The wolf nudged her, and she stared down at him. "They won't follow because it's not worth the chance of death or harm. Not many have successfully made it down it alive. I'm not saying it's ideal, but two miles west is a river, its miles and miles wide. To the south are the Winter Court warriors, the east is the Ice Horror Mountains, an un-scalable mountain that the immortal sleep within, and those who want to hide do. Then there are the Grayscale Cliffs. So you tell me, which one?" she asked as she knelt in the snow, feeling a certain hopelessness settle in. "If you leave me, I can make a stand against them. I can give you enough time and a distraction to reach the mountain."

The wolf growled, and the others joined him.

"You stupid dogs! They are at their most powerful following the storm. They will kill us all, and you can make it out of here. Go, get lost!" she shooed, her eyes filling with tears. Sinjinn nudged her, refusing to budge as she pushed him away. "Revenge isn't worth dying for."

He nudged her again and growled, baring his fangs. She stood up, staring the way they'd come as shouts started. It was now or never. She surged forward, kicking up snow as she made a last dash effort to reach the Grayscale Cliffs and pray to the Goddess that they all made it down them in one piece.

She ached, burning until her breathing labored and her legs turned wobbly. The wolves pushed against her, driving her with their sheer brute strength until she teetered on the edge of the cliff. Icelyn spun around, listening as the men behind them closed the distance. Turning back, she gauged her location and then stared up at the sky.

"Goddess, protect us please," she uttered as power rippled behind her, and she turned, finding a lot of naked men staring at her.

"Where do we go down?" Sinjinn asked, urgency driving his words.

"To the left, about thirty feet," she uttered breathlessly. "There's a tree that aligns with the edge, it's where I went down as a child."

"You said hardly anyone survives it," he growled.

"I was a stupid kid, my older brother dared me to do

it, and so I did," she shrugged.

"So you have a brother?" he smirked.

"Focus, angry warriors coming to kill us," she said as she grabbed his face and stared into his eyes. "Not the time, dog!"

"Show us where we go down, now," he demanded as he gripped her hand, holding it tightly, and moved towards where she'd said. "You're going down with me."

"You might want clothes for this," she pointed out.

"If we use magic, they'll be able to track us with the snow leopards they're using even now."

"Wait," she cried as she spun towards the tree line that they'd just escaped. Sinjinn yanked on her arm as the men broke through to the clearing. Giant snow leopards were following closely behind them. She exhaled, grabbing the minds of the wild beast that followed the men and connected to them. They stopped, heads tilting on cue as they felt her in them. She stepped closer and brought her hands together, sending ice shards sailing towards the men. The snow leopards rushed them, ripping the men apart as they followed her command. Sinjinn's head turned slowly, staring at her with suspicion.

"Snow, you want to explain how you did that?" he asked.

"No, we need to run. They'll only attack until someone stronger takes their minds from my control. Let's go," she insisted as she rushed towards the spot she knew by heart.

Once there, she paused, hesitating. The tree across the slate-face lay uprooted, on its ancient side. She leaned over it, slipping. Sinjinn caught her, bringing her back up against his heat as she shook with terror. This was suicide. She wasn't a child who could be teased until she jumped to prove her worth anymore.

She turned towards Sinjinn, staring at him as her head moved one way and then the other quickly. "This is stupid, it's almost right up there next to shooting you."

"It will work," he said as he smirked, showing way more confidence than she was feeling. "It has to, because right now there are thousands of men coming at us through those woods and we have no other way to escape. You can do this." He turned her in his arms and peered over the edge. "See you fuckers on the other side?" he chuckled.

"Who wants to live forever?" Cailean said.

"I kind of want to," Lachlan muttered. "I'd rather go out with a woman riding my cock than getting ripped apart by fucking rocks."

Sinjinn pulled her mouth around and kissed her gently, almost a goodbye kiss, almost. He picked her up into his arms as he sat at the edge, eyeing his brothers one last time before he said a silent prayer and sent them sailing over.

Icelyn closed her eyes, remembering the shock and awe in Lane's eyes when she'd went over the edge, and recalled the horror she had felt once she had. She screamed with fear, holding her body against Sinjinn's as jagged rocks missed them by the slimmest margin that she thought maybe she'd misjudged the correct spot.

It wasn't until they came to a full stop that she leapt to her feet and rushed to the bushes, retching up her guts as she realized they'd survived. Not all did; she could hear the screams and the bellowing of pain as the unlucky ones hit the jagged spikes.

She didn't want to tell them the truth of this cliff: that her father had created it to kill anyone fleeing the court. Spinning around, she stared and started counting heads. They'd all made it? Then who was screaming above? She looked up, staring in horror as one after another, the men of her court leapt, not slid, down the incline.

Dropping to her knees, she watched in horror as one after another leapt to certain death in the wrong spot. Sinjinn and the others viewed the horror as well. It was unbelievable, as if something was forcing them over....

"Run!" she screamed, lifting to her feet and forcing everything she had left into it. Her father was above, the only male strong enough to force his army to continually die for him. No other person would view their deaths as expendable or collateral damage.

Wolves exploded beside her, even as her last reserve expired. She felt a nip and then started to fall, only for the largest wolf to break her fall as the other nipped her ankle until she lifted and realized what was happening. He was carrying her, which was slowing them all down. Her eyes blinked back tears as she looked back, peering up at the merciless monster that stood on the edge of the Grayscale Cliffs. Unwilling to go over himself, and yet willing to throw his own men to their doom? And he thought she was the betrayer here?

She faced forward, staring at the edge of the realm, where winter became fall, and the warm autumn breeze washed over her. She closed her eyes, ignoring the pain as they surged forward, never stopping until they'd put miles between them and her court.

Luckily, they didn't stop until they were deep within the Autumn Court, away from the palace by two days' ride, at least. Sinjinn deposited her on the leaf-covered ground and then shifted again. He waved his hand, glamouring a large tent that he scooped her up and carried her into. Icelyn didn't open her eyes after her head hit the pillow, and then sleep claimed her and shut them once more.

CHAPTER THIRTEEN

Icelyn felt as if she was on fire. Her body ached, growing hotter with a need that stroked her from within. Lips touched hers, and she moaned, moving closer to the heat source that seemed to thaw her aching body. She opened her eyes, staring into the dreamy green gaze that watched her with heat banked in their depths.

She lifted as he urged her body forward, uncaring that he was stripping her bare. Icelyn moaned as her dress was raised and tossed aside. His greedy mouth sucked and tasted her pink nipple before he pushed her backwards, following her down as his teeth scraped the delicate flesh. Her sleep-filled mind allowed him to fondle and caress her, his mouth heaven against her needy flesh.

He slid down further, his mouth leaving a scorching trail of need as he nuzzled her flesh and then began licking it. Her spine arched as her hips flared and a low growl escaped her swollen lips. He moved like a man starving for her flesh; his groans were earth-shattering as he pushed his fingers into her body, demanding she give him what he wanted.

Hips lifted, rocking against what he was doing, her body growing slick with sweat as the orgasm fought to come out. He worked her until she was begging for release, his tongue flicking her clit as he fucked her with his fingers, pushing another in until it ached with fullness.

Her body jerked as he slid up, staring down at her as he rubbed his silken flesh against her aching need. Yet her body refused to find release, and every moment it remained just out of reach, her hunger grew.

"You need to feed. Yesterday took a lot out of you, little snow bunny. Use me," he encouraged with desperation in his tone that unraveled something deep within her. He rolled them, forcing her to stare down at him.

She swallowed hard as she tried to remember how to form words. He looked like a God, his dark hair spread behind his head, pooling around his shoulders. Sinjinn's body was ripples of hard, sinewy muscles that she explored slowly with the tips of her fingers, as he'd done to her.

Icelyn bowed her head, kissing his flesh as he hissed at the subtle contact. Her tongue escaped, drawing a pattern over his pectoral muscle and then up his neck. Once there, she tasted his pulse, enjoying the hammering of it as her tongue traced over it.

"Gods," he growled. "If you keep this up…" His threat hung in the air between them.

Her pussy rubbed over the hard, steel ridge of his

cock slowly, leisurely taking her time as she felt the orgasm building. Every move she made was clumsy, and yet he didn't say anything. He let her slowly discover his flesh. Her hand pushed between them, wrapping around his thick cock as she pushed it against her aching need. It was thrilling to hear his uttered groans, labored breathing, which she was causing.

She pushed it against her opening, feeling his hips moving with desperation as he pushed the head into her warmth, never adding more than what she herself had allowed. Her heartbeat fluttered as she turned her mouth towards his, but as he lifted, she pushed him back down, holding his throat with both hands as she stared down at him.

Sinjinn watched her, her grip tightening around his throat as she stared into his hungry gaze. The slip of his cock into her sweetness was playing with fire. He wanted to push her hips down, claim that sweet flesh for himself, and yet he wouldn't push her. Instead, he let her touch and explore his body, a dangerous move with how he hungered to taste and feel her as she came around his throbbing cock.

Icelyn scooted her body away from his, kneeling over his cock to lick the delicate edge that had him shaking with need. She tasted her own arousal on it. She cupped his balls, slowly kissing the thick ridges as she listened to his body's response to her actions.

The rich scent of burnt citrus mixed with embers of wood. As if he gave off more of the intoxicating scent the closer he got to his release. She wanted to know what he felt like buried deep in her body, for him to satisfy the ache that never seemed sated.

What was holding her back? She no longer had to save herself; she was marked for death by her own father. He was right here, willing to end the hunger that grew in her belly. There would be no wedding, of that she was sure, and her plans to escape him hadn't changed.

She climbed back over his hips, staring down at him as she leaned over, kissing her way to his hungry mouth. She angled herself posed over his flesh, pushing that crown back into her body where it so wished to be. Just once and she'd leave him.

Her mouth consumed his, and he allowed it. His hands cradled her hips, brushing those heated fingertips over her side to elicit a hiss of excitement from her lungs. She rocked against his cock, swaying as her body adjusted to the sensation of it, and then she pushed back until a scream stole from her lips as she fully took him into her body.

"Snow," he rasped as he lifted his head, staring down at where their bodies had fully joined.

She didn't dare move; pain was ripping through her as her body trembled with fullness. He took up every inch in her depths, stretching her body to accommodate his large cock. Her screams turned into mewling, her body shivering as she remained on him, unsure what came next. Tears rolled from her eyes, trailing over her cheeks as she continued to stare down at him. Pink tinged her flesh, her cheeks burning with embarrassment at her knowledge or lack of with what to do now.

Heaven; he'd fucking died on that cliff, and this was heaven. Her body pulsed, sucking against his cock as it struggled to adjust to his size. Shit, most skilled women flinched when he first entered, but here she sat, gloriously innocent, seated on his cock, all the way to the base of it. Her innocent eyes flared, revealing ice-blue eyes that seemed to turn the color of a freshly melted glacier filled with tears, and he swallowed hard.

He flipped her over, onto her back, and lifted himself up on his arms as he slowly withdrew from the paradise her body was offering him. Sinjinn winced as it tightened, his cock covered in the proof of her innocence. His forehead rested against hers as he felt her pulling away from him.

"Don't do that," he urged as his mouth crushed against hers, tasting the fear she felt. He deepened the kiss until she was groaning against him for more. His hips surged forward, pushing back through her tight core as he swallowed the moan she breathed out.

After a few more slow thrust of his hips, she seemed to relax as the pain lessened and pleasure took over. Her tiny hands touched his arms as her legs lifted, wrapping around his hips as she angled her body to take more, deeper.

"You didn't have to do this," he muttered as he lifted to stare down into her eyes. His thumbs pushed away the tears before he leaned back, grabbing her thighs to part her legs. "Are you ready?" he asked.

"Ready for what?" she whispered thickly.

"To scream for me," he chuckled right before he released the reins on his control and began moving in and out to a steady beat, his body grazing her pleasure nub as he continued fucking her as she whimpered and screamed as he pounded into her untrained body.

She was fucking perfect. Her innocence made him crazed, and the beast inside of him growled, wanting to make her theirs. His dark head lowered, licking her shoulder as she exploded around him. Her scream of intense pleasure echoed in his ears as his teeth sharpened, and then he bit into her creamy flesh, marking her as his. Her screams intensified as one after another, orgasms rushed through her as his magic assaulted her.

Icelyn was shocked to her core, a core he was pounding into without mercy. Her body milked him, rocking to the pleasure that refused to let her go. His teeth tore against her shoulder, but there'd been no pain, only shock and then absolute pleasure. Sinjinn released her shoulder, and then his mouth was against hers, kissing her with her blood on his lips, in his mouth.

Her body clenched against his, trembling as he lifted from their kiss, increasing the speed at which he fucked her. It was brutal, it was beautiful; it was everything and more. He didn't stop even when she'd felt his release deep within her body. The man just kept going, as if he feared he'd never get to be with her again.

Hours passed, and yet they rolled around, trading places as she discovered his body and her pleasure, feeding until she was sure she couldn't feed anymore, but then he'd prove her wrong, and they'd start all over again.

"You two done fucking? We got company," Cailean's voice cut through their blinding need.

"What?" Sinjinn shouted, uncaring that he continued to drive her body towards her next orgasm as Cailean waited outside their tent.

"Riders are coming in fast and hard," he called back. "Get your dick out of her and help us?"

Sinjinn stared down into her icy gaze, grinning as he

turned to stare back at the door of the tent. He pulled out of the tight sheath, gritting his teeth as she whimpered from the soreness. Her body clenched, as if it thought to keep him.

"Dress, be ready to run in case it's an enemy," he growled. "Stay hidden," he demanded.

"Don't go out there," she pleaded, her eyes filling with fear at the idea of her father being outside.

"Scared for me, Snow?" he asked softly as he pulled his shirt over his head.

"No," she whispered as she sucked her lip between her teeth, watching him.

CHAPTER FOURTEEN

Jcelyn listened to the noises outside of the tent as she glamoured on leather pants and a top that covered her arms. Next, she shuffled through the bag that Sinjinn had left, pulling out a dagger and working the chains that he'd placed on her before leaving. Once she heard the clasp release, she dropped the metal cuffs, pushed the dagger into her belt and peered outside.

The men were all deeper into the woods of the Autumn Court, staring at whoever was creeping up on them. She turned her head from side to side, knowing she couldn't stay here and chance them losing to her father in battle. Her father may be a lesser Fae, but he was powerful.

She silently moved to the edge of the clearing before bolting into the woods. Her feet crunched branches and other debris as she rushed towards the tunnels that led deeper into Faery, running like a maze beneath the lands. Once she was inside the tunnels, the scent of earth assaulted her nose.

Deeper and deeper she went, rubbing her scent over each tunnel entrance. It took hours to reach the corridor where it split off, running through four different main arterial tunnels that drove you deep into the four different lands.

One took you to the Summer Court, where heat was smoldering, and palm trees swayed over a welcoming oasis. She'd been there a few times, sticky from the heat that never let up or lessened by even a few degrees. It was a beautiful place filled with lush greenery that never died off, as the Autumn Court was plagued with. The scent of the ocean breeze mixed with the heat of summer, creating a soothing balm that excited the soul.

The second led to the Court of Dreams, where you ended up so warped in your own mind that everything seemed right, even if it wasn't. She'd loved the multitude of stars, filling with the aurora borealis. It was the human equivalent to the Northern Lights and bathed their endless nights in lights of every color you could imagine. Unlike the Court of Nightmares, only your wildest fantasies played out there, and though they seemed so real, you could be stuck in them forever. It was how they killed their enemies.

The third led to the Court of Seelie, which was also called the Court of Horrors. That was where the evil truly lay in this realm. It lay in the beautiful perfection that disguised the truest evil of the lesser Fae, even though they were High Fae by right. They were the unseen court, meaning those who ventured too deep never lived to speak about it.

The fourth one led into the Higher Courts, which was where she would go and hide among them until she could figure out a plan. She dipped into the Seelie Court tunnel, hiding the gown he'd glamoured her beneath a rock.

Once she'd pushed her scent into the cave, she backed up. Her heart raced as something moved, stepping out of the darkness to watch her. *Seelie*, her mind screamed. It continued, its beautiful iridescent eyes following her every move as she slowly backed up to the threshold of the crossroads of the cave.

"Pretty," the male said. Those eyes could see through her, see to her deepest, darkest fantasies. Its flesh turned darker, and away from the world that showed his true form, he looked more Unseelie than Seelie. "You're afraid of me, sweet ice princess," he murmured as he observed her, animalistic hungry banked his beautiful eyes. "It's been a long time since anyone used these caves, and yet here you are."

"I am heading to the Unseelie Court."

"And why should they get something as delicious as you, while the Seelie starve?"

"They don't get me," she shrugged, noting the way he inhaled her scent.

"Oh, my pretty, but they did. One tasted the pleasure of your sweet flesh. May I taste you? I promise to leave you whole. It's been so long since the princes of the court were allowed outside to feed, and I'm starving."

She took another step away from him. "And now you've been released?" she asked.

"We escaped."

"And the Queen and King of the Seelie Court?" she questioned, taking the last step into the tunnel she knew he couldn't pass through.

"Dead, I fear. We were so hungry after they had locked us away for so long," he purred, pushing his black hair away from the slithering brands that pulsed over his chest, marking him Seelie royalty. He was easily six and a half feet of utter male perfection, and if she hadn't known his game, he'd have caught her and consumed everything that made her into her before she could have prevented it.

"And the new king and queen," she uttered as she looked back the way she'd come. "Have they been chosen?"

"We're undecided, but since we killed everyone who thought we should be locked up like animals, we're out of options for mates. The only way for us to mate is to find our equal and become blooded with them. You're the first female who hasn't betrayed me that I've seen since I escaped, so can I fuck you?"

"I'm rather busy at the moment," she swallowed.

"Pity, I didn't want to resort to forcing my potential mate," he shrugged and started forward. Icelyn brought her hands up, sealing the cave entrance before she turned, running towards the safety of the Unseelie, how fucking ironic was that?

Irate screaming followed her as her lungs ached, burning the deeper she got into the cave. There was no turning back, not with the epitome of evil thinking he was her mate, or hunting for one in the way of rutting with every female he found to hurry his chances.

Her thighs burned, but she refused to slow as she sped towards the unknown. She'd never been past the lower courts, ever. She'd never been alone this long; her guards were ever-watching, protecting her, and now,

now she was alone, and someone had been crazy enough to help the Seelie escape their eternal prisons. The only reason the lesser courts stood free was because the king and queen had tired, desiring peace across the land.

She tripped and rolled, coming up on her feet as she looked down at the tree root that she'd been unable to see. Her eyes followed the roots through the dark as she stepped into the light, taking in her first view of Faery.

CHAPTER
FIFTEEN

Sinjinn snapped irritably as yet another tunnel ended up fruitless in his search. She couldn't have gotten that far, and it was apparent she hadn't gone back to the Winter Court, not when they were hunting her down. He stood at the junction of the cave, staring down each tunnel as if he could sense her. He couldn't, though, which was because being in this blasted eternal earth kept his hound from catching her scent to be able to track her.

He'd tasted her blood, knew her scent by heart, and yet this far down beneath the earth, he couldn't track her for shit. He turned slowly, looking at the Seelie Prince he'd found. His iridescent eyes burned as he stood inside the bars of ice as he watched the Unseelie before him. The bars of ice that held him were a good indication his little vixen had come this way. His arms were folded against the expanse of brands and muscle as he refused to tell Sinjinn anything.

"You are the male she let fuck her," he hissed and

inhaled deeply, as if it could smell her essence still saturating his cock.

Sinjinn stared at him coldly, eyeing the prince as he smirked. "She's mine, yes."

"If she was fully yours, why would she run, Unseelie Prince?"

"You know what, stay in there," he said crossly as he laughed coldly. "This world doesn't need you or your kind bringing the plague of Seelie back into it."

"Oh, but we're here. The Goddess has abandoned us. With her death, the cage was unable to hold us. We're free and hungry. I assure you, we are back already."

Sinjinn rolled his eyes as the prince sniffed again, probably trying to suck in the enticing scent of Snow that still covered him. He'd left her scent there, unwilling to wash her from his body until he found her again. The Seelie Prince's nostrils flared, and as he watched him, he tilted his head, turning his eyes into an endless starry sky as he gripped the bars and whispered.

"I think she found you lacking, Unseelie. She needs a true mate, one who isn't afraid to leave his claiming mark upon her pretty flesh. You didn't claim her, curious creatures you've become in our absence. When I was last free, we claimed our mates. Has this tradition stopped? Or has it been forgotten as we were, left to rot at the bottom of the realm in a cage made of sex and sin? One created to keep us alive, and yet never sated the endless hunger while you and your kind were left to run rampant over the world, unchecked."

"You should have stayed there," Sinjinn grumbled, wondering what else would escape now that Danu wasn't alive to hold their prisons closed.

Mating had changed in the thousands of years since the Seelie had been allowed to leave their realm. No longer did the Fae claim a mate, since most died in childbirth or soon after, when the loss of a child had become too great, and they gave in and either went into stasis or asked Ryder to put them out of their misery. If you mated, you mated once. It was for life. And when you were immortal, that was a damn long time. Most chose to remain untethered, free to fuck and feed from any they wanted.

"I'm going to ask you one last time, and you will answer me, creature. Which way did she go?"

"That way," he said, pointing towards the Summer Court. "No, it was that way," he amended, chuckling as those soulless eyes consumed the white and turned black. His skin began to change, growing as black as his eyes as he laughed coldly.

Sinjinn dismissed him, hating the idea that they were free but unable to change it or deal with them at the moment. Snow was out here, alone and unprotected. Her body had to ache, since she seemed able to heal his wounds, but not her own. Not to mention, this land was meant to kill anyone who wandered where they shouldn't, and she was far from home and unfamiliar with this portion of the world.

His eyes moved through the tunnels, and then he put himself in her place. The lesser courts hated each other for the most part. Meaning they dealt in trickery against one another, and while it had seemed to lessen with the newer generations, they still didn't help each other out. Probably because of the repercussions of his father tearing them apart... They wouldn't help her, which meant she wouldn't have gone to them. That left the Seelie and Unseelie courts' tunnel as her options of escaping him. He eyed the Seelie one last time, knowing she'd come face-to-face with the prince and had survived it, or so he assumed by the lack of her husked-out corpse being here. Knowing the princes had been freed, she wouldn't have gone into the Seelie Court, because that would be suicide. That left her heading right to his court and playground, which seemed to amuse him entirely too much.

"She's heading towards the Unseelie Courts," he announced, and then his eyes narrowed on the Seelie Prince as a new sensation ran through him. A familiar bond, one created from blood, ran through the monster before them. Fucking hell, it couldn't be. Not even his father would have been that demented to combine both races, right? He shook it off, staring at his brothers as he watched them to see if they, too, sensed the familiar bond with the Seelie Prince.

"You're sure? I mean, a lesser Fae rushing headfirst into the Unseelie Court is pretty damn ballsy," Lachlan muttered.

"She wouldn't be helped by the other lesser courts, not with the ice that runs through her veins. She's aware that he and his kind have been freed, and was smart enough to not allow him to touch her. She captured him, but she isn't dumb enough to run headfirst towards a Court of Seelie, the epitome of evil in these lands. They're what started the tithe being due in the first place. Them and the Horde feeding and fucking the lesser courts until our babes were all that were born into their courts. Alazander's father made the deal long ago.

The Horde would protect and remain away from the lesser courts, but only if the tithe was paid on time. That leaves her running right into our playing field."

"How is your father, princeling? My mother missed his visits. In fact, I'm sure you're aware that some of us are his offspring?" he laughed mirthlessly. "Imagine the monsters they created when they combined Seelie and Unseelie together."

"Not even he would have been stupid enough to allow that to come to fruition," Lachlan spat.

"No? Then how do you explain me?" he asked, his eyes turning tricolored with the mixed constellations of galaxies and prisms of light so jammed together that you couldn't tell where one ended and another began. Thick black wings extended behind him as he opened his mouth, revealing elongated fangs that appeared sharp enough to tear through the ice that held him. "I am both, I am everything, *brothers*."

"Family reunion aside, this is bad news." Cailean ran his fingers through his hair, staring at the abomination that watched them with cold detachment. "How could he think that sleeping with the Seelie Queen was a smart fucking move?"

"He wanted to create the perfect monster, and so he has."

"How many more of you are there?" Sinjinn asked the creature.

"Hundreds, maybe thousands? I lost count of the young they brought to us, abandoning them as she birthed the dirty bastards of the Unseelie King. Occasionally, she'd forget whose bastard she had birthed, and feed us one of her other consort's children. They never lasted long enough, though, and soon only a husk would remain. What can I say; we did what we had to do to survive that eternal hell."

"Endearing, feeding off your own siblings." Sinjinn swallowed the bile that rose to the back of his throat. "Not surprising, considering what you are. That's low, even for something as sick and twisted as a Seelie Prince."

"They were different than we were. You spend eternity in hell, never sated, and never fully fed, and see how far you are willing to go to survive it. Danu punished us for merely being born, like we were to blame for their coupling, their unclean union. Imagine being punished for simply existing, and you have our world."

"You fed from the lesser Fae," he argued. "You consumed them, mating them and leaving babes in their bellies before you left. You claimed women and damned them to hell with your touch. They died when you left them, turning to nothing more than a shriveled husk after their children were born. A bonded mate to a monster who didn't *feel* anything," he hissed.

"Not all are like that. Some of us just wanted to be accepted for what we were, which wasn't of our own choosing," he shrugged, as if it wasn't his fault. "Some just wanted to live. Others couldn't figure out why we didn't feel anything. It wasn't until Viloria, the Seelie Queen, had mated the King of Nightmares, who had abandoned her own daughter to the King's Court, that shit had begun unraveling and steps were taken to prevent her mating with others. Danu didn't like us messing with her world, or those she thought were better than us. I mean, look at me, I am the monster of both Unseelie and Seelie, and I was locked away simply because I was born wrong. Why weren't those who created us punished? No, instead they were rewarded with beasts that kept them protected from us."

"The beast was always inside him. It's what drove him mad. He wasn't gifted it, he was chosen to house it. I don't feel sorry for you, not knowing what you have done and will do once you escape these tunnels. We're leaving," Sinjinn spat, his eyes hard with malice as he considered how many women this monster had turned inside out, leaving them to wither to nothing more than a husk after he'd fucked them.

"Good luck finding her, she did smell so sweet. Although I could still smell the taint of you between her sexy thighs, I'd still have fucked her. I'll see you soon, brother, of that you can be sure." He grinned, watching the group as they started down a darkened tunnel.

CHAPTER SIXTEEN

Icelyn hugged her legs to her chest as she hid beneath the thicket to rest. Her body reminded her of her decision, as if he'd marked her by making love to her. It hadn't been love, of that she was sure. He was High Fae, used to fucking to eat, so for him, it was nothing more than casual sex. He'd probably slept with a million flawless, beautiful women in his lifetime, and she wouldn't even make that list.

After the sun finally broke across the sky, painting it in orange and pink hues, she left the safety of the thicket and meandered deeper into the High Court lands. She took in the wildlands around her, wondering which part of the Unseelie Court she'd entered.

It had taken her three full days of running to pass through the tunnels, discovering yet more winding paths that had led in every direction imaginable. It also gave her hope of escaping him, knowing that Sinjinn would need to explore every nook and cranny of it to figure out which direction she'd finally taken.

Her stomach rumbled and she frowned, staring around the open meadow as she took in the exotic flowers that beckoned her forward. Treacherous land, this place was, ever-inviting and promising to soothe your aches and pain with the lull of beauty. This place wasn't for the weak or wary, because it would offer you salvation and destroy you. The flowers would send off toxins, slowly feeding from you if you were naïve enough to get too close to their beauty.

The sound of a bubbling stream beckoned to her, and she slowly pushed through the thick foliage as she avoided the flower-covered fields. Her legs were bleeding when she finally pushed through the thorns, her eyes growing heavier with every step she took. Had the thorns been feeding from her as she lay among them? She let out a wispy sigh as she took in the damage.

Icelyn turned, staring back at the thorn bushes that hummed as they fed from her blood. She looked at her legs, finding them scratched up badly, her leather pants shredded from where the thorns had torn them to *feed* from her.

Fucking Faery.

She made it to the stream and walked right into it, praying to the Goddess that it healed her ravaged flesh. Whatever toxins the thorn had used was pushing through her system, trying to knock her unconscious so it could finish the job. The ice-cold water refreshed and washed away the blood as it cleaned the toxins from her body and woke her from the stupor of the poison.

Icelyn sat in the stream, uncaring that the entire world watched her. Smaller fairies danced upon the water's surface, pulling her hair as they played with her. Some landed upon her shoulders, and she realized they were sprites, but only because one began to glow as if it sensed she was slowly dying. Before she knew it, hundreds of them gathered around her as her heart thundered in warning.

Sprites could heal you or they could kill you. They were known for the latter, but then with them, it depended on the mood they were in or if they were hungry. She felt her head falling forward, and then weightlessness came over her.

She awoke in a berm, tiny sprites dancing over her flesh as they sucked the toxins out. She sat up, pushing the swarm away from her as she took in her green outfit, which they'd made of leaves. *Awesome.* Her body no longer felt sluggish, and she smiled shyly, thanking them as they danced in her vision, showing off.

"Thank you, little ones," she whispered, aware of their sensitive hearing.

Icelyn had read all of the books she'd found on this part of Faery, but obviously, it lacked knowledge of the treacherous thorns. Sitting up was easy, but the sprites seemed to become agitated as she did so. Looking around, she paused as the bushes on the other side of the river began to move.

Swallowing hard, she got to her feet slowly. The sprites vanished in a whoosh of wind that sent her hair sailing up above her head in a hiss of air. Her eyes strained, wondering what kind of beast would disrupt the tiny beings so. She didn't have long to wait, as a glorious stag stepped out of the bushes with branches of horns that stood proudly above its head, glowing blue... *Holy shit.*

Holy farting fairies! The White Stag stood across the river, staring at her through ancient eyes of infinite wisdom. Icelyn slid to the ground and bowed, her entire being trembling with the gravity of its presence. It only appeared to those it found worthy. Those he deemed privy enough to learn the secrets of his ancient wisdom.

Its coat was as white as the snow of the Winter Court, pure and clean. The endless branches that grew from its head seemed to expand as she watched it. Golden hooves clicked over the rocks as it slowly bent down at the river, drinking. Her eyes never left it, uncaring that she stared at him in wonder and shocked amazement.

This was one of the most mythical creatures of this entire world, and it had chosen to reveal itself to *her*. The sprites chattered excitedly from where they hid among the riverbank, and yet she didn't remove her gaze as she watched it lift its head to stare back.

Tears filled her eyes, burning them as she swallowed a sob. Her entire life, she'd dreamed of seeing this creature, of being worthy of its gaze. Now, it was mere feet away from her and slowly moving closer. It walked through the water, shifting to the form of a beautiful naked man. She should have looked away, should have offered him some sense of modesty, and yet she couldn't.

"You're a long way from home, my little Winter Princess. It is unsafe here, and yet you travel alone, unguarded. It is not wise of you. You're frightened of me?" he asked, his voice the sound of a lullaby of childhood that danced upon her soul. "No, you're pleased I have come to welcome you. You're not supposed to be here, though, but yet you are, which is curious."

"I can't go home," she whispered, still unsure how

close the sprites were.

"You will soon, and you will be where you belong, with whom you belong. Your king is sick, he will not recover, and you will be the one to help ease his passage into his next life."

"He hates me," she whispered.

"He is aware that you are not his daughter, and yet you are the heir. His children will never hold the land as he craved. You were the strongest of three, the three who were left. You were chosen to lead, to bring them into the new world. You run from fate, my sweet one. There's darkness in these lands, a poison that spreads even now. Destiny has marked you, and so you will follow the path she leads you to whether you wish it or not."

His dark hair caught the breeze, and he smiled, staring his cerulean blue eyes towards the sky. The sprites settled around her, staring up with wonder at the stag who had allowed them to come close to him. He was breathtakingly beautiful and alluring in this form, the epitome of purity and lust. He knelt down in front of her, uncaring that his cock hardened as he touched her legs, checking her wounds.

"I am male, first and foremost, Icelyn. This role chose me, and I am not immune to what perfection is before me. Your father called you less because you are more. He beat that lesson into you, but only because he knew who had planted the seed into your mother's womb. He is not immune to your purity either, and is crazed because of it. You need to be careful of him and his impure intentions for you."

"Dresden," she muttered as the memory of her

mother whispering her horrifying ordeal and the truth of her birth to Icelyn once her father had found her in a room with a boy and almost beaten her to death.

Impure, he'd whipped her with a belt until she was a bloody pulp, unable to move or even try to escape him. It wasn't until her mother discovered her, called forth by her nursemaid when the beating seemed to never cease. She'd been coming through her first woman's time then and found that she wasn't like those in her court. And things happened that she couldn't explain, and every day since, she'd hidden and repressed what she was until not even she knew it in her mind.

"He couldn't understand that Danu had forced the union, blessing it to bring forth someone of purity to hold the light. You are not impure or less. You are more, and you are blessed by the Goddess of this world. Never forget that. Stay to the path, Icelyn. Stay away from the woods and the brush. He will find you faster, and your destiny will play out." He leaned over, claiming her lips in a soft kiss that sent her mind thundering with pleasure before he ended it too soon. "Of women, I miss the taste of their pleasure the most."

Her eyes grew heavy as he smiled. "Rest, and heal, for I am watching over you, my little treasure trove."

Treasure trove? More like a cursed woman who was so mixed in her genetic makeup that she no longer knew where she fit in. Dresden was missing, sent from this world by the Horde King, his wife along with him. There wasn't a claimed Light Heir anymore or one they could find, and yet she'd been born of his seed with those cursed brands, marking her as such. Her mother had warned her of what it could mean, but she'd doubted it. She was hidden in the lesser realms, far beyond the reach of the Royal Fae and their treachery. But she'd never let it leave her mind entirely that Dresden had raped her mother during a summit, forcing himself on her. That was how she'd been conceived, and once her father discovered it, everything had changed between them. *Everything.* Thick laughter sounded as he slowly stroked her hair, whispering close to her ear as she fell into the healing sleep.

CHAPTER SEVENTEEN

Sinjinn inhaled the fresh air as they finally escaped the blasted tunnels. His eyes were aglow as he caught the enticing scent of his prisoner on the gentle breeze of the upper lands of Faery. He could smell the blood that had been spilled, along with the toxins of the plant that had caught her. His nose lifted higher, inhaling deeper. She'd been hurt, but she'd escaped.

"You do realize she may be dead before we ever catch her. Faery will fight to keep her, and make her a more permanent part of it," Cailean uttered as he shielded his eyes from the intensity of the sun.

Not that any of them voiced a complaint about the heat this realm offered after having been stuck within the Winter Court for so long. They'd stripped down to their pants and let the heat of the sun kiss their flesh.

"She's alive, and she probably thinks to disappear into the land," he grouched, his muscles burning from the endless rushing through one wrong tunnel after another, which he was sure she'd sent him down on purpose.

He smirked as he removed his shirt, tossing it aside as he let the familiar sun settle on his flesh, warming it. He stretched, knowing the others did the same as they prepared to track his little prisoner through the ancient land that was created of deadly beauty, made to lure its prey in and never let them go.

Sinjinn looped his thumbs through the jeans he wore, dropping them as he transformed into his hound form. The men followed his lead, sending the few who couldn't transform on their way to the stronghold, where they would be safe.

Endless hours inside the tunnels had drained them and given his minx a three-day head-start on them. Not that it would save her; she was on his territory now, his hunting grounds. There wasn't a single inch of the upper lands that he and his brethren didn't know by heart. One last deep inhale and he started off, trailing her by a feminine scent he knew by heart.

Icelyn heard the howls that seemed to echo off the mountain she was currently scaling. She slipped and then winced as the rock's sharp surface bit into the soft flesh of her hand. Peering around her, she could see animals moving through the bushes, and her heart sped up. Those animals had been trailing her for hours to this very cliff, as if drawn by her scent.

She climbed faster, knowing the top couldn't be that much further ahead. Of all the things to discover in Faery, a freaking mountain standing in her way hadn't been one of the things she'd enjoyed. She leapt to the next edge, teetering as the rock seemed to give out. Her air whooshed from her lungs as a scream tore through the mountain range. Something caught her, slamming her body against the rock's punishing surface.

A terrified screech bubbled deep in her chest as red eyes peered through a rocklike body of a creature. She lifted her leg, kicking it off the cliff's edge she teetered on before jumping back up, catching the higher ledge by the tips of her fingers as she increased her speed. She could hear the mountain rumbling, and tears burned behind her eyes as she climbed blindly, moving quickly as more of the creatures fought to reach her. The entire cliff face of the mountain was created of living creatures that looked almost like rocks.

The closer she got to the top, the more of them that appeared. Her muscles burned, and yet she refused to give up. Their scale-covered fingers seemed to stretch further, as if they could easily pluck her from climbing and suck the marrow from her bones.

At the top, she didn't stop. She hoisted her body up and rushed towards the thick tree line that offered a perfect retreat and hiding place. At the welcoming woods, she crashed, sliding down the trunk of an ancient tree as she struggled to control her breathing. She was just about to close her eyes and rest for a moment when the tree began to move.

"What the hell now?" she demanded with wide, horrified eyes as she stood, staring at the tree as it took an almost humanlike form.

It continued changing until a beautiful woman with thick brown hair and green eyes stared back at her. Icelyn stepped back, intending to run, but the entire forest began to change into people... No, not people.

Brambles. Her clothing was created of vines, bark, and leaves. Her sharp features were narrower than most Fae. Tall, frail creatures encircled her, and then a tiny bramble stumbled past Icelyn and rushed into the arms of its mother.

"Leave," she hissed.

"My pleasure," she nodded back, spinning around to do just that. It was going to be easier said than done. She was blocked by the rocklike creatures on one side, and the brambles on the other. "I need to go through. I will not touch or disturb you."

"No," it snarled, clear sap dripping from its gums.

"I will go through because I cannot go back," she growled back as the air kicked up, sending tendrils of her hair wafting behind her. The scent of an impending ice storm shot through the air. It grew colder; the temperature plummeted as she stared down the self-imposed leader who had refused her passage. Icelyn refused to back down, even as ice particles began to attach to the brambles, forming frost upon their flesh.

Everywhere the frost touched upon them turned their flesh black. They whimpered, backing away as they stared her down, as if she was some type of monster. A howl ripped through the air, slithering over Icelyn's flesh, and the brambles paused, no longer worried about her or her permafrost. She watched as the woman who held the childlike creature tilted her head. Another howl sounded, followed by a pack of wolves picked up, cutting through the air as others answered the call of the first. The brambles stepped away, turning into trees without another word.

Icelyn fought the shiver that trailed down her spine

as she listened to the howling that continued from every direction. As if she was surrounded by wolves and, unwilling, had become the Stag of the Wild Hunt. She started forward, peering around as she carefully stepped around the trees which she knew to be creatures. Branches slapped her, as if they were taking justice for the frost still marring their bark.

Once she'd escaped the forest, she stared at the open meadow with horror. This world was trying to kill her, of that she was sure. As far as her sight reached were meadows which were filled with flowers of every color. Poisonous flowers swayed, beckoning her to come to them. The wolves howled closer, and she sent a silent prayer to the Goddess and started through the flowers of Faery, knowing she may not survive it.

CHAPTER EIGHTEEN

Icelyn didn't stop running. Her feet barely skimmed the flowers that stretched and reached for her as she rushed through them. Every time they seemed to expand and grow before her, she flung ice towards it and trotted in the other direction. It seemed to never end, the meadow stretched further with every step she took. Just when she thought she was making headway, another flower seemed to grow, grabbing her ankle with a long, winding green vine. It took several attempts to remove the vine and the barbs that dug into her flesh.

Pushing off the ground, she swayed as she ignored the pain that once again bit into her flesh. Her fingers trailed in ice as she bent low, freezing the next vine until it hissed and released her flesh. A few more steps, a few more steps and she'd reach the cave and the safety it offered her. If she could just reach it, the blistering heat wouldn't hurt so much. The pain that ached in her legs would cease, and she could remove the clothing that offended her flesh.

The closer she got, though, the further away her mind went. It was as if the toxins of the barbs were slowly poisoning her, lowering her willpower to escape. The air around her was intensely smothering, thick with their heady scent. It stuck to her pores, sending a wealth of heat shuddering through her.

The steady footfalls continued behind her, and yet she refused to look back. Refused to see what or who was chasing her through the flowers. She knew she was being hunted; she could sense and feel it, the danger that trailed behind her. She just had to make it to the cave, and she could seal it behind her, at least for long enough to heal from the damage that she could already feel growing inside of her.

Her body ached, either from running for so long with little to no sleep or the toxins entering her system. The horrifying howling had ended, and yet the sensation of being hunted had yet to diminish. Everything inside of her told her to run faster, to not look back. Yet the horrifying reality of what was happening to her seemed to pulse in her mind, racing with the knowledge that she wasn't going to make it through this one unscathed.

Icelyn tugged at her clothes, the burning becoming too intense to bear. Her hands ripped at them, stalling her forward motion as she pulled them off forcefully. The cool breeze flittered across her bare flesh, and a moan of relief escaped her lips. She could feel the ache between her legs, the neediness of her flesh as arousal stirred to life violently as it dripped down her inner thigh.

Just a few more feet.

She'd be safe from those who hunted her.

One foot in front of the other, she stumbled, no longer in control of her limbs as her hands pushed against her wet pussy, the flowers begging her to play with it. Fucking Faery and their endless curses of creatures meant to lure you in and never let go.

Her feet scraped over rocks as she entered the cave, turning to throw her hands up to seal herself inside. It didn't happen. Something hot and all male slammed against her, pushing her against the cave wall with burning green eyes.

"Caught you," Sinjinn hissed, but his eyes were dilated, wrong. His brands pulsed, humming so loudly against her flesh that it echoed in her ears. Those eyes dipped to her heaving breasts, and then slowly rose to stare hungrily at her mouth. "Mine," he snapped huskily, his voice echoing inside of her. His head tilted as he watched her like she was a feast he intended to devour. "You shouldn't have run from me," he growled, pushing his lips against hers.

Sinjinn felt his cold, calculated control slipping as the aphrodisiac pulsed through his system, taking away both of their control. His mouth slammed against hers punishingly, and the sexy moan that growled from deep in her chest snapped whatever control he'd had left.

He'd prowled behind her in his wolf's form, watching her firm ass wandering aimlessly and without purpose through the meadow, already lost to the toxins that bathed her body in every hue of the rainbow. Instead of keeping his distance as he should have, waiting for her to reach the other side, he'd followed her into them. The intensity of the chase had held him prisoner, refusing to release him. He watched her fall, and those tiny fingers slipped between her thighs, touching her body where he wanted to join with her.

Then she'd begun to strip her clothes, and all images of his beast disappeared and in its place was a feral male with one purpose. Fuck her until she knew who she belonged to. Make a mark so deep that no other male dared to argue his claim. He stalked, like a mindless beast needing to rut that pretty little cunt between her legs, following her right into this very cave to do just that. To wash her in his scent, filling her womb until he was so deep inside of her that she could never dispel it.

The moment he'd made it through the meadow, he didn't pause, didn't think. He slammed against her, needing to be buried in her warmth. The urge was as deep inside of him as his own fucking soul. He felt the primal wolf pacing, wanting and craving her as much as he did. His mouth covered hers, demanding she open to his kiss, and he wasn't disappointed as his eyes took in her blown pupils; the same hunger that throbbed through him had taken her too.

The flowers' potent aphrodisiac mimicked the throes of Fae Transition, the absolute need to fuck and claim dangerously pulsing through him. Only where he could sense her needs through the Transition, the drugs of the flowers intensified it and made it worse. Primal, all-consuming, and deadly.

Sinjinn lifted her arousal-slick thighs, pushing his fingers into her tight, needy cunt and growled as he found her ready. He pushed against her opening, wrapping her hair around his fist to fuck her mouth with his tongue, as surely as he was about to pound into her sweet pink flesh. He entered her hard, without mercy.

Primal need drove him to abuse her tight cunt, to take her over the edge of passion to the darkness the flowers craved. Her needy flesh tightened around him, milking his cock as his tongue darted into the heat her mouth offered at the same time, mimicking the motion his cock took with his tongue.

Her noises were wild, guttural. Her throat tightened as he refused to give her air. He was the fucking alpha, and she was his fucking beta. The juices of her body allowed him to pound into her tightness without having to ready her, but then the flowers had wanted them to mate. They'd demanded he fuck her into nothing more than a pool of punished flesh upon the cave floor. Releasing her hair, he gripped her hips, grunting as her mewling noises mingled with the sound of her naked ass hitting against the cave wall, violently.

She screamed his name, demanding more as she raked her nails over his flesh. Her glowing eyes held his as he smiled coldly, planning to give her what she craved from him. He reached down, pushing her thighs further apart, giving him full access to the pretty pussy that was swallowing his cock to the base as he fucking destroyed her for any other man.

Snow was gone, and in her place was a needy little bitch who demanded to be fed. Her hunger leaked from her eyes, trailing down her cheeks through the yellow pollen the flowers had painted her with. The sound of their flesh meeting filled the cave. Those hungry eyes were beyond seeing, beyond understanding what had claimed her. Hell, she probably didn't even know who was fucking her anymore with the toxins in her system, but she would when he was finished with her.

He wanted to punish her for running from him, to work her pretty little pussy so hard that every time she moved, she felt him and what he'd done to her. Worse, he couldn't stop his own reaction to the flowers. Not even he was immune to them or could stave off the need to fuck that they fed him through their poison.

Her legs wrapped around his narrowed hips, hitting every thrust with a slow twist until she angled him right where she wanted him. He wasn't gentle; he slammed into her until sweat trickled from his forehead, dripping down to slowly move down her breasts. Her release was wild, her nails dug into his shoulders, and he fucked her like a rabid animal. The sweet noises she made only fueled his fire.

Icelyn whimpered breathlessly as her body, a slick mess of need, rocked against his. Her mind told her she was screwed, and her body relished it. He growled her name over and over again, and every time it rolled off his tongue, those hips increased speed. It was brutal and beautiful. Raw need, which threatened to consume them both as she yanked on his hair, fisting it until his mouth covered hers.

He growled something sharply and then slammed into something soft as he ripped her legs apart and dropped between them, lapping at her slick sex until she was screaming to the Gods. Blinding white light burst behind her eyes and her body bucked, legs pushing further apart as she tried to beg for more.

Sinjinn's mouth sucked against the soft nub, flicking it until she was writhing from side to side, trying to escape the madness of his mouth as the pleasure became too much to bear. He flipped her over, grabbing her hair hard as he pushed into her body harder.

It wasn't sex. It was ancient and deadly fucking, as if the Gods drove their bodies as they watched from afar. His growls were that of the animal inside of him, growling and hissing as he fucked his mate. His teeth grew, slipping easily through her flesh, marking her with a possession that would ensure she knew who the fuck had claimed her.

He slammed into her over and over until her body bucked against his, meeting him with every thrust of her own. It was the most erotic thing he'd ever seen, her tiny hips slamming against his hard length, unfearful of the pain he knew she felt as her body tightened with her impending release. Blood dripped from her shoulder, and she growled, her delicate frame trembling as she took his thick cock with ease. As if she'd been created just for him.

Sinjinn wasn't sure how many orgasms she had or how much time had passed, and yet they didn't stop. He flipped her over, filling her in a swift motion meant to keep her sated, keep her fed as he slapped her swollen flesh repeatedly until she was screeching with pleasure. He smiled down, his teeth a mass of sharpness as he lowered those teeth to her mouth, intending to take everything she gave him.

Something slammed against his head and he howled, tasting blood as it dripped from his forehead and dotted her snow white flesh. He snarled, before heading straight for her mouth again as something clawed into his arm, yanking it out of its socket. He spun around, dripping blood and saliva as he faced off against those who'd been drawn to the pretty pink cunt he'd claimed.

"Get away from her, Sinjinn. Look at her!" Lachlan demanded.

Sinjinn hissed, his inner wolf flexing its joints as it prepared to pounce on them and rip them apart. Something flashed in the cave, and he lifted his hands, noting the black flesh that revealed fire that oozed from the tips of his fingers. He saw red, saw them staring at his mate, and lunged.

Cailean and Lachlan spun away at the last second, escaping the fire that he'd sent sailing towards them. His fire was hot enough to melt steel. He stood to his full height, preparing to let yet another blast of fire loose, but something else had entered the mouth of the cave.

Something deadly, that even through the fog he sensed couldn't be killed. "She is mine, I claimed her," he warned the intruder as huge gossamer wings of the darkest obsidian entered the fray. Golden eyes watched him, ancient eyes with the knowledge to end his life came forward.

His king was here. No, not king, brother. His eyes moved to the others as his heart seemed to slow. What the fuck had he done?

"Kneel," Ryder demanded, and Sinjinn stumbled, his head turning to take in the damage to Snow's body. She was covered in welts, bruises, his mating mark... and *blood*.

What the fuck had he done? He knelt as his eyes flashed with horror before they lifted to his brother. "What did I do?" he demanded.

"What the flowers wanted you to do," he muttered as he rubbed his hand down his face, as if he could scrub the horror from it.

On the bed he'd created of poisonous flowers, she lay unmoving, her white-blonde hair colored crimson with her blood. Her back was mutilated; where he'd thought he'd nipped and played, he'd torn and destroyed. The gaping wound of his mating mark stood apart, as if his wolf had tried to protect her from the monster that had craved her blood and yet had failed.

Ryder moved closer as Sinjinn held his breath. She couldn't be dead. He didn't want that, didn't want to be the monster his father had been. A mixed sob and growl of horror ripped from his throat as Ryder flipped her over, revealing a dreamy smile on her perfect lips.

"Please finish it," she whimpered. "They're so hungry."

Ryder ripped her from the flowers that sucked at the pool of blood she'd laid upon his hands carefully avoiding the damaged areas where Sinjinn had bitten so deep bones were revealed. Tears of anger and denial burned the back of his eyes, and he stood.

"I'm a monster," he uttered as he sat on his haunches, staring up at the ravished female. "I'm just like he was."

"You were under a compulsion to make sure she didn't escape Faery alive. You didn't have the strength to ignore the poison, not even I can withstand it. Yet you marked her to protect her. Your wolf was trying to save her, even under the compulsion to end her life so they could feed from her corpse. Be glad he was present during the sex, or she'd be very dead right now."

"How did you know to come?" he asked as he dropped his gaze from where her blood was dripping to the cave floor. In the bed, thistles, flowers, and twigs had been used to create the love nest for him to rip her apart as the stronger Fae.

"Lachlan thought you were fucking, but the scent of blood and sex didn't bode well; when they couldn't reach you through the link, they knew it was bad. They have been trying to get you off her for a little while without you ripping them apart in the process or setting them ablaze."

"And how did you get me off of her?" he demanded.

"Eliran sent me with the antidote for the toxins. Once Lachlan knocked you up against the head with the branch, Cailean injected you. Now, we need to get her back to Eliran because she's losing a lot of blood."

"Go!" Sinjinn growled, his wolf pacing, demanding he take her from Ryder and protect her. But he wouldn't, because Ryder was the fastest in the group, and only he could sift into the newly rebuilt medical ward below the castle. He'd become a fucking monster, just like his dad.

CHAPTER NINETEEN

The endless beeping fractured her sleep, forcing her eyes to open. Pain assaulted her, red-hot pain that ripped through her mind as she opened her mouth and screamed deafeningly. Everything was wrong, too hot and too cold, wounds were being tended to, and something was hissing and cursing close by.

"Hold her down," someone demanded, and then hands grabbed and held her against the crinkling paper that she'd been placed on. "Gods, do you ever find a girl with just a broken finger instead of one that's been torn-up, stabbed, or shot? What the hell did this anyway?"

"I did! Fix her," Sinjinn's deep baritone hit her like ice water. Pain was etched in every word as he stared down at her with something lingering in his gaze. Regret?

Icelyn couldn't understand why he'd feel regret for anything. She turned, looking away only to lock gazes with golden eyes that stared back with an intensity she wanted to hide from. Of all the pain, the burning on the back of her arm hurt the most. She felt weak, as if she'd used too much magic and then drank for days on end and was currently under the influence of too much wine.

"What happened?" she whimpered, finding her own voice weak and scratchy, as if she'd screamed too much.

"You were poisoned, and then preyed upon."

"I don't understand."

"You were poisoned by the flowers of the meadow. Sinjinn was chasing you through them, but he isn't immune to them or their magic. The toxins made you both rabid; the need to breed or tear each other part became your sole focus. You lost." Those golden eyes searched hers until finally, she looked away to find Sinjinn staring at her, covered in bandages.

"It was you, in the cave?" she whispered thickly as memories assaulted her. She watched him, pounding into her flesh as she begged for more. His teeth biting through her flesh, needing more and more as she joined, intending to rip him apart with her claws. "Oh, Gods," she sobbed as every sordid detail replayed until she was trembling, fear ripping her apart as her claws shredded his flesh in the nasty nest of vines and barbs, the toxins holding them locked into the deceit of thinking they were making love.

What she'd thought had been a primal need to mate had been the flowers drinking from her body, bathing in her blood as he'd ripped her apart. Every time she'd come, she'd felt those flowers pushing in deeper, taking more until she couldn't stand it, and yet he hadn't stopped. He'd been drugged right there with her, an unwilling victim of the deadly land they lived in.

"Snow," he whispered as he stepped closer, watching

as she flinched and crawled into a ball. "It wasn't me, I wouldn't have done that."

"I know," she whispered, nodding and then crying out as something slipped into her skin, tying it back together.

It felt endless, the stitching of her flesh, the blotting of blood as she lay there, naked, surrounded by men who watched as the healer endlessly worked to right the shredded flesh. Once he touched the wound on her shoulder, a deep, horrifying growl erupted from Sinjinn.

Another growl entered the room, and she watched in silence as sapphire blue eyes held emerald ones. The rattle in his chest deepened, while the air in the room seemed to permeate with unease. Tension so thick that not even a knife could cut through it sat between the two males. It wasn't until the golden-eyed Fae stepped between them, letting a rattle of his own explode from his chest, which both men backed up from, dropping their eyes from him.

"He bit her, Zahruk. He marked her," the larger of them said.

"How deep?" Zahruk asked.

"Mine, she is mine. I made it so!" Sinjinn snarled with confidence in his tone. "We are one."

"Gods, Sinjinn. Are you fucking daft? This is the female who *shot* you. She fucking shot you. She's not yours. Undo it, you have a fucking fiancé. Remember? You vowed to marry into the Court of Nightmares."

Pain shot through Icelyn's chest as the words were shouted. This had to be a joke. What the hell did they mean he was engaged? To the Court of Nightmares? What the hell, they'd sent this asshole to her, to her court, with the intention of her marrying him. Had they changed their minds already? And even so, why did it leave a pain that seemed to grip her heart?

"What is the problem?" a blonde asked as she entered the room in a swift motion that was dizzying.

"We had an issue," the golden-eyed man explained, pulling her aside to whisper into the blonde's ear.

Violet eyes seemed to find where Icelyn lay on the bed, narrowing on her as he continued his hurried muttering into her ear. Once he'd finished, she pulled back before lifting on her tip toes to place a gentle kiss on his cheek. Even with his greater height, she seemed to make it look utterly graceful.

"Snow, I'm Synthia."

"And?" she said defensively as she realized her situation.

She was sitting in the infirmary of a stronghold, surrounded by the Horde. Her eyes narrowed on those golden eyes, and something inside of her mind clicked into place. Wings, he'd had huge, beautiful gossamer wings inside the cave. He'd been…larger.

"Oh, no," she uttered thickly through the tightness of her throat. She started to move, only to be pushed back down by the healer, who cooed gently, as if she was some child he wanted to soothe.

"You're safe here, Snow."

"I have to go home," she whispered.

"And where would that be exactly?" Sinjinn asked, his eyes narrowing as she swallowed hard.

"The Winter Court," she replied sharply.

"Yes, but *where* in the Winter Court?" he snapped, his mark upon her shoulder burning, as if it sensed something from his anger.

"Why don't we let her get dressed and allow Eliran to finish bandaging the seeping wounds before we interrogate her?" the woman asked.

A few hours later, Icelyn was directed to the main hall, where several men had gathered and were arguing with Sinjinn, who all seemed to pause as he noticed her presence and calmed. As if he'd been unsettled without being close to her. She exhaled and started forward when a soft voice met her ears.

"Icelyn?"

CHAPTER TWENTY

Frozen in place, she turned on her heel, staring at Lilith, Queen of the Night Court and heir of the Shadow Court. Her blood turned to ice water, coursing through her veins. She shook her head, uncertain which course to take. She couldn't run; she could try, but it would be seen as a retreat. She was the heir and princess of the Winter Court, and she didn't cower.

"You're mistaken," she said forcefully as her chin jutted up in a coldness that filled the room.

Lilith watched her, her eyes narrowing as she shook her head and opened her mouth to speak, but then noted something was off. Icelyn was beside two massive Fae bodies, both staring between her and Lilith. Her heartbeat pounded violently, and her shoulder burned, but she refused to acknowledge either one.

"My mistake," she offered, but somehow, Icelyn knew it wasn't the end of it.

"Tell us who you think she is," Sinjinn's deep voice rumbled.

"I made a mistake," she said, her own eyes dropping to the floor with her lie. The red head beside her pulled her close and whispered something into her ear, and then the golden-eyed guy was there, between them.

"Who is she, and do not lie."

"She is Icelyn, Princess of the Winter Court and heir to the throne."

Icelyn's heart dropped to her stomach as her heartbeat pounded in her ears. She gasped as that mark on her shoulder burned like a red-hot poker had been pressed against it.

"You fucked my bride?" Cailean snapped, and everyone turned around to stare at him. "Even worse, you fucking claimed her, Sinjinn. What the fuck?"

Sinjinn turned Icelyn around, staring at her and the shock that lit her eyes. His gaze moved between Icelyn, Cailean, and then settled back to Ryder.

"I didn't know," he offered in explanation as everyone waited for someone to explain what the hell had happened. "Ryder, we didn't know."

"*You?*" she spat at Cailean. "I shot the wrong one?" she groaned.

"Wait, you shot Sinjinn?" the beautiful blonde demanded.

"I'm his prisoner," Icelyn muttered as her eyes settled on him.

"That's a new low. Even for you, Sinjinn," a man with dark blond hair covered a laugh with his hand as everyone looked between them. "That fucking mark isn't just going to go away."

"I didn't know she was the heir, she pretended to be someone else. She kept everything from us. I thought she was a high-born lady of the court, not the fucking princess," he snapped accusingly as he stared at Icelyn, as if she owed him some explanation.

"But she is, and now we are at war with the Winter Court for what they did to the men. They have committed an act of war that will be dealt with swiftly," the one with the golden eyes, Ryder stated.

"No, no you can't," Icelyn pleaded. "The people had nothing to do with this! My brother and sister, they've done nothing wrong."

"You lied to my men; you shot the Horde Prince, and kidnapped him. Tell me, did you intend to murder him like your spineless father killed the others?" Ryder asked as his eyes flashed gold and power rippled through the room. There was no more remorse for what had happened in the cave, nor understanding in those golden eyes; just murderous anger that pulsed through him, stifling the air in the room.

It was so thick that her knees wobbled, threatening to give out. Her nape grew slick with sweat as the room seemed to close in on her. She struggled to keep her eyes from rolling back in her head, because this power, this suffocating power had been felt before. The day the Horde had infiltrated her kingdom and ruined everything.

"I wasn't going to kill him," she cried. "I just wanted to make him go away! I didn't want to be stuck with anyone from the Horde."

"And we should just forgive you for what you have done? I remember the Winter Court starting a rebellion once before, what was it that my father did to them then?" he asked, and Icelyn went vacant, empty.

Her mind rushed with the memories, the atrocities that had befallen the court. Her hands sweat, her spine threatened to give out, but Lilith answered for her. Her body swayed as nausea pushed against her throat and tears burned hot behind her eyes.

"He killed the heir and then the next who took power. Once he'd finished with them, he raped the third, putting her deep into her mind, which killed her as well. After he'd finished, he forced the parents to eat their children, which he'd prepared over a fire as the entire court watched. The siblings were forced to be witnesses and then endure the feast Alazander had prepared for them. When he'd had enough of watching them consume their young heirs, he raped the queen." Lilith watched Icelyn flinch with what she knew would be said next. "When he'd finished, the queen begged him to take her, to finish it. She wished for death, and even to this day, the king has not touched her again. It is why the Winter Court has only three heirs when others have fifty or more in their lines."

"Jesus H, Christ, are you fucking serious?" a redhead asked, her startling eyes landing on Icelyn, who trembled so severely that her teeth ached.

"And yet you would enrage the wrath of the Horde again?" Ryder demanded.

"Kill me."

"What, wait, what?" Sinjinn demanded as he tried to turn her around.

"I am the heir, I knew what would happen if I got caught. Kill me, not my people. My brother and my sister are good. They'll follow your rules. Once I die, the heir powers will pass to another, and Cailean can have her. Frostine is everything gentle, she's demure and beautiful. So I'm begging you to kill me, not them," she cried as she fell to her knees. "Please, not them."

The entire room was so silent that you could have heard a pin dropping. She remained there, bowed before the king, knowing her death would be swift, but it would protect her sister, gentle Frostine, who was afraid of her own shadow. Lane, her brother who fought to undo what her father did by helping the people and feeding the starving masses.

"That isn't fucking happening," Sinjinn growled, and her head whipped up and around.

"Shut your lips, idiot. He is the king! He will murder you," she hissed.

"He's my brother, and you're mine to punish, *Icelyn*," he barked. "You also carry my mark upon your shoulder."

"She's to be my wife," Cailean uttered, and everyone turned to look at him.

"I slept with her, *several* times today. And I fucking bit her, so she's mine!"

"I fucking heard it, *several* times today," he winced as he scratched his neck. "We're under a fucking blood oath, man. This is some twisted fucking shit."

"You're given to the heir of the Court of Nightmares, if they ever fucking respond." Ryder's tone was irate, and Icelyn didn't blame him for it. "The Winter Court will pay for the men we lost, and the way it happened. The Court of Nightmares has yet to respond, but the papers giving Icelyn's hand to Cailean are written in *my* blood."

"So undo it!" Sinjinn demanded.

"It's not that fucking simple! It's a blood oath. Meaning the king would have to agree, or whoever ruled would have to, and then and only then would the contract become null. I gave my word. My word is law. I can't change it."

"So I will still marry Icelyn," Cailean groaned as he looked at her where she was still trembling on the floor. "What a fucking mess."

"And me? She's my prisoner. And I fucking claimed her; it's not something I can take back even if I wanted to."

"She is no longer your prisoner, Sinjinn. She is mine and therefore will be treated as such. Guards, remove her from my hall. Find a cell in the dungeon, make sure she is comfortable and her needs attended. Find her clothes befitting her station, and have a bath taken down to her. Sinjinn, Cailean, rest. Once you have, we will find a solution to this fucking mess."

"That's it?" the blonde asked, her eyes narrowing on the king.

"Do not question me right now, woman. You should have told me this was a bad idea to begin with."

"Oh, I did. I warned you that sending them into places your father ravished and destroyed wasn't an ideal situation, and you argued it. I told you that while the people rallied with us, it didn't mean that we should turn our back to them. Trust is always earned and never given. Trusting someone who showed you their hatred and expecting them not to put a knife in your back is exactly how it gets into your back! Considering she watched your father feed her siblings to her parents, I'm surprised she didn't intend to murder him, and if she truly had him at her mercy and yet didn't, she never planned murder."

"Synthia, not the time or the fucking place. I am the king, and if we intend to fix what has been done, we have to make sacrifices, all of us. I offered to accept a tenth of what was owed, and they handed me their fucking daughters for my harem. My *harem!* As if I was the bastard my father was. And in turn, I offered them a Prince of the Horde. If I had refused, the Horde would have rallied against us when we needed them. We would have looked weak in the eyes of our enemies, and we cannot afford to do that right now. If no tithe were paid, the Horde would have once again begun ravaging and destroying the lesser courts. What would you have me do?"

"I understand," she said, cupping his cheek. "But she is terrified, so tell her that you don't intend to feed her brother and sister to her parents and that they will not pay for her crimes. Then throw her ass into the dungeon for shooting Sinjinn and be done with it. We will figure something out, we always do."

Icelyn's heart raced as she stared at the aura that surrounded the woman. No; not woman. *Goddess.* She was the Goddess of the Fae, the one who had inspired even her own mother to join the call to arms for Faery. She'd messed it up; she'd assumed her intended would be as cruel and awful as their father, and panicked.

Now, now she'd die for it.

CHAPTER
TWENTY-ONE

She sat upon a feather-soft mattress, her hands folded on her lap. The dress they'd sent down was ridiculous and gaudy, but at least she was covered. Her mind raced as thoughts of home plagued her. Her father had wanted her dead. The Horde wanted her punished, and she had no idea what she wanted. Home sounded good, but she'd never be welcomed back.

Icelyn jumped as the sound of a door opening reached her ears. She watched as men entered the cell, pouring buckets into the large round tub that had been carried in earlier. Backing up against the wall, she watched them as they finished and left the cell as silently as they'd entered it. The scent of burnt citrus and embers touched her nose, and she closed her eyes against the memories that scent provoked.

"You could have told me, and we wouldn't be here right now," Sinjinn said from the shadows.

"Come to gloat?" she asked as the men left the dungeon, closing the door behind them. She waited until they were alone before she touched the water, closing her eyes as the cold of it bit at her flesh. Most people wouldn't find the cold comforting, but to her, it had always been.

"Came to see how you're doing," he said with a shrug. "I know you're in pain from what we did, and I'm sorry for that. The flowers are deadly, and what I did… I wouldn't have hurt you had it not been what they wanted, demanded of me."

"I'm alive. I don't hold it against you. I felt it too, that primal need to let you do those things. I felt the pain, knew I should scream, and yet I couldn't. It didn't hurt when it happened, not on a level I could feel or understand. I just knew I had to do what they wanted us to," she said as she turned her back to him and began to strip, unsure how long they'd leave the water in her cell. He hissed as she slipped out of the robe and into the tub. Her arms wrapped around her shoulders, barring him from viewing anything that might be visible.

"You're safe here," he said, but it wasn't a promise.

"To marry Cailean," she reminded.

"To marry Cailean," his tone was rough, almost guttural, when he spoke.

The bars opened, and he entered, slipping beside the tub to dip his fingers into the sudsy water. Heat whirled from him, heating the bathtub. She didn't shy away from him; instead, she turned to stare at him.

"I wish things were different," he muttered as he covered his mouth and stood. "I wish I could fix this and remove that mark from your flesh." He watched her as she lifted from the bath, closing the distance to stand before him.

She stared into his eyes with hunger, but it really didn't matter in the greater scheme of things. He'd seen her naked, he'd done things with her that no one else ever had. She reached for the towel, brushing up against him by accident. She stiffened, but he didn't. Instead, he pulled her against him, kissing her with everything he had. His mouth was demanding, devouring her fears as she let him take them all from her.

He picked her up, moving towards the bed, but a muffled cough from outside the cell made him stiffen. Like two thieves in the night, they turned to stare into golden eyes that gave no mercy. Sinjinn glamoured clothing over her before stepping away from her slowly.

"You won't seek her out again."

"Ryder," Sinjinn started.

"I said, you will not seek her out again. Do you understand me?" he said it so quietly that Icelyn shivered at the violence it promised.

"I understand," Sinjinn said as he disappeared, exiting the room without another word.

"You will not lead him on. Do you understand? You are betrothed to his brother, and I will not allow you to come between them. Your hand is given to another, see that you do not slip and land on his dick." Black took over the whites of his eyes, blanketing the gold until something feral and deadly peered back at her. "I understand that because of you and what you did, my brothers are alive. Your deed is erased, but it won't be forgotten. Your father cannot be saved."

"He doesn't deserve to be," she said watching as his eyes narrowed.

"No love for your father?" he asked coldly as his

brows shot up in surprise.

"I am nothing, I am less, and I am ugly and unworthy of being loved. I learned that by his fist. Your father turned our family into one that others pitied and feared. I once had a father that I loved very much, but something changed after he watched his wife fucking the Horde King for endless hours and begging for more. Or, it could have happened when he ate his children. It's really a toss-up as to what changed him into the monster he's become. I don't know, as a child, watching it unfold, I'm surprised we're not all fucked up like they ended up." He flinched, and she smiled. "I didn't seek him out, obviously. I'm not even sure why he did, since I'm plain compared to the women of this court. I'm sure he could do a lot better."

"He beat you," he said gently as he touched the bars and they disappeared. "Your father, he beat you?"

Icelyn wasn't sure what she had expected, but it wasn't for the Horde King himself to sit beside her on the bed, resting his arms on his knees as he turned his head, staring at her through the most beautiful golden eyes she'd ever seen before. Galaxies banked in their hypnotic depths as he studied her closely.

"What my father did to your siblings was…" he stopped.

"Atrocious? Terrible? Devastating, that is what it was. It ripped the entire court apart. It ripped *me* apart. I was terrified of your brothers. The idea of being mated to one for an entire year, and he being anything like his father, forced me to be rash, unpredictable."

"You weren't alone, though, when you brought him down."

"No, but I'll take those names to my grave even if I see it sooner rather than later. I am the princess, and I forced them. They couldn't say no."

"One was there because he is in love with you; the other was there out of his own selfish gain."

"One wants power, the other wouldn't let me do stupid shit alone. He refused to let me since I left without my guards."

"Loyalty isn't bad, but he broke the law. He saw a member of a royal house wounded, and left him to die."

"He knew I'd heal him, and I am the guilty party here. I held the power, and I made a choice."

He reached over, gripping her chin as her eyes went wide. His thumb trailed over her cheek. She had to look like a snow owl caught in a snare. He released her, turning to look on the other side of her.

"Pet, make yourself visible before she thinks I intend to molest her, or worse," he growled as a snickering laugh sounded from beside her.

The Goddess appeared beside her, her violet eyes staring at her with sadness. She tossed an irritated look across the bed to the king. Icelyn wanted to run, to throw herself across the room before she ended up being a Horde and Goddess sandwich.

"We're scaring her," she said as she patted her leg. "We don't swing that way, Icelyn. We came to see what is driving Sinjinn to drink tonight, and well, he ended up here, so we did too. You're betrothed, so please, act like it. I'm sure the mark he gave you is going to make that slipping part a lot harder, which I'm sure you are strong enough to ignore?"

"I slept with him," she uttered thickly.

"And? You're Fae."

"I'm lesser Fae; we remain pure until we reach our marriage bed."

"Oh, oh shit," she laughed as she slapped her leg. "He took your virginity and marked you. This is going to be harder than we had thought, Fairy."

"It's something we do to honor our intended husband. So that he is the only man who knows us on that level. I thought I'd die or escape and then die, so being with him was a choice. Cailean deserves someone pure, someone who can love him."

"Do you love Sinjinn?"

"I'm...I was his prisoner."

"And yet you gifted him with something you've protected for hundreds of years."

"I didn't think I'd live long enough to have to deal with it becoming an issue. My father, he wasn't just trying to kill them, I was his target. I'm now soiled, unworthy of ruling his court. The moment he discovered what I had done, he tried to stop us with an ice storm. When that failed, when we'd gone down the Grayscale Cliffs, he knew I'd told them where and how to go down. Only a few had ever gone down them and lived to tell about it, and I was one of them. He began throwing men over the edge, forcing them to their deaths over and over until a pile had been made, and he did that for me, knowing I adore the court and those who protect it. So when Sinjinn started to feed, I allowed it. I wanted it as much as he did, but I kept telling myself to stop him before that day, and honestly, I don't regret my choice. I'm not the kind of girl who gets a fairytale ending, I know that. I'm okay with whatever happens to me."

"So you're not opposed to marrying Cailean?" she asked, standing to watch Icelyn.

"If that is your wish," she said dutifully, even though it hurt to say it. Her chest ached, burning as the words escaped passed her lips. That damn mark upon her shoulder throbbed, as if it was somehow connecting her to Sinjinn or what they'd shared.

"I'm not asking you what my wish is; I'm asking what you want."

"The blood oath will be called in by my father. He'll want me to suffer. I don't want you or him to suffer for my failure to follow the oath. My father has no mercy and would enjoy harming us both if he could find a way to do it. I'd prefer not to allow him to have his way. The oath stated that, should it be broken, a life will be forfeited. He'll want mine."

"That's something we both can agree on," he said as he patted her leg and she jumped, almost tripping over the bathtub to escape him.

"So smooth, husband," Synthia snickered. "Come, Icelyn, I will take you to your room, which is nowhere even close to Sinjinn's. I'm pretty sure Ryder picked the furthest location away from his just for you. You will be allowed to wander, but the family chambers will be forbidden for a while. If I catch you even close to them...well, you've heard rumors that the dragons are back, right?"

"Your children are safe around me, Goddess. Any babe is innocent in this mess of a world, and believe it or not, I hope they are the cure to healing our world and would defend them with the last ounce of my blood. They're legends even to the lesser courts, but not all think they will do good."

"My children are not in residence, but others are. We protect our own, even those who marry in once they've proven they are worthy of being family."

"But I'm not. I'm less, I'm unlovable."

"And your father deserves to die the slowest, hardest death beside Alazander for ever teaching his daughter such lies. You're beautiful, Icelyn. You're not less unless you decide to be. You saved people because you have good inside of you. You could have let them go down wherever and taken the correct path for yourself, yet you chose to save them."

"Or I didn't think of that," she shrugged.

"But you did, because you just showed me the truth, in here. Let's get you into a bed and some clothes that match your status."

"Please stay out of my head," she uttered. "And no gaudy dress, burgundy really isn't my color," she winced.

"Let's go, my beast is famished from stressing over his brothers."

CHAPTER
TWENTY-TWO

The bedroom was gorgeously done up in soft hues of silver and baby blue. The large bed was inviting, and yet her eyes seemed to settle on the bubbling pool that sat off to the side of the room, gurgling as water fed it from below. Next to the pool was a fireplace that burned wood, filling the room with a heady scent of comfort that she wanted to believe. Yet she wasn't stupid enough to think she was a guest here; no, she was their uninvited, unwilling hostage as they decided her fate.

There was also the issue of the bite that adorned her shoulder, throbbing endlessly as if it was somehow tied or bound to Sinjinn. She'd heard of mate marks, but the fact that she now had one both bothered and scared her. It wasn't unheard of for men to mark the women they pursued, claiming them to warn of any other male and scare them away from her.

His scent still clung to her body, as if he'd gone even further and somehow become a part of her. It worried her, and she couldn't help but wonder if by adding his scent, he'd marked her even deeper than his bite.

Icelyn didn't want to think of the repercussions of it or acknowledge that it thrilled and excited her that he had claimed her. He'd been primal in that cave, unhinged, and hadn't held anything back as he'd fucked her so raw and hot that her flesh was still singed from it. Of course, it had turned violent in the process, but to begin with, the male that had strolled into that cave and taken her, she'd wanted that.

Once the door lock clicked into place, she stepped further into the room. Her hand grazed the bed, testing it by bouncing on it before she stood, moving to the wide glass doors of the balcony and throwing them open.

Below her was the most beautiful garden, with flowers of every hue of the rainbow dazzling her eyes. Outside the endless chatter of happiness continued, and fires were strewn in the fields, as if the guard were out there, warming themselves against the cold of Faery in winter, and yet her soul craved that cold, demanded it. The crackling fire inside her room was the only noise that escaped from within, and yet her mind returned home.

Her father was enraged, and she worried for her remaining siblings. Then there was Amira, the princess who lay silent and unmoving inside the glass box in the family crypt, believed to be dead all these years. Her mind fractured, her body endlessly wasting away and yet somehow she lived. No one knew how since Alazander himself had raped her for hours, forcing her to retreat so far into her mind that she barely drew air into her lungs. Amira was so deep into stasis that the world felt her loss, and yet she lived. Frostine—her gentle, demure sister who was often afraid of her own shadow—would miss her, and Lane, the brother who preferred to be away from their court, was he safe?

She missed home, but more so, she worried what would befall her beautiful kingdom should the Horde descend on it, extinguishing the beauty with those who sought to defend it. Her transgression against them would force her out, or at least turn them against her. But hadn't they been poisoned already by her father?

He'd always acted differently towards her, from the moment the Horde had entered their kingdom and Alazander had whispered against Gerald's ear, he'd changed. The way they'd both turned and looked at her afterwards had sent a chill racing down her spine. She'd assumed he had offered for her, prayed for it, even though she was merely a child. It would have ended what unfolded, but whatever had been said, it wasn't that. Instead, the horrors had unfolded and everything that had changed, everything. He'd changed the way he looked around her, acted around her, sexually.

Her father had beaten her afterwards, as if he wanted her to die. He'd told her she was less than any other creature in the entire realm. He'd told her she was vile, unworthy of love. He'd beaten the lesson into her mind until she'd been bloody and defeated, nothing more than bruises and broken upon the throne room floor. No one had tried to stop him, not her mother who had begged the king to never cease fucking her; her desire to be as mindless as Amira made Icelyn vomit, and yet her mother had screamed it.

That was her first introduction of sex, watching

the king as he brutally took her older sister and mother violently. She'd screamed and begged him for more, her legs slick with his semen from where he refused her his seed. His beautiful rainbow-hued wings spread wide, barely blocking the view from where she'd been held, forced to watch what was happening. The sound of skin meeting and the cries of the court had made her skin crawl, but the coldness, the cold dead eyes of her father as what little love he'd held for her mother died was the hardest of it to watch.

So as she'd lain upon the floor, beaten and bloody as Gerald had beaten her beside the crumpled form of her mother, no one stilled his hand. No one spoke up on behalf of her; they'd just watched it unfold. And since that day, her father had barely spoken to her. Other than her reporting to him on the summits or advances of the other courts, she was dead to him.

Of course, she knew why now. She'd known since the first changes of her delicate body had begun. The subtle signs and the brands that had danced upon her flesh. She wasn't even his child, but besides her, her father, and her mother, no one else had understood why their princess had royal brands that pulsed upon her flesh. She hadn't been less, she wasn't his at all. It almost made the way he lusted after her explainable, almost. Except to her, he was the man who had raised her, and that meant something to her.

Her heart pounded as the memory of that day played out in her head. He'd wanted to kill her, to murder the child he'd raised as his own, because he no longer loved her. He'd waited for a reason, for any justification to end her life, and now she'd handed it to him.

The day she'd become a woman, though, when he'd stood staring down his nose at her with disgust and hate filling his blue eyes, she'd wanted to die. Those slithering silver brands had danced on her flesh, pulsing which only had intensified the anger that filled the room. Her mother had sobbed, bowing her head as she recanted what had occurred when Icelyn was conceived.

Dresden, the Light King, had found her mother alone during a summit where he'd demanded a similar tithe as the Horde received. He'd been enraged when the lesser courts had refused, and when he'd found her alone, he and his wife had raped her. They'd brutalized her, and Dresden had left a child growing in her womb. Icelyn's father had backhanded her mother, sending the queen across the room with his rage. It had been violent, and yet he couldn't outright kill either of them. Not without answering for his deeds to the Horde.

And so she'd lived, a daily reminder that she was not Gerald's child. Her glamour use began to happen by accident, first when she'd thought someone's dress was rather pretty, and wish she'd had one of her own, and then she'd screamed as she found herself redressed in it. Then it couldn't be stopped, so her parents had begun to spin the tale of how there was High Fae blood in her mother's lineage, which wasn't a lie per se, but it was so watered down that it wouldn't have manifested powers to Icelyn. The people bought it, and so the whispers had ceased, but then her body craved more. Her eyes started to glow ice-silver in color, and that would make the brands pulse, but still, no one questioned it or dared to point it how strange it was that their princess and heir was so akin to the Royal Fae in the high courts.

So she hid them beneath leather, her hunting garb her daily wear. She became the princess they had needed, a force like none before her. Icelyn spent hours away from the court, skirting accidents her father had laid for her, turning her world into her own hunting ground. She'd trained endlessly with the guards from afar, watching how they trained and moved, learning to defend herself for the day her father would stop sending his personal guards to end her life and do it himself. She'd known he tired of her, of her mother who had sided with the Horde against his wishes when the Goddess had called upon them. For the better of Faery, she'd said.

And then the announcement of her impending engagement had come, and she'd been enraged. He'd found a way to send her to the very beings who had destroyed her perfect world. She was to be given to the monsters who had murdered the heirs who should have sat upon the throne beside her parents. He'd found a way to kill her that no one could question.

Gerald had smiled cruelly when he'd announced the union. His mouth had twisted into a horrifying grin as he'd told her what her fate was to be. How, if she was lucky, they'd just rape her like they had her sister and mother, and plant a babe within her belly. How he hoped they broke her so that his own heir could take her place.

He hadn't hidden his hatred of her. Instead, he'd allowed the entire court to see the animosity behind the normally careful king. But then he'd never been the actual king, more of an imposter dressed up to play the part. He was of noble birth, sure, but the family themselves were poor, inbred among themselves as they tried to keep their line pure. He also came from a family of known usurpers, and as a way to end their problematic family, her mother had been handed to him. So all the royal blood he craved, all the power he had wanted hadn't passed to him at all. Instead, Icelyn carried it in her veins, veins that carried another's blood in them. What Gerald held wasn't even one-tenth of what she did, and yet she'd cowered before him, afraid that her court would pay the price, or that war would grow from the discord it would create.

And even now, without removing him from his throne, she'd continue. If she opted out or broke the oath, he'd call for her blood to end her life. Of that she was sure. He'd figured out the one way he could kill her without it being questioned, and now, she had to allow it to play out to keep him from getting his wish.

Her eyes darted to a shadow that watched her from below. Her shoulder began to throb, and she knew without having to see who watched her that Sinjinn was below. She stepped closer, as if an invisible thread pulled against them, and then he vanished.

She exhaled sadly and moved inside. Icelyn intended to sleep for at least a week after everything she'd endured. Life was moving around her, and yet she felt as if she stood in place, watching it go by without her. She craved his kisses, the heat of his touch, but worst of all? She missed arguing with him or hating him when he was close, because at least he'd been close.

Icelyn felt so utterly alone here, terrified of her predicament, and though she probably deserved it, it didn't ease the tinge of regret that pulsed through her. Nothing eased it, not Cailean and his natural ability to smile and ignore that she'd lain with his brother or the knowledge that Sinjinn watched her from afar, even though his brother and king had forbidden it.

She was being pulled in two different directions. One was out of a sense of duty and oath, and the other was the craving she held to be touched by a man whose scorching heat threatened to consume her. One ended with a babe swelling in her belly to create an alliance and keep her court safe from the others, the other ended in certain death. Death seemed the one she wanted to grasp onto, and that scared her more than anything else running through her mind tonight.

CHAPTER
TWENTY-THREE

Sinjinn stared up at her as she gazed out upon the land. Her white hair caught the light from the fires and glowed like that of a fire goddess. She was oblivious to the bitter cold as she stood there in her nightgown, her delicate curves bared to his hungry gaze. Her eyes had glowed with unfed hunger, which caused his cock to jerk beneath the confines of his jeans to fulfill her needs.

He could smell his scent on her, aware that he'd claimed her more than just the mark that would tell others she now belonged to him. He'd imprinted on her, sending his seed deep into her cunt to claim it and her soul. He hadn't held back his inner monster in that cave. Instead, he'd let it out to play, to claim, to imprint his name to the depths of her very being. And she'd never been his to claim. She'd belonged to another the entire time, his own brother's intended bride, and he'd claimed her until they were both damned from it.

He wanted to pummel the smugness from Cailean's

face. Sinjinn had never wanted to hurt or harm a brother before; sure, they had their ins and outs, but this, this was fucking primal. His wolf paced, demanding he take her away and nest with her. To claim her until his child grew within her, a sure way for the world to know she was his.

Zahruk's wolf had scented it; his alpha wolf had lifted those blue eyes, and there'd been sorrow in them. As if it sensed what he wouldn't admit. He was mated to someone else's betrothed. If it hadn't been for the blood oath or the fact that it would give that evil prick power to demand who paid it, he'd have argued against it. He'd have made them aware of the facts of his mark and claim.

Fact: He'd claimed her. Fact: That mark that burned on her shoulder was doing the same shit to his heart that she currently felt, only worse. They'd sealed that mark as he'd pushed into her body, leaving his overpowering scent inside of her. He'd fucked her savagely, yes, but that did little to undo what he'd done to their souls. That wasn't even the worst part; no, he'd mated her, endlessly allowing his seed to feed her womb with the intention of breeding her. His wolf was an asshole, primitive and wild. It wanted, and it took whatever that was, and now, now he would stand aside as she married his brother.

Sinjinn wasn't even sure how they'd gotten here, or why they had. The wolf he carried as a part of him didn't care, didn't follow the king's decree. Zahruk, though, he was the alpha in their pack. He was the one they followed when the Wild Hunt began, and he wouldn't win that fight. He knew it, knew his older brother would fight him to force him to fall into line with what the king decreed.

Blood oaths were a promise, and if not followed to the exact specifications, one or both parties could die. But there was always a loophole; they just had to find it. It would take time he didn't want to spend away from her, time his wolf would endlessly pace in his mind, demanding he continue until his babe was buried deep in her womb.

He stepped back, blending into the darkness around him as he let his armor materialize. The material was created to blend in, to let them move around without being detected when the need called for it. Her eyes seemed to search for him, those red lips tightening as her grip tensed on the railing. A soft gasp left her lips, and he inhaled, breathing the enticing scent of freshly fallen snow and winterberries deep into his lungs.

His eyes opened as he scented something else; something that shouldn't be there. His cock grew incredibly hard. Sinjinn's eyes bulged, his mouth dropping at the familiar wild scent that drifted down to him as she spun on her heel, disappearing into the room.

Sinjinn sifted, appearing in the great hall where Ryder was bored to tears as he listened to complaints of the people. He passed shapeshifters still shedding the human forms they'd stolen. Werewolves growled or snarled while others stepped back as he moved by them with long strides. The moment he turned those feral green eyes towards them, they bowed, sensing the wolf that prowled beneath his flesh.

"We have a situation," he hissed as he reached the dais and gained Ryder's attention.

"It can wait," he said, indicating the next complainant

to step forward.

"It can't," he argued.

"What the fuck is so pressing that it can't wait?" Zahruk snapped from where he stood beside Ryder.

"Clear the fucking room," he continued as he stretched, his body aching with the scent he'd caught earlier. If these assholes caught what he had, it would be a fucking race to claim her. Every red-blooded being here would kill to claim her, and he wasn't about to let that shit happen.

"Fine, clear it," Ryder said as he watched Synthia entering, her lithe body moving with purpose towards him. They were connected on a level that warned her when he was angry, which also went both ways. Once the room was cleared, he rested his eyes on Sinjinn.

Sweat beaded his brow; his eyes glowed with something deeper than hunger. There was also the wolf that Ryder sensed pacing, uneasy about being here instead of out hunting. His teeth morphed, elongating as Ryder watched. He was off, but the reason wasn't immediate. Sinjinn had never wanted anything, never asked for anything from him, and now, the one time he wanted something, it was the one thing he couldn't give him. He hated it as much as he hated the Mages.

"Mind telling me what the fuck could be so pressing that you interrupted this shit show of bowing and cowering for?" Ryder snapped, watching Sinjinn's hands that balled into fists only to loosen and repeat it. He waited to hear about the need to claim, knowing Sinjinn was going bugfuck to claim the little princess, but he wouldn't change his mind when too much dependence on it not happening.

"She's in Transition," he growled. His fingers pushed through his dark hair as he shook his head. "I smelled it, which means so will others. She's in fucking heat."

"Impossible, she's lesser Fae, and they don't Transition."

"Listen to me, I don't give a fuck what she is, she is sending off the scent of an impending Transition, Ryder. Enough that it took everything in me to come here instead of to her room and end that ache. I feel her, here," he said as he pushed his hand against his heart. "Within the next few hours, she will go into full-blown Transition, and you'll have a big fucking fight on your hands with this many alphas on the castle grounds."

"It's impossible. That would mean she's High Fae, Sinjinn. She's the heir to the Winter Court, which makes this impossible. I know that everything inside of you is scratching to get to her, and if there were anything I could do to change this, I would."

"I fucking know that, but it doesn't change what I scented from her, now does it? Go fucking check and then tell me it's impossible. Get the fucking guard up there to protect her. I'm not fucking wrong, I know it."

"Where is Cailean now?" Ryder asked as he turned to Zahruk.

"Hunting the Court of Nightmares to cement the contract and figure out who is supposed to be collected for Sinjinn to marry," he disclosed sternly. "He left this morning. I didn't see any harm in sending him since there was no pressing matter to attend to, and his wedding is days away."

"You sent him away? If what he says is true, you

need to call him back now," Ryder snapped.

"I can't, there's been no communication since they entered the edge of the Court of Nightmares. I've sent more to check on them, to ensure nothing like what happened at the Winter Court has befallen them, but he won't be back in time if she is in Transition."

"You're saying we may, and I mean may, have a High Fae in heat and her intended is somewhere else?" His hand scrubbed down his face as he rose from the throne. He stared at Sinjinn, golden eyes sparkling as he shook his dark head.

"If Icelyn is High Fae, we need to know which caste she belongs to. Each one experiences Transition a little differently," Zahruk offered.

"We're about to have a massive brawl erupt if she is. We're wasting time speaking of it," Synthia offered as she crossed her arms and stared at Ryder.

"If she is, we will need to drug anyone who isn't immune to the scent. It won't be a brawl, Pet, it will be a bloody fucking fight to the death to be the alpha who takes her. Several may be needed to achieve full Transition."

"Why now? I mean, if she is High Fae and as old as we think she is, why now?"

"She wouldn't have needed to feed or change without the pheromones from other males nearby. She'd have fed from what is available, but she's not home, she is here where men who ooze testosterone or pheromones that initiate Transition are closely gathered. Like yours, you started changing once you were around us. Your body sensed it was safe to Transition with us around you. Plus, you were hidden and had a tattoo that stopped the progression of your change from happening. Once you were close to creatures that could fulfill the need, it didn't matter what you had, it was started. Same with Adam, you were around us, and we set off the reaction. If what Sinjinn is saying is true, she's been with men who could handle her body's changes, and it would force the changes."

"So because she's here, she could be evolving without knowing it?" she asked.

"Why don't we go ask her why she's evolving?"

"About fucking time," Sinjinn growled from where he'd been silent, following the conversation as he fought his most basic needs. Everything male inside of him wanted to slam into the men who stepped forward. The primal need to fight them for the right to claim her was fierce, unbending.

"If she is, she's yours. Without Cailean here, she will be mauled by men who seek to fuck her, which I'm sure she isn't going to want. If she chooses you— because make no mistake here, it is her choice who will bring her over," Ryder warned. "There's also the fact that if she decides to forego it, we won't interfere."

"She'll die."

"If she decides to go through this alone, yes," he agreed. "I don't think she is suicidal. I think she wants to live."

"She isn't as strong as she appears. When my wolf claimed her, I saw shit that turned my stomach, Ryder. She's been through hell, and she's tired of fighting. That prick spent his every waking moment trying to murder her; the reason was never clear, but he hates her."

"Then maybe we don't give her a choice. We adlib

the situation and downplay it. We tell the facts, but still, Sinjinn, the final choice is hers to make. She chooses what happens next."

CHAPTER
TWENTY-FOUR

Icelyn paced the floor, her body heating and cooling as that ache inside of her grew to an almost unbearable level. Her nightgown clung to her flesh as she rolled her neck, her eyes heavy with a need she couldn't pinpoint or express. Something was off, her skin was on fire, and it felt like a million tiny pins were pushing into her skin, only to be pulled back out.

A knock sounded at the door, and she shook off the fear that slipped up her spine and settled in her mind. Slowly, she walked to it and opened it. The king and queen both stared at her, and Sinjinn growled as the other man from earlier stepped closer, his eyes aglow with hunger.

"Bloody hell," Ryder snapped.

"You can say that again," Synthia groaned. "So, what are you?" Synthia demanded softly, her eyes slowly settling on Icelyn and searching her face.

"What?" she questioned. Icelyn was uncertain what the question actually asked since what she was should be clear to them.

"You're High Fae, so who are you really?" she continued, her eyes narrowing as she watched her.

"I'm Icelyn, Princess and Heir of the Winter Court. I don't feel right," she uttered thickly. "I think I'm sick."

"You're not sick, Icelyn. You're in fucking heat." The king looked pissed, and Icelyn's mouth opened and closed.

"Because of my father?" she asked

"And who is that if not the king of the Winter Court?" he countered.

"Dresden, he raped my mother at a summit," she whispered, ashamed that the truth was coming out.

"Holy fucking fairy fucks," Synthia whistled and then frowned. "Wait; if she's Dresden's...is your mom really your mother? Or are you Tatiana's and Dresden's?"

"I just told you that he raped *my* mother," she swayed as something slithered through her, sending slick heat pooling to her core.

Sinjinn and Zahruk both snapped and growled, but only Sinjinn entered the room, staring at her. "I need a room, Ryder."

"I need questions answered before that happens," he argued.

"Her pussy is soaked, which means it's sending out pheromones to every fucking male here that it is slick with need, and in heat."

"That's rude," Icelyn muttered as she stared at him. He wasn't wrong, but did he have to announce it to everyone?

His eyes glowed as bright as emeralds beneath

sunshine. His lips opened to reveal blunt white teeth that promised pleasure. His body tensed, as if sensing an attack at any moment. Icelyn smiled, her body pooling with more heat as she stared at him with a hunger that wouldn't be ignored. She stepped forward and caught herself.

"Dresden fathered you, and yet he never claimed you as his," Ryder said.

"Not a question." It escaped on a hiss of air as her pupils expanded, dilating with her need that seemed to be laser-focused on Sinjinn. "He caught her at a summit when he requested the lesser Fae to pay him a tithe to match what they offered to the Horde. It was ill-met, and he was told to leave before they notified the Horde of his treachery. He was supposed to leave, but he found my mother alone in a room. Tatiana held her down, and they took turns raping and harming her."

"Tatiana is a female, how could she do such a thing?" he asked.

"She had…things she used and did, I think. I don't know the details, only that once her husband was sated, and I was planted, they left. He didn't stick around to see he left anything behind."

"And your father, he figured it out?" Synthia asked.

"No, I think Alazander whispered it into his ear the day he destroyed my court. He sensed it, knew I wasn't my father's child somehow. That was the day he stopped looking at me as if I was something he loved, and I became something he loathed. When the brands formed, it cemented it. I became the unwilling Light Heir and the Heir to the Winter Court. I've spent my entire life trying to ignore one to claim the other."

"That's not good," she uttered as she turned to Ryder.

Icelyn's head whipped back to Sinjinn's hungry stare with a smile marring her lips. Her hand smoothed over her stomach, uncaring that the others remained in the room. Sinjinn's nostrils flared, his lips moving, and yet no sound other than a wild growl escaped. His hands balled and clenched at his sides, as if he was fighting something that pulsated through him.

"She's the fucking Light Heir," Ryder growled and then narrowed his eyes. "Icelyn, when did the brands show up?"

"Twenty-two years ago," she mumbled as she stepped closer to Sinjinn, her hunger becoming unbearable.

"She belongs to Adam," Synthia muttered.

"No, she's just a stand-in heir. The world found what it was missing and claimed her. It doesn't mean once the other heir enters Faery, that those brands wouldn't choose the other to replace her; it depends on who is stronger. They belong to a full-blooded High Fae. They chose from what they had, meaning since they couldn't sense the other, they slipped into what was available. If the Light Heir isn't found, she may become Adam's."

"She is mine," Sinjinn snarled.

"The dungeon, Sinjinn," Ryder growled, his own eyes slipping from golden to that of his beast, obsidian death. "Use the wall behind the third cell, and don't let her out until she's fully changed. Ask her, now."

"Choose me," he demanded. His tone came out gentle, comforting, as if he was asking her out on a fucking date instead of asking her to fuck him. After their last encounter, he wouldn't blame her if she wanted another, even if it fucking stuck in his craw.

"For what?" she asked.

"You're about to need to be fucked for hours, days even. Choose me," he demanded, his pride pricked as he waited, watching the emotions that displayed across her face.

"I am under oath to belong to Cailean. I can't let that bastard win."

"He isn't available, and no one has the right to question Transition, not even an oath given. You can't be held responsible for what happens right now. This is the most primal fucking time in a Fae's entire life, and no one can deny it. Your...your betrothed isn't here. *I* am. You will die if you deny it, Icelyn. Your other option is to stay here and let those who are unable to fight the call to mate have you. It could be several who fuck you, do you understand that?"

"I want you," she uttered as she stepped into his arms and rested her head against his chest. "I choose you."

His heart thundered at her words, and his wolf howled from within and then bowed his head like a hunter sniffing out its prey. He would have her for days on end, and no one would have the right to say otherwise, not even Cailean if he returned. He didn't waste time, gripping her hand and holding her as he sifted them to the darkness of the unused dungeon and slipped behind the secret wall, preparing for the wildest fucking sex of his life.

She'd be the first woman he brought through Transition, and the knowledge that he may have to call for help didn't sit well. He'd do everything in his power to sate her hunger, and though he smiled as the image of her naked and spread out before him with a small smile, he couldn't help but worry with the memory of what Ryder had said. If the Light Heir weren't found, she would remain it. Meaning, if they wanted to heal Faery and cure the land fully, she'd become the Dark Queen of the Fae by marrying Adam, Prince of the Dark Fae. Because being stuck with Cailean hadn't been stressful enough? That was a mere year and one day, but the other? The other would be until eternity if Adam chose her.

CHAPTER
TWENTY-FIVE

The room was clean and hidden behind a false wall in the dark dungeon. The moment he opened the door, she groaned as something throbbed deep inside her stomach, sending a wealth of heat surging through her. Icelyn moaned loudly as she struggled to remain standing upright. Her hand skimmed over Sinjinn's arm, and she growled from deep in her chest, letting the noise resonate through her throat before it rolled from her tongue. It sounded wild, as if she was part animal.

"Inside, little princess," he urged, his body bristling with strength as he smirked, not bothering to hide the excitement at knowing she was at his mercy.

He could feel the pull from the bond they now shared, the ache in his chest that tied her to him. He'd been unable to deny it, the inevitable pull to mate. Staying away from her had been hell, but he'd reminded himself that he had to. He would never go against what Ryder wanted or stand in the way of them fixing the wrongs of the past, but Icelyn? She was like a balm against the festering wounds of his soul.

Sinjinn had never craved anything before her, never this raw hunger that blurred his vision with red. Cailean was duty bound to keep his word, but fuck, Sinjinn had bit her, obliviously, yes, but his mark was visible, and it pulsed with proof. He'd felt her fingers as they'd danced over the angry red scar, her sex as it responded to the curious caress. The fucking oath had been the only thing standing between them, and now, now not even it could naysay him where she was concerned, because the consequences would be death.

He stood back, leaning his long frame against the doorway to the room as she searched it. Her icy blue eyes lowered demurely as she surveyed the bed, and then the ropes that hung from the ceiling. Did she know what they were for? That he could tie her up and use them to control her body in any way he decided to? Sinjinn pushed from the doorframe, closing it behind him as candles leapt to life, filling the room in a heady scent of rich musk and amber.

"What happens now?" Her voice came out tiny, scared, and yet there was a hint of sex in it, her fear scenting the room as the beast within him paced.

"Soon your body will need to be fed, and the hunger will consume your mind. You will be helpless to ignore it."

"And we…we do it to feed? Isn't there another way?" she asked, her eyes somehow managing to avoid his as he walked in a predatory circle around her slowly.

"I don't think you'd like what that would entail," he admitted as he stopped in front of her, lifting her chin with the tips of his fingers. A shiver of hunger rushed through her, and he smiled as she reacted to his touch. "In order to feed off emotions with the amount you'd need to make it through this alive, you'd need hundreds of people being tortured. That's why we feed off each other during it, and not humans. They wouldn't survive it, nor would we be able to stop. Usually, they have multiple Fae lined up and prepared to bring one of us over into adulthood, Icelyn. You may need more than just me, but I'm going to do my fucking best to prevent that."

"I don't want to be shared, or with anyone else," she answered thickly as she hugged her stomach and pulled her chin away, as if his touch burned her. "I don't want to do this. I don't want to change."

"You obtained brands twenty-two years ago, Icelyn, and yet you never went through Transition. Your bloodline is mixed, but I can smell your sex pulsing with the need of your impending transfer from youth to a woman. That means every fucking male in this place has as well. This is happening, whether you want it to or not."

"And if I refuse? If I ignore it and ask you not to touch me?" she countered.

"Then I'll be here when it becomes too much to ignore, and you need me."

"I don't need you," she argued, her body becoming slick with sweat as she moved towards the bed. She crawled on top of it, hating that she knew she lied. But if she was changing, and she was becoming one of them, she'd soon be unable to utter lies. "How long does this take?" she asked, as if she had somewhere else she'd rather be.

She had nothing left, no home, no one who could challenge her father's words on her behalf. It was as if she'd ruined her entire world the moment she'd let the arrow sail through the air to find its mark in Sinjinn's chest.

Now even more was being taken away, as if she hadn't been punished enough. Her mother had promised she wouldn't have to endure this since she hadn't felt anything as her body changed. That her lesser Fae parentage was dominant, and what a total lie that had been, and yet she'd swallowed it right up as fact. The day the brands had spread across her flesh, burning their way over her arms and flesh, they'd waited in horrified silence for the tremors of pain to begin, and yet again, nothing happened. Not until him.

There was no High Fae inside the lesser courts, which was true. They preferred to remain among their own, as if the idea or thought of being around them was beneath them. So what they'd said could have been what had set this off, which once again, lay the blame at her feet. She'd also provoked the sex between herself and Sinjinn, and now it could end up backfiring and ruining the oath they'd given.

"Days, weeks, no one can pinpoint how long each Transition will take. Some need more, some need less time and feeding to become full Fae, but you're an Heir of the Light Court, and heirs sometimes take longer. Your body is going to be powerful, and that takes time to change once you begin."

"And the ache?" she asked as her body released slickness from her core, as if it was preparing for what was about to unfold.

His nostrils flared as his green eyes dropped to stare at where her body ached to be filled. As if he knew what was happening. His lips curved into a sexy smirk as those beautiful eyes began to glow with unhidden hunger.

"That ache is only going to worsen the longer you ignore it," he said as he snapped his fingers and then sat down in a chair, kicking his feet up onto the bed as his shirt disappeared. His own brands slithered as he watched her, not heir brands that moved with power, but that of the man in control of a beast that pulsed within him. "I'm here to use, so use me, Icelyn."

"I don't want to change," she cried as she hugged her legs to her chest and rested her head against them. "I've lost everything, and now I'm going to lose myself too. It was the one thing that couldn't be taken from me."

"You think you'll be different?" he asked as he dropped his feet and sat beside her. He stared at the white-blonde hair, so light that it appeared to be tinged blue in the dim light of the candles. "You'll be you still, just stronger. Your eyes will change, but unless something else from your lesser Fae becomes dominant and effects the outcome, you shouldn't change that much."

"I won't be able to lie, nor will I know how to control my own magic. I'm not a child, Sinjinn. I'm a woman, one who has spent the better part of the last one hundred years honing skills so that I could survive a murderous king who wanted me dead. I won't be the same, don't you see that?"

"Talking or arguing isn't changing what is happening to you. Your pussy is wet; it's aching to be filled already.

Your eyes are aglow with hunger, and you're sweating. This is happening. My dick hurts because it's ready to fill that sweet flesh because that's what it does to the males who can scent your body's needs. I'll do my best to be gentle, but this is happening no matter what. You hear that?" he asked, tilting his ear to the sky.

Icelyn stared at the door that he'd closed, locking each bolt soundly before he'd entered the room. She could hear it, scuffling and grunts, as if something was happening outside the room that not even the soundproof room could fully block out.

"They're fighting to get to you, for the right to claim you. Every full-blooded Fae in this stronghold is itching to fuck your cunt because you're putting out the scent of a woman in heat. It's ingrained in their genetics to bring you into womanhood. And right now, it's taking everything inside of me not to part those thighs and take that tight pussy. I've tasted it, Icelyn, and I crave it."

Her body jolted, and he moved, pushing her down as he watched her face contort into a frown. His hand blazed with heat, and he lifted it, watching as tears slipped from her eyes. His hand pushed against her sex, adding heat to ease her discomfort, and she groaned as her tiny hips lifted, legs spreading wide as she growled in response.

The noises outside the door intensified as the flesh of her sweet pussy coated with need. She was soaking wet, her flesh slick with sweat as her pupils dilated and then went to pinpricks before another moan escaped. The arch of her spine lifted, pushing her needy cunt closer to his hand that offered an escape from the pain.

She was so close to saying screw it and throwing her

fears aside to demand he give her relief. Yet there was something feral in his gaze. Something that told her this wasn't going to be just her transitioning into High Fae; he was about to destroy her world and ruin her for any other man alive.

CHAPTER
TWENTY-SIX

Icelyn rolled her hips, her eyes growing heavy with the relief his heated touch offered. She felt wrong, as if she was burning from within and couldn't dig through her flesh to get to the itch to stop its incessant discomfort. Sinjinn grabbed her hands, pushing them beside her head the moment she'd begun tearing at her flesh.

"Stop fighting it, it's natural," he murmured as he dragged his heated lips over her flesh.

His fire was uncontrollable with his need to consume her, to leave her singed by his touch. He waited for her signal, any signal to tell him she was done fighting the inevitable. For hours she'd lain on the bed, twisting in pain and agony as her magic burned through her bones, fusing to become second nature to her. Yet still, she shook her head as moans and screams slipped past her lips.

Watching her was agony on its own. She was strong, strong enough to last hours through the endless torture he remembered going through long ago. The endless burning and feeling of utter starvation that not even sex fully sated at first. Bones that felt as if they were being broken, and then fused back together with no medication strong enough to dull the pain.

It was her noises that broke him the most. Her silent screams that never fully came out, yet the tears seemed to endlessly flow. Sinjinn ran his thumb over her cheek, capturing the tear before he leaned over, placing a gentle kiss against it. She leaned into it, her hand lifting to push through his hair as her mouth lifted, searching for his even though her eyes were closed tightly.

"Rest," he urged, even though it was the last thing he wanted her to do.

"I can't take it anymore," she whispered thickly as her fingers sent ice tendrils onto his flesh.

"You can, and between the pains, you'll need to rest. This isn't going to end quickly," he explained softly, even though his voice escaped huskily. He was hard as fuck, an endless ache that seemed to throb worse as those sexy-as-fuck moans escaped her full lips.

Her lashes dusted against her cheeks before they opened. Glowing eyes peered through the haze of lust that stared back at him. Her eyes were silver, the hint of blue lost in the murkiness of her tears as Transition held her prisoner. Her hand smoothed over his hard chest, slowly exploring the contour of the muscles.

Those fingers left ice in their wake. Ice his body melted but not before it shot straight to his cock. He smiled softly as she lifted her head, licking the tendrils of water. She was making it really hard not pin her against the bed and show her how much her actions were affecting him. He captured her face in his hands, trapping her as he pushed her against the bed, trailing his heated kiss over her frozen flesh.

She was unable to prevent her use of magic in this state, oblivious that her lips were blue from it, yet he pushed his heated mouth against hers, and she struggled to take control. He chuckled as he lifted up, staring into the most beautiful eyes he'd ever gazed into before. She was his walking fantasy, the woman who had starred in every dream he'd ever had of his perfect match.

Maybe that was why his wolf had claimed her. Maybe, just maybe it hadn't been the aphrodisiac of the flowers, but his wolf knowing she was his equal? His wolf had never cared who he fucked, had never shown his teeth in bed until Icelyn. Sinjinn had assumed it was because she'd harmed him, and his wolf wanted to dominate her so she knew who the alpha was.

"You're so beautiful," he uttered as he continued to gaze into her eyes. "I've met so many women, so many beautiful girls in my lifetime, Icelyn. But you, you stare at me with your bare soul exposed. You look at me, and I see the beauty that is so fucking deep and pure that nothing impure could ever touch it, and yet I crave to. I crave to taste your mind, to know shit that I've never cared to know or discover about other women. I fuck them, and when I'm done, I'm done. I've never slept with the same woman more than once, but you, I crave you and can never get enough."

"Liar," she uttered as she tried to close her eyes against the honesty she saw shining in his eyes. "You don't have to lie to me; we both know I can't take any more pain."

"I'm not lying. You know that I cannot lie."

"I'm not pretty, not like the women you're used to. I'm fair, but I'm not beautiful," she uttered hoarsely and then winced as fire rushed through her, settling between her legs where her body clenched.

"You are wrong, Icelyn. You're fucking gorgeous. You may not look like High Fae, but who cares? Looks can be altered, and those who are vain are shallow and deserve pity if they think it is all they need. The most beautiful creatures are not those who shine from the outside. They shine from within, their minds are a thing of purity and beauty, and you are that. My wolf doesn't care about looks, it senses what is inside, and it wants you. So take the fucking compliment," he smirked, his eyes burning as her body flushed and even more arousal built in her soaking wet core.

"It's starting."

"I know," he said as he stared into her cloudy eyes. "Do you trust me?" he asked, watching as her eyes seemed to grow wide as a frown marred her lips. "I need you to relax, but I also need you to focus on what you feel instead of what I am doing. You're about to lose control, and I need you to be secured when it happens. Your body needs release, but it also needs to be fed, and what I plan to do will make you focus on what you feel, not anything else."

"How?" she asked, unsure she wanted the answer.

"I need to secure your hands above your head and take away your sight. You're straining your eyes already, and they need to rest to change. I'm going to put a blindfold on you, and then I'm going to play with your pretty pink cunt and give it what it needs. After you come, you will rest until the next wave hits. We will repeat it until it allows you to rest for longer periods of time. Then, I may untie you and let you fuck me."

"I won't be able to see, though."

"That's the point," he laughed as he lifted up and stared down at her sweat-covered body. "Ready? You have about…" She screamed as her body buckled, her spine arching as her head shook from the force of her need. "Less time than I thought," he muttered as he removed her clothes with a single thought and pushed his fingers through her wet cunt.

Icelyn groaned, her legs dropping open to give him access to the one spot that she needed him in. Fire blazed through her, an inferno that threatened to consume her from within. His fingers pushed into her pussy, and she trembled so hard that the entire bed shook from it. His other hand smoothed over her flesh, moving up to pinch a nipple as his head lowered.

His tongue drew a pattern over her clit, pushing hard and then flicking it until she was screaming her need to come. Her entire body was pain mixing with pleasure, and the moment his teeth scraped over her nub, she exploded in a mass of cursing and cries as tears slid down her cheeks. Once she was out of the throes of pleasure, she whispered to him.

"I'm not going to survive this, am I?"

"You're not going to die on me. You hear me? I won't allow it."

"This isn't normal, I am not normal, am I?"

"Waiting this long to change is unheard of, but that doesn't mean you won't make it through this, Icelyn. I'm right here with you. I'm the fire to your ice, and I'll do whatever it takes to see that you make it through this alive and whole."

"Has there ever been a lesser Fae who survived this?" she asked as they waited for the next wave to hit.

"We don't know, there wasn't time to search the records. I smelled your flesh, your body changing, from outside your room. I knew it was you and that it was coming quickly. It doesn't matter anyway, no two Fae Transition the same," he said as he sat on his knees and collected her hands.

She swallowed hard as he captured one hand and then the other, holding them in his large hand as he wrapped a cloth around them, and then rope as he secured them to the bed. She didn't back away or fight; instead, she followed his sinewy muscles as he moved, noting the dark patch of hair that ran from his belly button to the waist of his jeans.

Icelyn bristled as the hard, thick cock pushed against those jeans, straining to be freed from the prison which held it hidden within. Licking her lips, she stared up, finding him watching her. That sinful smirk covered his lips as she gave him a nervous smile.

He didn't give her time to think, he manufactured a silk blindfold from thin air and wrapped it around her head, forcing her eyes to rest. She opened her mouth to speak but his mouth brushed against hers, the slow, soft exploration sending a new need coursing through her.

Ice skimmed over one nipple, and she yelped. Just as fast as it had been there, his fiery touched replaced the cold and sent shivers of need racing up her spine. Her bent knees dropped open, showing him her needy flesh. If he took notice, she didn't know. Adjusting to the darkness and the sound of him moving took energy.

He lifted from the bed; his fingers trailed heat over her curves, as if he was learning each one, memorizing it. It was terrifying, to not be able to see his movements or to gauge what he would do next. Those fingertips, though; they danced on her flesh, sending goosebumps up her legs and down her body.

She sensed the ice seconds before it skimmed over her stomach. A small moan escaped before she worried her lip with her teeth. Breathing became difficult as his mouth brushed against the same trail the ice took, sending scorching heat after it. A trail of warmth was left everywhere he touched and seemed to uncoil something in her stomach. Icelyn gave up trying to hide the moaning that escaped as she let him hear how his actions affected her.

His other hand sent tendrils of heat through her slick flesh, pushing something cold and thick through the sheer magma of her flesh. The fire eased, but the pain didn't lessen. She was addicted to his attention, to his touch, the way his fire melted her ice. He was right, he was fire, and she was ice, and unlike other men, she'd never have to worry or be careful. He could withstand her cold, and she his flames.

His mouth kissed her stomach at the same moment the ice pushed into her body, sending her over the edge without warning. White light exploded behind her eyelids, and she screamed his name as her back arched, lifting from the bed as it ripped her apart. The only other noise in the soundproof room was his deep growl of ownership. The sound left no question as to who owned her orgasms.

He didn't stop; instead, his movements increased until she was lost to the passion, her mind an endless crest of dancing pleasure as he took her over the edge until she pleaded and begged for it to cease, to end the never-ending pleasure. The orgasms turned painful, but the ice within melted further as her body released her orgasm, melting the thing driving her over the edge. Once they began to abate, his flesh touched hers, poised at her entrance, ready to plunge into her welcoming heat.

Sinjinn waited, knowing her body would need more, even if her mind said no. She was wild in her heat, her flesh ready to be pounded, and yet he wanted her ready. He enjoyed her begging, and his name on her lips had his cock so hard he feared he'd lose it before he was ready. Those pretty red lips opened, and he leaned over, placing ice between his lips before he drew upon them with his. Her tongue escaped, seeking his but he only let her touch the ice and drip it over the heat he knew burned within her.

Tossing the ice, he claimed her cold lips, letting the heat from his Djinn replace it. Her tongue captured his hungrily, devouring it with a need that drove him crazy. That primal growl that escaped them both was erotic and addictive, as if she held her own inner beast who craved him as much as his craved her.

Pulling away from her lips, he kissed her scared shoulder, nipping at the bite which was his mark of ownership. His tongue traced the raised flesh, kissing and nipping it, knowing she felt it to her soul. He felt her there, her ice against his fire. Her drifting snow scent that was filled with winterberries, driving him crazy from the moment his eyes opened until he drank himself to sleep. He'd never felt his wolf prowling unless it knew it was closing in on the hunt, and he would be freed. Now, now he prowled, strutted and bided his time as he had waited for her to be his. Like it had sensed this coming and knew who would bring her over into his world.

Fucking Light Heir, right, as if he was handing her over to Adam. His teeth grew, and he pulled back, staring down at her mussed hair, splashing across the silk sheets as her head turned in his direction. Her full breasts were amazing, more than he could fit into his hand. Her pink nipples were hard, begging to be sucked and nipped. Once his teeth retracted, he bent his head, touching nothing until his tongue heated. Slowly, he traced a circle around the peaked flesh, listening to her response to the heat.

She didn't back away as most women had before, afraid to be burned. Hell, he himself had never used his heat in sex because mistakes happened in the heat of the moment. He moved to the other, glamouring ice to use on the one he'd just used his heated lips on. Her response was wild; the noises she made were sweet and hot as fuck.

He lifted, staring down at the pink flesh, and then as the heat of her body rose, he watched her twist in pain before he pushed into her tight pussy. He rolled his hips, awaiting her move to tell him when she was out of the pain and ready to dance flesh to flesh. He could smell her tears and wished to see the pain in her eyes, but she needed to rest them, to let them evolve. Her head thrashed as she spoke muffled words and he paused, lifting his head to watch her. His hands flew to the blindfold, pulling it off.

Sea-blue eyes framed in silver stared at him; her hair started to turn a darker blue as if it would fully become a hue of blue, but stalled to enhance the color of her white-blonde hair. There was a piece highlighting it blue in one thick tress that matched her eyes; eyes which stared up at him as if seeing him for the first time. He leaned in, kissing her lips as she growled and slowly started to writhe beneath him, demanding he give her what she craved.

Icelyn stared up into his tricolored eyes, taking in the delicate art of them. His hair was mixed shades of browns, and utter perfection. She lifted her hands to explore it, yet couldn't move them far enough. His mouth grazed hers, and she moaned, feeling his cock as he started moving to meet her hips movements.

"Faster."

"No." He watched her, the word slipping from his lips infuriating her, and then she ripped her hands from the rope he'd tied them in, turning them over until she was posed on top of him. Her hands grazed his flesh as she leaned over, kissing the top of his collarbone as she let her teeth and tongue nip and lap over the bone. The moment she reached his shoulder, she bit into the tissue and smiled as he growled from deep in his chest. The taste of copper filled her mouth, and she licked it, knowing she'd barely broken the skin, but it had been enough to draw blood to assure he understood what she had wanted him to.

Sinjinn rolled her over onto the bed, unwilling to wait another moment to teach her who the alpha was in their relationship. He held her legs apart, watching her lips which were covered in his blood, and he smiled coldly as he increased his speed, driving her to the edge before he pulled back, watching her struggle to reach it. Her hands moved, and he captured them in his, locking her wrist together, pushing them against her stomach.

"I don't think so, princess," he smirked as his words escaped huskily and thick, watching the glow brighten in her eyes until he felt it like a punch to the stomach. Icelyn was beautiful, even without her full Transition finished.

Sinjinn turned her over onto her stomach, grabbing her arms as her face dropped into the sheets. One hand held hers trapped against the sexy-as-fuck arch of her spine. The other spread her legs apart as he settled behind them. He pushed into her without mercy, enjoying the moan of absolute pleasure that expelled from her lungs as he filled her until her cunt gripped him in protest. He watched her bucking her hips, demanding he give her what she craved, but she was at his mercy, and he was going to relish every fucking moment of this.

He wouldn't fucking move. He'd denied her what she craved, her body ached for more, and it ached to be filled by him. She could feel her body trembling, her womb aching for what only he could give her. Yet he moved so slow, sending his cock so deep into her body that it quivered and touched her right where she needed him most, but too slow. She needed him to lose control, to let the monster inside of him off the leash to give her what she craved.

"Move," she pleaded.

"Who do you belong to, Icelyn?" he asked.

"Please?" she begged through the longing of need that whimpered her words into a plea.

"Who do you belong to?"

"You, I'm yours," she uttered breathlessly and then moaned as he moved faster, the sound of flesh meeting flesh filled the room, and she exploded.

Lights flickered behind her eyes as her orgasm tore through her without warning. Rainbows danced before her eyes as his own grunts followed, his body stiffening as he thrust a few last times and yet continued to move into the tightness of her body. He burned her from the inside, and yet her body kept it from being painful.

Once he'd freed her arms, she turned, staring up at him with a satisfied smile on her lips. It wasn't over, it was far from it. Yet her body ached, as if she'd ran up a hundred mountains and back down them hunting her prey. She watched him pull out and pull her body next to his.

"Sleep, Icelyn. You have less than an hour before you will need to feed again."

"I'm glad it's with you," she whispered to him. She was amazed at how sharp everything was now, how crisp and clear the world was. It was worse than she'd thought. High Fae saw everything better too, which meant they saw flaws better, and imperfection better.

How bad did she really look to him?

"What are you doing?" he asked when she started to pull away from his touch.

"I...I...I can't lie!" she cried as she placed her hand over her mouth and sat up, staring down at him.

"No, little princess, you can't lie anymore," he agreed with an amused grin.

"I'm a mess," she said as she hit the pillow with her head, hard.

"You're a beautiful mess, and I like messy people. They don't fuck around with trivial things. You bit me," he said after a moment had passed.

"It was only fair," she muttered as heat filled her cheeks.

"Go deeper next time, and we will add some salt to it. Then it will be fair," he chuckled as she rolled her eyes, watching him. "I'm glad it's me too. Because I'd have fought to have you, and I wouldn't be able to live with myself if I hurt my brothers."

"I'm not worth fighting for."

"You're wrong; you're worth killing for, Icelyn. That's what scares me the most."

CHAPTER
TWENTY-SEVEN

Icelyn wiggled her hips, rubbing against Sinjinn as she groaned. Every part of her body ached, and that hunger that never seemed to be filled growled as it gnawed on her stomach. Sinjinn moved, his body on autopilot as it had been for days now, waking only to feed her and be fed. Transitioning was brutal, all-consuming, and apparently, never-ending.

She pushed him over, letting her fingers trail over the ripples of muscle that lined his abdomen. Her eyes reflected in his, proving how strong her hunger was. Her other hand grabbed his cock, wrapping her small fingers around it before her mouth began kissing a trail across his belly, placing heated kisses as she made her way to the one thing her body craved.

"Icelyn," he warned in a thick, husky growl that only emboldened her more.

Her hand stroked his cock, enjoying the silken flesh that grew tight with need. Her mouth kissed and licked slow circles into his flesh, spreading ice over his heated flesh until her tongue found the sensitive underside of his cock and licked up and down it. His body tensed as a growl erupted from his lips.

Sinjinn lifted his head, watching her as she held his eyes. Heat pooled to her core, clenching with need as she took him into her throat, enjoying the heated growl that escaped before he could stop it. Her hand worked his cock, while her lips clamped over it, along with the tip of her tongue that tortured him until he started to sit up.

Icelyn pushed him down hard, her magic a palpable thing in the room they had nested in. She wasn't an idiot; they were hidden, and all they did was fuck, mate, and sleep in it. It had been days, and the entire room smelled of magic and sex with a hint of winter and embers. She rose up onto her knees, her body slowly positioning over his chest, and she pushed her hair away from her face as she kissed him, claiming his mouth hungrily. Icelyn straddled him, never breaking the slight contact she held.

Her own animalistic growl reverberated through her, disappearing with his kiss. Teeth nipped and pulled at his full swollen, bottom lip before she pushed her pussy against his thick cock.

"Do you want that?" she uttered hoarsely.

"Like I want the air filling my lungs to live," he answered thickly. His hands brushed down her sides, catching and holding her waist. He didn't move her; instead, he watched as she slowly pushed back, taking every inch he had to offer and then threw her head back as a scream of pleasure released from deep in her lungs.

She was fucking wild and beautiful. Her enticing

scent of winter mixed with his, and every time she found her release, he'd inhale it so deeply that he knew he would never forget it. Those breasts bounced as she lifted and dropped back down, riding him as if she'd been born to do just that. He filled every inch of her cunt, and yet she never complained that he was too big, or of being sore. She took, and she gave, and he was covered in her marks, her blunt teeth marking him as hers, and he fucking loved it.

Silver brands moved with delicate blue ones, marking her royal and that had made the coil in his stomach tighten with what it could mean. Not only was she not his, but she was also part of the prophecy to save Faery. He didn't want it to be true, but the moment those brands ignited and began to pulse, there was no denying it.

Her moans intensified as he flipped them, taking her over the edge with the precision of his hips, knowing right where that place was that he pounded against with his cock. Her eyes glowed silver and marine blue, which reflected the green in his eyes back at him. His name was whispered from her lips like a fucking benediction. Tears slipped from her eyes, as if she was feeling the same turmoil as he was. His own release followed hers, his power pushing against her as he fed her what little he could, and a vise tightened around his heart at the thought of being too drained to continue. The idea of having to bring in help left a sour taste in his mouth.

He rolled off her and rested his elbows against his knees as he placed his head in his hands. The soft sound of her even breathing told him she slept again. Sinjinn rose from the bed, staring down at the white flesh that was covered in red marks and bruises.

Sinjinn sat on the other side of the room, staring at the sleeping beauty that carried his mark. He'd imprinted on her, claiming her with a power that he hadn't understood until now. His wolf craved her, more than it craved to be let free to run and hunt. That was a fucking problem.

Adam, the kid wasn't even over his dead girlfriend and hardly knew his dick from his finger, and he was supposed to watch him walk away with Icelyn? Fuck that. She was his; it was as simple and complicated as that. She deserved a man who looked at her like she was his fucking moon, and he was the stars that lit up the sky to honor her. He loved the softness of her curves, and how she fit perfectly against the hardness of his muscles. How her tiny form fit cradled and protected by his much larger frame. He craved to savagely corrupt that softness with his touch, and yet he would be asked to walk away.

And he would, because no matter what he'd done, or the fact that he would always feel as if he was missing a piece of his soul, he'd taken an oath. He'd stood before Ryder and promised to do what was best for Faery, to help heal what they'd done under their father's hand. Sinjinn, along with everyone alive during Alazander's reign of terror, had vowed it.

"Sinjinn," her tiny voice whispered as he watched her. Her hand smoothed across the bed, searching for him, and yet he was frozen in place. For the first time in his entire life, he wanted something more than he had ever wanted anything else before.

Icelyn stretched, her hand finding only crumpled

sheets where he should have been. Her eyes opened with effort, and she searched the bed beside her, lifting to look through the dark room. Fear sliced through her and she sat up fully, rising from the bed as she peered around it, searching.

He sat in a chair studying her, his eyes filled with something that made her stomach coil and churn. She walked towards him with slow steps, slipping into his arms as he lifted them to pull her close.

"You're upset with me?" she asked.

"No, no, I'm upset with the world," he uttered as he inhaled and closed his eyes as he rested his head against her stomach. "You've finished," he supplied.

"Finished?" she questioned.

"Transition, you've finished needing to be fed."

"I don't want to be," she admitted softly as she pushed against him, crawling into his lap as he held her in the dark room filled with sex and magic. "Can't we just stay here a little longer and pretend I'm not?" she asked, surprising him.

"I don't think we should," he growled. "I need to go. I need to walk away from you, and you need to let me."

"Then don't, don't walk away from me, Sinjinn. In one year I will be free of the oath," she explained with an innocence he envied.

"I need you to get up," he ordered, pushing the coldness into the words and knowing he was about to leave her broken. "I've had enough of this."

"Enough of what?"

"Enough pretending that you're enough for me."

"What?" she asked, and his stomach tightened as nausea swirled inside of him. "What do you mean, I'm not enough?"

"I thought you'd be more, but you're not."

She backed up, scooting off his lap with a look of confusion marring her sharpened features. Fuck, she was beautiful. Too beautiful by far, with delicate features made sharper and even more beautiful with her High Fae features. Her ears, though, the slightly pointed tips had confused him, but then he'd chuckled. She had ancient blood running through her, from another time when fey land creatures had mated with the lesser Fae.

Fat tears filled her eyes as she glamoured on a gown, not bothering to wash her flesh or his scent from it. The wolf inside of him lifted its head, as if it too sensed what he was about to do and disapproved. He dressed without using glamour, drained from feeding her without taking so she consumed enough to survive the changes.

"I don't understand," she whispered through tears that choked out her words.

"You wouldn't," he shrugged. "Look, it's been fun, but I fucked you out of my system, little one. Don't get clingy; no one enjoys someone who doesn't understand a casual fuck."

His stomach tightened further until it ached, and those tears, those fucking tears that fell unchecked sent a knife twisting through his heart. He turned, intending to leave the room, but the atmosphere shifted, and ice crystals covered the door and walls. The air grew thick, burning his skin with the intensity of the coldness in the room. Sinjinn turned, finding her covered in ice particles, as if she'd become a living statue.

Thick lashes lifted, ice covering each and every one. Her skin matched her hair, blue from the frost that coated it. Those silver and blue eyes glowed as tears continued to fall, freezing in the arctic air that she was creating. He stepped back, watching as she stared through him. As if she was beyond hearing him, or seeing that he hadn't left.

It took everything he had inside to walk away, to open the door and leave his princess to her freezer that mirrored what she felt inside. He didn't stop when the others lifted their eyes, watching him and then gazing back at the room where snow had begun falling from the ceiling as if she'd brought the Winter Court storms with her.

"Sinjinn?" Ristan asked. His hand reached out for his brother, and Sinjinn slapped it away and continued forward.

"Stop." It wasn't a request, it was an order. Ryder's tone held command of the king, and he paused, turning to stare at the golden eyes that watched him carefully.

He didn't say anything, didn't move other than to stare back at his brother. The one man he'd trusted above all else. The one man he'd follow to death if asked to, and this was the one who stood between him and Icelyn.

Golden eyes dropped and gazed back at the door before he moved closer to Sinjinn, sniffing him. Those eyes changed from golden to black as the beast within his brother smelled the change in Sinjinn.

"She is finished," he said, and Sinjinn snorted at his astute observation.

"She's the Light Heir," he confirmed what he knew they'd waited for.

"And the ice coming from the room?" he asked.

"Her response to my rejection," he growled. "Can

I go? Or do you want to know how tight her pussy is too?"

"Careful," he snapped as his eyes took in what he tried to hide.

"Or what? You'll end me? Ask me if I care right now?" he seethed, and Ryder's eyes narrowed, flinching as he stepped back.

"Go, we will handle it from here."

CHAPTER
TWENTY-EIGHT

Icelyn was placed into the bed, and a fire was built. It didn't matter. She felt as cold as the air around her, numb as his words replayed in her mind. She could hear the others speaking, hear them as they spoke about Sinjinn's departure from this realm. He'd left after her Transition had ended, and not even Ryder's orders had brought him back.

Day turned to night, and nights turned into a week as she lay on the bed, unmoving. There were no needs to be met, not one other than the hunger which often made itself known, which she did her best to ignore.

"She isn't getting better," Synthia said as the worry in her tone grated against Icelyn's nerves.

Why they lingered or cared, she didn't know. She just wished the world would forget about her, move on without her presence in it. There was a deep hollowness in her chest that ached, as if he'd reached in and ripped her heart out with his words. She couldn't stop the storm that raged around her and knew the Fae worried about the snow that now drifted outside, a part of her emotions attaching to the land around her. As surely as the king's storm raged, Icelyn's own version of it stormed here.

"There's three feet of fucking snow outside. The arctic winds have played hell on preparation for war, and no one can find him. This needs to end now."

"It won't," Synthia said as she stared at Icelyn. "She's the center of it; whatever happened in that room, it took something from her. This is her reaction to that pain. It's also why you don't meddle in other people's love lives. You get this when you do."

"How was I supposed to know this shit would happen? It's supposed to be simple, they take them, breed with them, and afterwards, it ends. How fucking hard is that?" Ryder demanded.

"You're taking broken females who have been through hell at the hands of your monstrous father and expecting them to just be fine with it. Your brothers are still damaged from what they were forced to do, and it is a mess. Not to mention, that now we have to bring her to Adam, who is missing, mind you, and tell him he may have to marry her and breed the children you thought he and I would make, to save Faery. While there may be another heir out there, she's the one currently wearing the brands, which is another mess. All of that and you still have to figure out how to void the oath and murder the man who raised her. I warned you that this wasn't something to be done yet, and you did what you had to do as king. I get it, you have to hold the balance together, but we need to find another way. If they come at us and try to attack as we defend this world, we will handle it."

"Who is Adam?" Icelyn asked, and the room went silent. "What do you mean by I'm supposed to be his?" She'd heard it mentioned too many times in reference to her, and she was done hearing it.

"It means you have a destiny," she explained. "You're tied to the land, as is he."

Icelyn snorted, pulling the covers over her head to block out the world. She had no idea who Adam was, other than he wasn't who hurt her. Rejection was a cold bedfellow. It left her more than frozen; it left her exposed, open to the pain she'd once endured as her father spewed hatred at her. Now, now it was all she could hear echoing through her. The pain, the uncertainty of not knowing what was to become of her, and she couldn't dig herself out of the darkness.

"Icelyn, you cannot just lie down and die. It doesn't work like that," Synthia groaned.

"Watch me," she said as sleep overtook her, and oblivion settled in.

There were hours of restless dreams where she was a child, rushing through her land to escape the assassins and guards her father had sent after her. But unlike the dreams where she escaped, a green-eyed wolf caught her, devouring her.

No matter how many times in the night she woke up or tried to ignore the dreams, it always ended with his teeth buried in her throat. His words reverberated through her as she drew in her last breath, right as she awoke, drenched in sweat and need.

Drenched from the nightmares, she rose from the bed, moving towards the fireplace of the new room they'd placed her into. Her fingers skimmed the cast-iron top, listening as her flesh sizzled. The smell of it was obnoxious and the fact that it healed before she'd pulled it up to look at it both bothered and amused her.

Her entire hand pressed against it and she screamed as it melted flesh to the iron and shocked her. The door was thrown open, and men came rushing in, staring at her as she held her hand up to her chest, protectively.

"Gods damn, what the hell is that smell?" Zahruk asked, and then his eyes flashed as he looked from the stove to her hand. "Slow death by fire wouldn't be a good choice, now would it?" he asked as he moved deeper into the room.

Icelyn frowned as she lowered her eyes to the floor, filling the room with ice as her emotions flowed through her. Her eyes lifted to hold his, glowing with unfed hunger that she watched shining back at her as his lit up.

"You want to go, sweet thing, we can go toe-to-toe, but I don't think that is what you're looking for here," he purred as he closed the distance between them. His finger trailed down her cheek, and a devilish grin lifted his lips. "You are a sweet thing, princess," he uttered thickly as his other hand flicked a blade open.

Icelyn stiffened but didn't back away as he trailed the blade to her cheek, watching her as it pressed against her flesh. He moved it lower, cutting through the shirt she wore. She could feel her heart thundering in her chest and knew he could hear it as well. He bared her shoulder with a flick of the blade and hissed as he took in the damaged flesh.

"He mated with you too fucking deeply," he growled as his fingers traced over the raised flesh. "You feel him, here," he said as he pushed against the mark. "Don't you?"

"Zahruk," Ryder's deep voice held a warning.

"He mated her, which means he feels her. He feels everything she does, and worse, he's fighting it and so is she. You want him back? I can do that," he shrugged.

"How?" Ryder asked.

"I cover his mark with mine, and make him feel everything I do to her. His wolf won't give him any other option but to protect its mate. He'll come back to her, even if he doesn't want to."

"You're wrong," she hissed sharply. "He doesn't want me."

"I'm not wrong," Zahruk returned with those sinful blue eyes watching every move she made. He carried his lethality like a second skin. His power exuded into the air, slithering over her flesh as it tried to beckon her closer, seducing her senses with a mere look that promised carnal pleasure. This man was made to kill, and he did it well. His lips curved into a wolfish grin, promising to rip her apart and then, piece by piece, slowly put her back together. "It's in his genetic makeup to crave you, to want you. His wolf claimed you, and they mate but once in a lifetime. I know, because right now mine wants to cover his mark and show you the difference between them. We may look like other men, but I assure you, sweet girl, there's not an ounce of mercy inside of us. He claimed, and he conquered you. I can smell his wolf on your flesh, and so can the one within me, and he's clawing to show you which of us is the alpha."

"Are you trying to scare me, or piss on my leg?" she asked, and his eyes widened before a beautiful smile played across his sexy-as-sin lips.

"I'd piss on that leg if I thought it would bring him running back, but it will take more than that. I have to make his wolf feel it, and with everything happening, I need my brother here. So what you're going to do is get on that bed and let me awaken his wolf."

"No," she argued as she crossed her arms over her chest and glared at him in challenge.

"Did you just say no?" he asked, as if he couldn't believe she would argue it.

"Read my lips, no. Was that clear enough for you?" Laughing sounded behind them, and he looked over his shoulder, glaring as Synthia smirked.

She lifted her brow as those dark blue eyes swung back towards hers and he shook his head, and then power ignited in the room. Sinjinn's power was palpable, but Zahruk's was ten times that. Her body grew heavy as he watched her, tilting his dark blonde hair to stare into her eyes with unflinching desire. He knew what he was doing; the air no longer carried the chill of winter, and instead, it was heated to an uncomfortable level. Her breasts felt heavy as her spine arched, no matter that she didn't want to want him, he was old, powerful, and he was using every advantage he had on her.

She moaned loudly, uncaring that they had an audience, or that she didn't want him. Icelyn moaned as his thumb trailed over his lips, and that pesky mark on her shoulder throbbed. He pulled her closer, nipping her shoulder as his lips trailed over the mark. Heat grazed her neck and then his mouth was brushing against hers, tasting the sweetness of it. He walked her towards the bed, pushing her onto it.

Icelyn watched him, her body on fire with a need that pissed her off. No matter what her mind screamed, her body ignored. He knelt beside her, leaning over to lick her collarbone, sending a growl of arousal pulsing through her that ignited a fire in her center. His hand cupped her cheek, turning her mouth towards his.

Once he had her where he wanted to, his mouth crushed against hers. His mouth consumed, destroying any fight her mind held the moment his tongue found hers and dueled against it, proving he was one hundred percent male. He leaned against her, pushing his thumb against her shoulder, marring the mark as he fucking destroyed her mouth. He didn't claim, he took ownership by right. The moan that exploded was felt through her entire body, clenching her legs together as it prepared for him. As if his tongue had gone through her, sending her legs a demand to open for his touch, but the moment his hand lowered, he disappeared, and crashing noises ripped through the room.

Icelyn shook her head, clearing the fog as she stared up at the ceiling, unsure where he'd gone; she sat up, turning towards the noise. Sinjinn was enraged, his hair was disheveled, and he wore no shirt. She exhaled, pushing the last of whatever Zahruk had done to her away, and moved to the side of the bed, stumbling towards them. One glance at the others told her that they had no intention of breaking the fight up.

She moved between them, uncaring that they were posturing as they both growled at each other. The moment she was between them, she punched Zahruk without warning, her fist stinging as he snapped his head back at her in surprise. Sinjinn snorted, and she spun towards him, slamming her knee into his groin fast and hard before she stepped back to watch him fall to his knees as he held his offended appendage.

"Fuck you both!"

"I see why you like her," Zahruk said as he righted his nose with a wicked grin marring his lips that were covered in blood. "But you fucked up, brother. You mated her, and that can't be undone. I get it, I get the fucking pain, but pushing her away isn't going to make it stop. I can't train men in the fucking snow while they're slipping on ice, so handle it. You get me?"

"I did handle it," he snapped.

"Like hell you did! You fucking left, you don't get to leave us. One fucking unit, Sinjinn. Us against the world, remember? We're in the last hour here, and you're my brother. So if getting her a little wet got you home, so what?"

"Don't do it again," he snarled.

"She isn't yours," Zahruk said as he swiped away the blood from his lip with his thumb. "She's got a purpose that benefits this world that's greater than you and me both. If Ryder could leave Synthia with Adam to marry him, then you can too."

"About Adam," Synthia groaned. "He's gone missing with Kendra's corpse. He hasn't been seen since."

"Then call him back, or have the Dark King call him back. He's got a responsibility to this world. He has to sire a child with the Light Heir," Ryder snapped.

"Good luck telling him that," she said as she glared at him.

"What the hell could he possibly want with a fucking

corpse?"

"He wanted a vessel, do the math, Fairy."

"That isn't good," he groaned as he turned, staring at the three who all glared at each other. "Neither is this. This shit is a mess."

"Maybe we should slowly leave the room? Think they would notice?"

"That you assholes just started a fight and are trying to sneak away?" Ristan said from the doorway, his silver eyes alight with laughter.

"Demon, not the time," Synthia said.

"Flower, when is it ever the right time?" he chuckled.

"Get out," Sinjinn snarled as he watched Icelyn moving towards the bed.

"But I just ordered popcorn," Ristan groaned. "I wanted to watch the smackdown play out."

"Icelyn," he started.

"You can leave too," she stated as she crawled into the bed, uncaring that her clothes were ripped. The air turned brittle, filling with ice as she pushed them out by force. She didn't care if he was back, or if he hurt, because the things he'd said had cut deep and were still fresh.

CHAPTER
TWENTY-NINE

Sinjinn paced outside her door, knowing she was an emotional mess because of what he'd done. He'd been out hunting, releasing the wolf to slaughter anything he'd caught a whiff of as they'd prowled through the mountains. He'd done the only thing he could to stop it from seeking her out. His wolf craved her, demanding they return until he'd offered him the only other choice: Hunt for the kill, releasing the beast within to be free of the flesh that held him.

It had worked for a while, right up until Zahruk had licked his fucking mark. He'd known the trick; his own wolf had issued a challenge to his. He'd known that it would alert the wolf to his mate being pleasured by another. He'd felt her loss of mind, her will slowly slipping away, and everything inside of him snapped. Sinjinn knew exactly who she was with, and how much she craved what was happening.

She'd wanted him, not with her mind, but he'd removed the issue, and her body had flooded with arousal. She wasn't even hours out of Transition, and he'd abandoned her. Selfish prick that he was, he'd walked out, making sure she hated him. Making sure she knew he found her utterly lacking, which wasn't even close to the truth.

He'd forced himself to walk away when all he'd wanted to do was curl her sexy little body against his and forget the world. He craved her scent. The wildness of her eyes as she'd awoken with that insatiable hunger igniting in their bluish-silver colored depths. The wicked smile she'd give him as she'd begun to touch him, exploring him as if he was a treasure she'd searched for endlessly and had finally discovered. Sinjinn stared at the door, sensing his brother's easy approach as he tried to mentally make himself walk away again.

"She's hungry," Zahruk pointed out as he folded his arms across his chest, thumbs pointed towards the ceiling in the hall with confidence as he stared Sinjinn down.

"So she is."

"You going to assist, or do you want me to handle it?" he asked with a sneer on his lips and glowing sapphire eyes that Sinjinn wanted to gauge out of their sockets.

Sinjinn rolled his neck as the bones cracked under the pressure. His teeth elongated as the wolf paced, prowling just beneath the surface. He shook it off, turning his head to take in his older brother. Zahruk wasn't pretty, far fucking from it. He had sapphire eyes with a thin black line around them. Unlike the rest of them, no one had any idea who Zahruk's mother was; only that Alazander had brought him home, claiming him. They sensed him, which alerted them to the parentage of his father, but nothing was known about his mother. Nor was the wolf the only shape Zahruk took. While the rest could easily change to wolf form, Zahruk could become any animal he wanted to.

"Fuck you, Zahruk," he snapped.

"I'm about to go in there and fuck her," he returned sharply. "Don't worry; I'll make sure she screams loud enough that you can hear it as I wreck that pretty flesh of hers. I bet she fucking comes undone before my cock even enters it. Care to wager?"

"She's beyond us," Sinjinn warned.

"How you figure?"

"She's the Light Heir, created to save Faery."

"So? She's hungry, and I don't see Adam rushing in to claim her. Cailean hasn't reported back, and right now, this fucking moment, she's hungry. You're here, and they're not. She doesn't know what the fuck is happening and she's alone. You marked her, Sinjinn. Pony the fuck up and ride her, or I will. There's too much riding on her surviving, and letting her starve to death because you're afraid of getting attached, that's bullshit, and you know it. You're already attached; the moment your beast smelled her and marked her, it was a done fucking deal. Cailean left to give you a chance with her. Do not fucking waste it."

"He left because you sent him away."

"Are you that fucking gone that you can't see shit clearly? He asked to go, to be sent to another court to retrieve your bride so that you could have time with her before he was called to follow through on the oath. He doesn't want her, not like that. He wants to honor his word, same fucking thing we all want. Ryder told you to stay away, yes, but he also told you which room she was in, and why the fuck do you think he did that?"

"To torture me," he groaned as he rubbed his hand down his face, covering his mouth as he exhaled the torturous scent of her needy flesh that drifted to him even thru the closed doorway. "I can't control it with her, like I'm losing my fucking mind. I crave her, Zahruk."

"Because you mated your beast to her," he said with a loud snort as he dropped his arms and stared at him. "Your wolf mates only once in a lifetime, and it chose her for whatever reason, but it chose. There's no easy fix. No off switch is going to fix this shit. You can't fuck this one out of your system, because she is your fucking system now."

"And if the child of Dresden and Tatiana never returns, she will wed the Dark Prince and become his wife. And I'll get to stand there and watch it happen, so you tell me, what the fuck am I supposed to do about it when the only thing I want to do is grab her and run as far as I can from him?"

"And that's the real fucking pickle, isn't it?"

"Adam doesn't want her, Cailean doesn't want her, and she's bound to both in ways she doesn't understand. I'm the only one who wants her and I can't have her."

"Cailean is an easy fix, and you know it. The oath states she is to marry him, birth a child, and then after the year is up, it's over. If we can't find the other Light Heir, that could be an issue. But we've got everyone on that shit, you know that. We've sent runners out in search of their daughter, but she's somehow managing to remain under the radar."

A moan sounded from inside the room and both men paused, turning to stare at the door. Zahruk shivered as power pulled to him, wafting through the air in the passageway as his monster within growled with hunger.

"She's mine," Sinjinn snapped as he started forward.

"I know, but my beast within really wants to lap at that sweet pussy after tasting her lips. If you need help, I'll be training the men."

"I don't need your help to fuck her," he snarled.

"Pity, she smells delicious."

CHAPTER THIRTY

The bathwater was growing cold, and yet she refused to leave the sudsy paradise of the tub. Her hands traveled over her stomach, slipping between her legs as she imagined his hand there instead. Her breasts ached; the burning hunger that rolled through her was endless, as if she was still locked inside that room with that heartless prick.

The door opened and then slammed as she stood, twisting to see who had entered. Their eyes locked, and she opened her mouth to speak and then closed it. She sat back down, turning away from him as the temperature dropped inside the room.

"Get out," she ordered.

His only reply was a growl as he walked over and sat in the one chair the room bespoke of. His eyes dropped to the suds that barely offered her a shred of coverage. The heat pooling in his green eyes did not help the hunger which chose that moment to release a loud growling noise. She hugged her legs up to her chest and glared at him over her knees.

"I said get out," she tried again.

"I heard you, I just chose to ignore it," he shrugged as he leaned over to rest his elbows on his knees as he stared at her intently. "You need to be fed, Icelyn."

"I'm aware, but you can send anyone else besides you to handle that."

"I don't think so," he growled hoarsely.

"I don't remember it being your choice anymore," she fumed as she stood up and turned, letting him see her heart-shaped backside as she headed for the towel she'd set beside her. "Send in someone else," she repeated, and then paused as his breath fanned against her neck.

"I said no, and I meant it," he warned as he kissed her shoulder, sending a wave of heat against her flesh.

A shiver raced up her spine as her body heated, igniting as if his lips were the flame and she was the wax that heated and pooled in the aftermath. She stepped away, glamouring on a soft, silver nightgown that showed the heavy tips of her breasts as she slowly backed up.

"You don't want me, remember? You rejected me."

"I'm aware of what I did," he countered with a wicked smile on his wicked mouth, his tongue jutted out to wet his lips as the glow pulsed in his hypnotic depths.

"Then why are you here? Why not send someone else to take care of my needs? Where is Cailean? Isn't he the one who should be here with me?"

"I'm here," he said, and his eyes moved to the mark on her shoulder, *his* fucking mark.

Everything inside of him screamed *mine* as if it was

a record skipping, repeating it inside of him until the wolf preened, gloating with that mark he'd left on her as his proof. He'd fucking bit her, and she was his. To the animal within, it was as simple as that. He didn't care about the complications, or understand that the land they called home was in peril. The only thing it cared about was that she was his. It was as fucking simple as that.

"I don't think you understand how much I loathe you right now."

"I don't think I care," he smirked. "I get it, I was an asshole. I said shit I didn't mean, and forced myself to believe it enough to get it to roll off my tongue."

"Don't get clingy, Sinjinn. No one likes clingy."

He smiled, and she had to force her face to remain uninterested as it softened his features, making him appear almost boyish. She shook her head, dismissing him as she moved to the bed and crawled back into it, uncaring that it seemed to be a retreat, but then that was precisely what it was.

"Are you hiding?" he asked as the bed moved, telling her he'd joined her on it.

"I'm pretending you don't exist," she muttered as the blanket was lifted and he crawled beneath it to stare are her.

The glow from their eyes lit the darkness, and the fact that he was close enough to kiss her only made her senses heighten with need. He pulled her closer, touching his lips against her shoulder as she pushed against him.

"I don't want to need you," she uttered thickly as tears choked her words.

"I need you," he replied huskily. "I'm sorry I was an asshole. I'm sorry, Icelyn."

"That's not enough," she whispered as she turned away from him, hiding the tears that flowed from her eyes, wetting the pillow beneath them.

Sinjinn smelled the tears, knowing she was hurt deeper than he had wanted her to be. It wasn't something he could wish away, or undo. He'd wanted her to hate him because if she had, walking away would have been so much easier, or so he'd thought. But he felt it, her inner turmoil and the need warring with her emotions.

The bond held nothing back. He felt everything she did and more. He knew her hunger was reaching a dangerous level, meaning he'd smelled her sex and assumed she'd finished Transition, but she hadn't been fully out of it. Had she been, she'd still be sated from how many times he'd taken her. Hell, he'd felt like the one starving for her flesh.

"You can always use me," he said softly, his fingers slowly traveling down to rest on her hip. "I can wait you out, because there is me, and then there's Zahruk. So unless you want me to go get him…"

"Just shut up," she growled as she turned around, glaring over her shoulder at him. "I don't want to feed."

"Didn't ask if you did, and neither did your body. It's not finished, or you'd be sated. Gods know I fed you plenty of times, so this hunger tells me there is more needed. Zahruk smelled it on you as well. So I'll be here until you need me, and you can use me."

Icelyn turned the rest of the way over, continuing to glare at him. She hated the hunger pangs that gnawed at her, but she didn't want to cave and give in to him. He'd hurt her, deeply. His words had been made and chosen to inflict pain, and she was worth more than that. She had more pride than that.

He leaned in closer, kissing her shoulder where his teeth had left a scar, one that hadn't disappeared as her body changed. As if that mark was deeper than she could understand. The moment his lips touched it, everything inside of her shot into overdrive. Her entire focus was him, to take what she needed and return it to him tenfold.

His lips trailed over her neck and a throaty growl resonated from deep in her chest. Those devilish lips skimmed her jawline, slowly kissing his way over it. The man knew his way around the female body. Hands touched, drifting fingers over the curve of her hips as he continued kissing her jaw and her eyelids with those feather-soft kisses that sent her heart thundering into a dangerous tempo.

Sinjinn touched, kissed, learned every inch of his mate as she mewled and moaned softly, unwillingly participant in her own seduction. His fingers slipped up, pushing through the silk strands of her hair. He pulled her closer as her mouth opened to protest. He didn't allow it, closing his lips over hers as his tongue searched and dueled against hers. The sound that ripped from his throat was anything but human. It was animalistic, the need that ripped through his abdomen that painful, as if the wolf was trying to force the change.

He broke away from her and pushed her against the bed, staring down into her beautiful eyes that tightened the need burning in his cock. Those fucking tears, the tears she cried because of him, he slowly kissed away as he glamoured her clothing from her utterly perfect body. It was covered in scars, a mix of her blood that had retained them through Transitioning. It was fucking perfect to him. His lips sucked against the vein that pounded wildly, perfectly in tune with his.

Icelyn was lost in the passion his lips kept her prisoner with. Her body heated, burning for what only he could give her. Their breath misted against the ice-laden air, her emotions forming it as his heat kept her warm. His clothes disappeared, and she felt him there, pushing her legs apart with his knees as he continually kissed her, drinking her in like a man with an unquenchable thirst.

"Sinjinn," she whispered huskily.

"Icelyn," he murmured.

"Don't get clingy."

He stared down at her, his eyes burning. "Too late, princess," he warned, his thick cock pushing into her body as he fed her inch after inch until, painfully, he was buried deep in her pussy. There was no time to adjust to his width; instead, he fucked her like he was starving, a man possessed.

Her legs wrapped around his back, tipping her ass up to give him further depths as he touched every nerve ending, shooting her over the stars with ease. He licked her shoulder over and over, kissing it until his teeth skimmed it as he emptied his cock deep into her body. She exhaled, sated, but just when she thought he was finished, he lifted his eyes with black consuming the green irises and growled thickly down at her.

"Mine," he said as he watched her, already moving his hips as he gazed at her with possession burning in those inky depths. "Mate."

"Sinjinn," she whispered, but that wasn't him watching her, it was something older, something inhuman that was claiming ownership. Teeth extended as she watched, unwilling to close her eyes as the man became beast. His hair thickened and his cock grew painfully larger, forcing a scream from deep inside her, as if he was locking them together in a way that was primal, *more* somehow.

She lifted her throat, baring it to the wolf who watched her. His teeth skimmed it, sending a ripple of fear racing through her, but instead of ripping it out, he licked it, trailing his tongue over her flesh until he found his mark there. Teeth pushed through her flesh as a scream bubbled up, but it wasn't painful. It was white-hot pleasure that shot through her entire body without warning, and then he let loose.

His body pounded into hers without mercy, as if he couldn't fuck her hard enough. His teeth released and he turned her, pushing her leg up to prevent their bodies from detaching. He thrust into her, and she whimpered as he fucked her deeper, harder, until all she could do was let him. Icelyn felt complete for the first time in her entire life; with this beast fucking her core like she was his, she felt whole, and it terrified her.

The moment he found his release, she hissed as her body cooled his come as it poured into her like molten lava. As if they were meant to be together, his fire to her ice, the unending coupling that continued until both were nothing more than a mess of limbs and sweat in the crumpled sheets on the bed.

CHAPTER THIRTY-ONE

*He stared at her, his beast a never-*ending wealth of pride and snarling animal that boasted about her being theirs now. He'd asked him over and over what he'd done, and yet it just growled and watched the sleeping woman, as if he knew why she wouldn't wake. It was hours since the sun had risen in Faery. The birds chirped as they sang of spring. No longer did grey clouds fill the skies, sending hail and sleet down to cover the land.

For what felt like the thousandth time, he tried to question the animal within with what he'd done to her without result. He had tasted her blood, found his cock thick and pounding into her flesh as he'd come back from being forced to ride passenger in his own body. That had never happened before without him allowing it to. Yet this time he'd been forced into blackness, a void of emptiness where he could hear, but couldn't see.

He'd felt her tight cunt pulsing against his cock, a cock that had been larger and harder than ever before.

He'd heard her sweet whimpers of pain as his body pounded against hers until it sucked his cock dry over and over, orgasm after orgasm. Right as he'd started to come back from the void, he was slammed back, and the beast who fucked her started again.

Sinjinn sniffed the air again, uncertain what had changed in her scent, but knew something had. While his own scent was mixed with her winterberry and musk, there was something else that he couldn't place. Something that was wrong and yet sweet.

A knock sounded at the door, and he turned his head, glamouring clothing onto her naked form before a pair of old sweatpants covered him. He moved to the door, opening it just a crack to stare into Zahruk's blue depths of curiosity. Zahruk sniffed the air, his eyes going over Sinjinn's shoulder to where Icelyn slept, crumpled on the bed.

"Tell me you didn't let him out to play," Zahruk demanded.

"I couldn't stop him," Sinjinn admitted as he ran his fingers through his wild hair. "It was like being in the hunt, he took control, and I had no idea what the hell he did to her. She won't wake up, but she's breathing still. I'm guessing that's a good sign."

"He wouldn't have hurt her," Zahruk said as he closed his eyes, inhaling her scent deeply. "Do you know why we don't speak of the beast we hold?"

"Because it chose us?" he asked, stepping aside as Zahruk pushed his way through.

"Because it's a primal beast with only a few needs," he said as he sat beside her, pushing her ice-blonde hair away from her face. "Feed, fuck, and mate," he continued.

"Sounds about right, so why the fuck you frowning," he asked carefully, watching as Zahruk lifted her satin nightgown and skimmed his fingers over the hollowness of her belly.

"She smells different, does she not?" he asked, lifting a brow as he whistled through his teeth.

"So what?" he scoffed, uncertain he liked his brother touching his woman. The wolf in him definitely didn't like it. He'd stilled, watching him with a predatory gaze as if, at any moment, he'd explode into fur and attack Zahruk outright.

"You were stuck in her flesh, weren't you," he spoke softly, as if he was thinking out loud. "Your cock was constricted in her pussy, resulting in you being unable to leave it, right?"

"The fuck you care about that?"

"Because *he* fucked *her*," he hissed. "He fucking knocked her up. You knocked up the Light Heir, Sinjinn. Congratulations, asshole, you're going to be a dad!"

"No," he said, shaking his head as his heart pounded painfully in his chest. "No way, asshole," he said in confusion, and then noted the smugness of the wolf inside of him. "Gods, this isn't happening."

"It is, and we're fucked," Zahruk snapped as he stood, righting her nightie as he pushed his fingers through his dirty blonde hair and then looked at the ceiling, as if it held answers.

"I knocked up Cailean's future wife."

"Excuse me?" Ryder growled from the doorway. "I don't think I fucking caught that right."

"Oh, you did. He knocked up Cailean's soon-to-be

bride," Synthia said beside him. She slapped him on the shoulder and chuckled. "You're going to be an uncle, congratulations. So, this is bad. I mean, how worse can it be than telling Adam, who is downstairs by the way, that the woman we called him back here to claim is now pregnant and not only that, she's mated. But oh, hey, we found her, so I mean, there's that at least."

Sinjinn stared at Ryder, his pride and duty clashing into a chaotic mixed up mess that made him want to throw up. He'd never betrayed his brother before, and now he'd fucked Faery. He needed to get out of here, to get fresh air before he lost his ever-loving shit all over the floor.

"Don't you even fucking think about it," Ryder snarled, his golden eyes sparkling with fire as he watched the panic rush through his brother. "She's going to need you around after she marries one of the males downstairs."

"I don't deserve her, or you. I betrayed your trust."

"Your wolf did this, not you. You have never let me down, and you've always chosen to stand beside me no matter what. This isn't you, brother."

"It's the same fucking thing! I lost control of it, and if I'm being honest, I wanted to. I fucked up."

"You did, but there's someone else involved in this mess now. Someone you chose to create, and he or she will need you."

"She hates me, how do you think she's going to respond when I tell her my wolf fucked her until she was pregnant?" he shouted as he yanked on his hair in frustration.

"Why don't you ask her, she's awake," he said.

Sinjinn's eyes swung to hers, finding them full of fear and unshed tears. She sat up with accusation in her eyes, her mouth moved, and yet no words escaped as she stared at him.

"You son of a bitch," she uttered hoarsely, her voice scratching from the endless screaming she'd done all night as he'd taken her from behind. "I'm pregnant?"

"We don't know that," he said as Zahruk spoke at the same time.

"Definitely pregnant," he said.

"I can smell it on her," Ryder announced as he sniffed the air.

Icelyn lifted her arm, smelling, and then looked around the room as everyone agreed. Her heartbeat increased as she put it together. "I'm going to need that wolf to come back now."

"Why the fuck would you want that?" Sinjinn snapped as he stared at her in uncertainty.

"So I can break his fucking neck!"

A growl sounded from Sinjinn and Icelyn narrowed her eyes on him. She felt sick to her stomach, her mind and body unable to process anything other than the throbbing ache between her legs. She'd felt him stuck inside of her, rutting like a crazed beast, and she'd gone with it, oblivious to the one fact that she'd stared it right in the eye. He'd been Sinjinn's beast, and he'd done this on purpose.

CHAPTER THIRTY-TWO

Pregnant! Jcelyn stared around the room full of people who looked at the wall, or the floor, anywhere but at her as she glared at Sinjinn. Why the hell were they in her room anyway? Had it been nominated as the meeting room without her being warned? She couldn't be pregnant, she just couldn't be! There were entirely too many things wrong with being pregnant this quickly. They were sniffing her, as if by scent they could detect something as life-altering as pregnancy.

"Stop it!" she hissed as Sinjinn inhaled, his nostrils flaring as that growl started deep in his chest. His earth-altering green eyes lifted, holding hers with something akin to dismay. "I'm not pregnant."

"You're pregnant," he argued as he scratched his head and sat beside her. "Look, I'm not sure how or why he did it, but he did it."

"Well then undo it! You understand that oath is ironclad, right? If I am pregnant, it doesn't just void it out. And you can't know that I am pregnant! No one can tell this soon, and definitely not by scent alone."

"Um," Synthia interrupted; her violet eyes staring at Icelyn's middle sent a chill racing down her spine. "How common are twins in lesser Fae?" she asked the room in general.

"In lesser Fae, I'm uncertain of that. You know how rare it is for them to be born to High Fae; I'd assume the lesser Fae were suffering a similar issue." Ryder turned his golden eyes on his wife, staring at her as she exhaled. "Why?" he asked.

"Because Icelyn has three heartbeats," she shrugged.

"What?" asking hastily, he exploded up from the bed to pace beside it. "That's not possible."

"You're Fae, she's Fae, and pregnancy is accelerated by breed. What isn't possible? I mean, your wolf claimed her and obviously decided to plant a litter in her womb while he was at it," Syn chuckled as she took in his distraught face. His mouth opened and closed as she snickered and watched him.

"I'm not pregnant," Icelyn growled as she stared at Sinjinn. "Whatever you did, undo it. I can't be with you, or my father wins and this ends violently. I assure you, he will want my life for breaking the oath. He has wanted me dead since I became the heir, chosen over his children."

"He can't call in the oath if you still marry Cailean," Ryder admitted.

"The fuck? She's carrying my child, Ryder. You want her to still marry him?" Sinjinn snapped harshly, his anger palpable in the confines of the room.

"Unless we can find another way to be released from the oath," he nodded. "We have no idea where the Winter Court is within their borders. Until he is removed as king, his oath will stand. As it also came with a timeframe of his choosing, she will marry Cailean to avoid either of our sides being held accountable for breaking the oath."

Icelyn sat there, frozen as she listened to Ryder speaking. A *baby*? *No*, babies. *Plural.* Her heartbeat was thumping so loudly it sounded like war drums pounding in her ears. Weeks ago she'd made a plan, and it had been a great plan. She'd planned to send a message to the Horde fast and hard. It should have been simple, and yet here she was in their castle, far away from her home. If what they said was true, she was about to marry Cailean while carrying the babies of Sinjinn.

"Am I pregnant with puppies?" she blurted as tears built in her eyes, burning them as they threatened to fall.

"No," Sinjinn laughed, but it was hollow. Green eyes the color of leaves in the early spring months stared down at her. "They'll be normal, Icelyn."

"Fire and ice, and nothing nice," Erie snickered from the door as her eyes seemed to cloud as if she saw something no one else could. "I'm leaving, he comes. Congrats on those babies, though, they're going to fuck some shit up when they get older."

"Who comes?" Icelyn asked.

"Callaghan; he is relentless. That Templar needs to find his God again, because I tire of being hunted. And if he had his way, we'd be having puppies together, you and I. I'd make a horrible mother, but you…you'll be great. Maybe after I blow him up, we can do some girl time, yeah?"

"Um, okay?" Icelyn replied, uncertain the fiery

redhead was sane.

"It's a date, in a non-sexual I'm-not-going-to-lick-your-face sorta way."

"Erie, be careful," Synthia warned. "They are running out of time. He won't be able to prevent the others from hunting you any longer. You've reached the ten-month mark for the extinction of two races. They will be working together to capture you."

"They'll try," she nodded. There was sadness in Erie that settled in her eyes, something she couldn't hide as she turned to leave. "If I don't come back, thank you for allowing me to be here," she said thickly before she laughed and chewed her bottom lip. "It's been fun."

"You could stay here, with us."

"And bring yet another fight to your gates? You have enough going on, and this is my fight. This fight is one only I can wage against them. No; if it happens, it happens. Know that I went out smiling, and they just went out with a bang."

"We'd fight for you, Erie. You're one of us now."

"Synthia, that's sweet, but this is war. Don't go ruining my glory with this mushy shit. I've lived by the sword, and I will die by his sword. I've always known my fate and never feared meeting it head-on. I'll go out on my terms." Synthia moved closer, hugging Erie awkwardly as they all watched. "What the fuck are you doing? We don't hug, hugging isn't badass. Eww, that was just awkward."

"Come back, Erie, come back to us alive," Synthia said, undeterred by the other woman's bravado.

"Not if you plan to hug me again. That's a hard limit for me."

Icelyn watched as the redhead waved with the tips of her fingers over her shoulder as she disappeared down the hallway. There was something else going on here that she wasn't privy to. The entire room held their breath until magic pulsed, and just as quickly as it started, it ended.

"She isn't coming back," Sinjinn pointed out.

"She already knew that," Synthia said, a frown creasing her brow. "She said when she showed up this time that we'd better make the best of it. However she knows, or figures things out, she saw her end playing out."

"How would she know that?" Icelyn asked, forcing everyone to turn and look at her.

"She's a druid," Synthia said, as if it explained it all.

"Druids do not birth females, it is not possible."

"Erie was created from the cauldron of the Dagda, born of two races to save them both. She's special, but she is unaware of just how special she is."

"She isn't sane," Icelyn said pointedly.

"Erie was raised with people who resented her and loathed her differences. They made sure that she knew she had only one use in this world. Callaghan is her best hope for survival, but I fear that even he can no longer hold the others at bay. If she doesn't give birth to a child of Templar blood, both races will begin to become mortal and die out slowly."

Footsteps sounded down the hallway, and Cailean stuck his head inside the room. He smirked as he entered, pausing as he inhaled deeply.

"What is that smell?" he asked as he smiled. "It's intoxicating."

"That would be the scent of your fiancée pregnant with your brother's child, or in her case, children."

"What?" he squeaked in a high-pitched tone.

CHAPTER THIRTY-THREE

Icelyn watched Cailean pace as he was caught up to speed on what happened, and how it would play out. He looked as if at any moment, he'd get up and walk out. Those blue eyes kept moving between Sinjinn and Ryder and back again.

"Your wolf claimed her? That's rare, right?"

"Very," Zahruk answered as if he held a stake in this mess. "The last wolf that resided in one of us to claim a mate was before Alazander took the throne. In fact, they'd been dormant for so long that we assumed they couldn't, or that the bloodline was so diluted that they were unable to. Some thought the magic of the hunt had lessened their power as they chose a host for the hunt. Two thousand years ago, the last wolf chose a mate, and since then, none have ever claimed another, until now."

"And yet you still want me to marry her?" he asked, his ocean blue gaze holding Icelyn's before he swung them back to Sinjinn. "She's your fucking mate, bro."

"She isn't my mate," he uttered as his eyes refused

to meet Icelyn's. "She's the wolf's mate. Not that it matters, because her father will want her death for the oath being broken. So it doesn't really matter now, does it? If she dies, so do my children, Cailean. Until we can find the king and eliminate him, she is yours."

"You're fucking joking," he snapped.

"No, we're not," Synthia said offhandedly.

"You know what that means, right? How's your wolf going to respond when I fuck my wife to seal the deal?" he snapped.

Sinjinn punched him without warning, sending him sailing across the room to slide down the wall. He started forward, but Ryder and Zahruk blocked his path, pushing him back with a warning as Synthia moved to check on Cailean, who shook her off as he glared towards Sinjinn.

"I know where the court is." Icelyn's tone was soft, so soft that she feared they hadn't heard her.

"You'd give up your own people?" Ryder asked.

"I'd want your oath that none would be harmed if I gave you the location of the palace," she said, then quickly held her hand up as he began to argue. "I'm not asking for those who stand against you to be spared, only those who do not. Among those who you will not touch are my mother, my brother, and my sister. If you cannot promise me that, you can continue searching and having the scouts come back empty-handed. That is what is happening, is it not?"

"They've made progress," he countered.

"They've been unable to find it because it is off pattern. In cases of duress, it skips three locations. Meaning your people are looking in the wrong location and are more likely to perish in the harsh climate than return with the location. I'm sure they've encountered many storms by now, have they not?"

"Icelyn, if you know the location of the palace, you need to tell me. I can put you back into the dungeon until you do."

She smirked as she held the Horde King's eyes and said the last thing he expected. "Fine. Do it."

"I'm not fucking playing, princess. This isn't a negotiation."

"You're wrong, it is. I'm not asking you to not kill the king; I'm asking you to spare those not guilty of treason against the Horde. Meet me halfway or don't meet me at all. Don't threaten me with your solitary dungeon because at least I can think down there. You're not asking me a simple thing; you're asking me to betray my people. Right now I am not Icelyn. I am the Princess and Heir of the Winter Court, and those are my people who will suffer."

"Take her to the dungeon," he snapped.

Icelyn squared her shoulders and eyed the guards who moved to follow through with the king's orders. She didn't blink or show an ounce of fear as they nodded for her to follow them. She did, her head held high with no trace of fear that he may change his mind and assault her. Those were her people, people who were innocent other than having the misfortune of being born unto the Winter Court.

"Ryder," Synthia uttered as she moved towards him.

"I am the king, she is under my roof. If I ask for the location, she will give it to me."

"And that worked out so well, didn't it?" she

countered.

"He slaughtered my men for no other reason than to do so! I am King of the Horde, Synthia. I rule by strength and fear, and that little girl isn't afraid! She should be fucking cowering, and instead, she's smiling."

"Oh, boy," she said with a frown marring her utter perfect features.

"She's also carrying my children." Sinjinn watched Ryder, who turned onyx black eyes in his direction.

"And am I supposed to marry her in the dungeon?" Cailean asked with a snicker. "Could make the honeymoon rather interesting," he shrugged as his voice trailed off at Ryder's angry glare.

"Guards, follow them. See that she has food, water, and adequate blankets. She is, after all, carrying the nephews or nieces of the Horde King. See that Eliran is made aware that she is expecting twins, and that she may need supplements. Adam and Ristan previously secured some for Olivia, and some can be given to her if needed. Ryder, bedroom," she finished with a pointed look.

"I'm not going to be talked out of this, Pet," he warned.

"Ryder, you just threw Sinjinn's baby momma in the dungeon. You need to feed," she snapped angrily. "You're hangry, boy."

"I'm not hungry, woman."

"Then I need to feed."

"You don't feed from sex anymore."

"Then I need to fuck your frustrations out of you. Stop arguing and let's go."

"She knows where that castle is right now. If we

don't move quickly, they can move before we find them. I will find them, Pet, with or without her."

"Then meet her halfway. She's the future queen, and if she hands them over to us, she won't ever be accepted by her people. You're seeing it from your perspective, but what about hers? She is going to betray the current king and dethrone him, which means she will then become the ruler. Icelyn, who gave you the coordinates to the palace, will then be their queen and their enemy."

"I hate it when you make a fucking point."

"I know, but you're used to taking things. You're the King of the Horde, the most feared and hated race of the Fae, Ryder. You think to rule them as you have known, but change starts with us."

"Now I have to get her out of the dungeon, don't I?" he snorted as he pushed his long fingers through his thick, midnight hair. Shit was so much easier when he could just take shit, or kill shit, and it would be the end of the discussion or subject.

"No, because then you'll look confused and we can't have it getting out that you're uncertain of a punishment."

"Maybe I should just send you out to deal with the Horde. They fear you now."

"Only because I bit one's throat out and chewed on it," she smirked as she pushed her fingers through his, twining them together. "You're a good scary king, but there has to be some give to these people. They've been through hell, and so have we. Only we know what we've endured, because we have yet to let them know it."

"For only being twenty-two, you're pretty smart, woman."

"Are you wooing me, Ryder?"

"No, I'm taking that ass to bed and then I'll show you wooing."

A cough interrupted their lovers' banter, and Ryder turned to look at Sinjinn, who looked about ready to bolt towards the dungeons. He nodded and then held his hand up.

"It's not like you can get her any more pregnant… right?" When Sinjinn just stared at him, he turned to look at Zahruk, who was frowning. "Right?" he chuckled.

"I'm pretty sure she's Fae, with Fae sexual organs for reproduction."

"So no?"

"I highly doubt it."

"You got her pregnant enough; maybe remind your inner wolf of that? While you're at it, remind him that her life depends on her fulfilling her end of the oath, pregnant or not. She has five days before it will be called in, and I'm pretty sure your wolf will want her and your children alive." Ryder frowned, staring at Sinjinn before he shook his head.

CHAPTER THIRTY-FOUR

It was darker in the cell she sat in this time, her heart thundered against her ribcage as she considered her next move. It wasn't that she feared for the king, quite the opposite really. She wanted them to tear him apart, mostly because he'd never stop trying to kill her, and if what they'd said was true, she would soon be a mother. In her condition, she wouldn't be as agile or able to fight off the assassins he'd sent after her.

Her mind wandered to her siblings, and if they missed her as much as she missed them. Were they safe? Had their father abused them, as he was often in fits of rage that they endlessly endured the brunt of? How many times had she dreamt of murdering him to free them of those fits? Every night since he'd beaten her, but they'd stopped when she'd shot Sinjinn, and in the place of those dreams of rage was something white-hot that left her dreaming of things she would never know.

A noise brought her eyes to the bars of her prison, and she watched as he emerged from the shadows, as if conjured by her racing thoughts. Her hand moved to her flat stomach as his eyes fell to it, as if she'd already become protective of what he said grew within.

Babies; they'd created life together according to him and Synthia. Icelyn felt numb, as if she was stuck within a dream and couldn't awake from it. She'd never even given thought to becoming a mother, since she didn't think her father would ever let it happen, and now, now everything had changed.

She'd known why she was chosen to fulfill the oath instead of her sister. Why he'd force her, the heir of the Winter Court, to marry into the Horde. He hadn't expected her to survive it, and yet with the heated touches of this male, she let the hope of surviving it sink in.

"You're pregnant," he said, as if he couldn't quite believe it either.

"So you think?" she replied softly as she took her hand away from her stomach and curled onto the bed, staring at him through her thick lashes.

He entered the cell, closing it as he did. He didn't move to the bed right away, but when he did, she shivered at the heat that entered his emerald stare. His body lowered, pushing her over as he curled around her, trapping her in his heated embrace.

"I didn't mean to allow him to do this. I had no knowledge of his plans, or that he could even do this. For that, I am sorry. I'm not sorry that you will bring my children into this world, Icelyn. I will keep you safe, and if after you give birth to them, you want to leave, I will allow it."

"I wouldn't leave my children," she said softly, her

voice a mere whisper into the darkness of the cell.

"You won't take them from me," he argued, and his arms tightened around her. The growl that escaped was primal, as if he was warning her that he would fight her.

"I will become the Queen of the Winter Court, and my children...our children will be in line to rule it as well. You cannot take that from them."

"I can," he countered as he pushed her against the bed, staring down at her with an intense look that she wasn't sure how to process.

His mouth lowered to brush against her jaw in a gentle caress that sent her heart pounding against her breasts. Sinjinn traced a trail to her ear, burning her flesh as his tongue and teeth played with the tissue.

"You will marry Cailean, but you will never fuck him," he warned, his cock hard against her belly where it rested in the low-hanging jeans he wore. "Your flesh is mine, your mind is mine. You are mine, Icelyn. Do you understand me? If you will be the queen, then I will be your king. My wolf chose you, which means I feel you to the depths of my soul. We will never let you go, you need to understand that. The sooner you understand it, the sooner you will accept it. You are my mate, little ice princess. He chose you, but even worse, so do I."

"He didn't ask," she replied as she moaned against his words and lips that ravished mercilessly. Their clothes disappeared, and she gasped as he entered her without warning or preparation. Not that he needed to; his mouth had sent heat pooling to her center, allowing him unhindered entrance to her most private place.

He stretched her until she cried against his mouth, rocking her hips to adjust to the sheer size of his cock.

Sinjinn wasn't small by any means, or any standard. The man was meant to devour, to pillage and leave you breathless. Her core clenched against him, as if it fought to keep him there forever.

His words pissed her off, but she couldn't deny the pleasure of the flesh that he offered so freely. She knew if what he said was true, feeding was a must, and the idea of feeding from anyone else left her bereft and cold. She rolled them, staring down at him as his eyes watched her. Those big hands cupped her breasts, forcing a cry from her lips as he tightened his hold.

"You're beautiful," he murmured before he lifted his mouth, flicking the pink-tipped rosebud with his skilled tongue. His hips never stopped moving, sending her rocking to the endless rhythm of pleasure that only he could give.

She was so wet for him, so tight as her body clenched and took what it needed from him. But they weren't alone in that bed, there was someone else just beneath the surface of his being that watched her, craved her. His cock grew until it became uncomfortably large. Her feet touched the bed, and she lifted from his cock, slowly moving until only the tip remained cradled in her flesh.

"You're playing with fire, woman," he warned, and then moaned as she slid him back into the welcoming depths of her body.

"Fire doesn't scare me," she uttered hoarsely.

Icelyn felt powerful, driven by a need she couldn't fully comprehend as she lifted and dropped, uncaring that his length ached and hurt her as she dropped onto it. His eyes glowed as he raised his head, staring at the point where they joined, watching as her pussy took him slowly into its heat, and over and over again she lifted adding another inch until she slammed his massive cock into her tiny cunt.

She screamed as her body was sent reeling into the pleasure of her climax. It was so forceful and unexpected that she visibly shook from the orgasm that ripped from her. His eyes glowed, staring at her wet pussy that coated his cock in her release.

One solid move had her pinned beneath him, and he growled with approval as he began fucking her slowly, knowing she wanted it fast and hard. His wolf knew what she wanted before she'd even decided it, and knew she was being held in her own orgasm. He felt the pain it created, the violence of it that had her mewling and begging to be released from the throes of passion.

"Who do you belong to?" he queried roughly, watching her exquisite breasts as each pump of his cock sent them shaking against her chest. He'd never been one to care of the size of a woman's breasts before, but watching hers jiggle as he fucked her made his balls ache to release in her welcoming flesh.

The way she responded to his touch made the beast within sated, knowing she craved this thing between them even if she refused to admit it sated it. The fact that it could scent her pregnancy had it growling and staking its claim on her over and over again.

"I asked you a question," he snapped as he sat back on his haunches, staring at her flesh that stretched to accommodate him. She'd been a virgin, unexpected but welcome.

There was something pleasing about knowing only he had brought her pleasure. The mere idea of another man touching her made his mind see red; anger flashed in his eyes as he watched her lips part as he pushed deeper, harder.

"Sinjinn," she cried out, his name her fucking benediction as the orgasm threatened to take her mind to the soaring height she craved to reach. He pulled out, leaving only the tip in her wanton flesh. She knew he craved her vow of ownership, but Icelyn feared admitting it out loud. His flesh pushed into hers, and she uttered his name over and over, as if he was her savior, her God.

His hand lowered, slapping against the center of her being. The hood of her flesh was rubbed, soothing the ache he created, and then he pushed her legs up, holding them apart as he leaned over, claiming her lips hungrily.

"I can do this all night," he warned heatedly. "I *want* to do this all night," he amended.

"I won't be owned," she seethed as she bucked her hips against him, trying to take what she needed from him. "Feed me."

"Not until you admit what we both already know."

"Make me," she growled huskily as she rocked against his impressive length, knowing a few well-placed thrusts would send her over the edge.

Her hand moved to rub against her flesh, and he captured them, pushing them against the bed above her head. His laughter was husky, brushing against her flesh as if he'd become one with her. His cock withdrew and yet never left her flesh, which she knew wouldn't happen for hours to come, because he wasn't fully in charge here. His wolf was claiming his stake. He'd grown until he couldn't pull from her body without tearing her apart.

"Say it."

"And if I do, what then?" she asked breathlessly. "You think if I say it, it would make it truth? I could say anything you wanted me to right now, and it would be empty. I don't belong to you, I belong to my people. I have nothing to give you, only a kingdom of those who choose to follow a crown."

"You're wrong," he crooned as he sucked a pink nipple between his teeth, letting them scrape over her delicate flesh. "You, I want you. Not your crown, not your people. I want you, the woman beneath me who makes the most delicious fucking noises when she comes, to want me. Crowns come and go, but this thing between us? I want it. I want to spend the rest of my days fucking your heat, knowing you want me too. I want to watch your belly swell with my babes nestled in it, and to watch them blossom within you. I want to hold you as you feed our children from these perfect tits, and watch them grow. That isn't something your crown can give me, now is it, Icelyn? I have a title, one that means more than any other to me, but I want you to want me," he purred as he turned his attention to her other breast.

"No one has ever wanted me before you," she admitted, crying out as he pushed into her body hard and swiftly. "I'm yours," she admitted, knowing it was the truth, and yet not fully understanding her need to say it.

In her entire life, no one had ever wanted her for anything other than the crown. No one had ever spoken to her as he did, or cared what was within her mind. Choices weren't made because she had wanted them or craved them; it was out of what the crown she'd inherit would need. But this man? This beast that had taught her pleasure and took her mind to places she had once feared to even dream of, he wanted her?

"Say it again," he demanded, and she did. Her mouth opened and she repeated it until he was driving into her body hard enough to steal the words from her lips.

Her words undid him, and he took her hard, fast, and no mercy was granted. He wanted her sore, so that every time she winced, she was reminded of her words and what she'd discovered as she writhed beneath him. He wanted her to remember that she was his and his alone.

He grunted as his cock released, filling her with his scent as he watched her eyes rolling back and her mouth opening to scream her own release. Fuck, she was beautiful. So fucking beautiful that it hurt him. Her hands formed ice, ice that was meant to hurt, and yet his heat absorbed it. They were covered in sweat; steam from his heat mingled with her frost and filled the cell that he'd claimed her in.

His head rested against hers, and the wolf released his hold, allowing his cock to shrink enough that their mating wasn't as painful. Yet he didn't withdraw, not when he was already growing hard again to take her.

"You're fire," she uttered thickly as she started moving beneath him, wanting more.

"And you're ice," he moaned thickly as he watched her blue eyes begin to glow with hunger. "You're the first woman I can find release with without burning her from within."

"Feed me, I can't seem to get enough of you."

And he did, several times, until they were nothing more than boneless pleasure that continued into the early morning hours, sated and well-fed. Once he'd pleasured her and assured she couldn't take any more, he pulled her slick form to his and held her close. He'd never allowed a bedmate to remain past sex, and yet he craved her closeness.

He was so fucked, and he knew it. Sinjinn knew that he'd move mountains to keep her with him. He'd go to war to keep her and their unborn babes safe from her murderous father. Long after she'd fallen asleep, he pushed her tousled hair from her face and placed a kiss against her forehead.

"I'm going to kill him for you. I'm going to be the one who claims you and your kingdom, and together, we will rule it. I'll protect you, my fierce little queen."

CHAPTER THIRTY-FIVE

Ryder paced outside the cell as Sinjinn pretended to ignore him, but he knew. He knew what he needed, and hell, Sinjinn wanted it as bad as his brother. He lifted his eyes, glamouring his woman into a soft, baby blue dress that made his balls ache as he slowly, carefully lifted from the bed. His body was sore from fucking, but he loved it.

"Did you get the location?" Ryder asked as he maintained eye level with Sinjinn, refusing to drop his golden gaze to see his brother's cock, which hadn't been satisfied enough, apparently. "Do you mind?" he asked when Sinjinn strolled towards the cell door and walked out, naked.

"No, do you?" he countered as he stretched, smirking when Ryder waved his hand, dressing him in his armor. "She's mine, she isn't fucking marrying him. There has to be another way."

"Would you watch her die?" he asked, and a pang started in his chest at the idea of it happening. "Didn't think so. The scouts returned again with no knowledge of the palace's location," he disclosed as he watched Sinjinn pacing outside the cell, his eyes drifting to the sleeping woman within.

"It can't just vanish," he growled as he pulled at his hair, his anger palpable as he strode towards Ryder. "Alazander had no issue discovering the pattern, why are we unable to?"

"Alazander had spies in each court and never allowed them the freedom of moving without his knowledge. I don't care that they move, as long as the tithe is paid in a timely fashion. I don't want them to fear us as Alazander craved. I want them to need us, as it used to be."

"The Seelie may know how to track the court."

"And what would they want for it? You think the Horde is bad? They make us look like fluffy fucking fairies. They were locked into that cage at birth, or most of them were. If they have been freed, we have bigger problems than then just the Mages being at our door."

"I still can't believe he did that," Sinjinn admitted as he paused in pacing, throwing a curious glance towards the cell and his woman, who slept within. "I can't believe I did it. I'm going to be a father, Ryder. I don't know what to do to protect her, but I know everything inside of me is screaming that she is mine now. I know I fucked this up, but we can't let him claim her for the oath, which may have been his intent all along. She isn't his child, and he won't hesitate to claim her life. He now holds three lives in limbo with that oath. He has to die before the time is up."

"Four days, Sinjinn. In four days, Gerald will call in the blood oath, and we think that is why the court is moving still. All he has to do is stay out of our grasp until then, and pull on that thread to see if she has fulfilled her end of the bargain. If she has not, he can cut the cord that is tethered to her life or mine. So you will allow her to fulfill her end of it, and we will hunt that bastard down and pull him apart, limb by bloody limb. Unfortunately, she will have to consummate the marital vows with Cailean, and you will allow it to happen. Not because you want it to happen, or because you may want to kill him afterwards, but because she does carry the lives of your children in her womb and the only other alternative is death."

"I'll feel it," he snapped, his teeth grinding together as the idea of it sent red-hot rage pulsing through him. "My wolf will go insane if she takes him to her bed."

"You'll be chained through it," he offered with a shrug. "It's not ideal, but the alternative is losing her. Cailean doesn't want her, or this, but he is willing to go through with it knowing he would save her life. I'd do it for Synthia in a heartbeat, which is saying a lot. Do you understand me? If you have to choose between losing your mate and taking a hit to your pride, you take the fucking hit, and you man up. You hear me, brother? You take the hit because losing them after we've mated to them will destroy you more than knowing she did what she had to do to stay alive. I handed the love of my life to another man when I assumed she was the Light Heir, and now you may have to do the same. If Icelyn ends up being the Light Heir, you will walk away from her, but at least you'll have a piece of her."

"It isn't happening!"

"So you'll let her die? You will let Faery die?" he

countered.

"This isn't right, and you know it."

"I never said it was right, or that I agreed with it. I won't let your children die, Sinjinn. I won't let your mate die, and I sure as fuck won't let that bastard win. Our father may have wrecked her life, but we won't. Your wolf isn't going to like it, but he won't reject her over it. Hell, he may decide to walk away from her if he sees it as a betrayal, but you house him. He doesn't control you. Those are your children in her womb. Not wolves, not beasts that will need him. Your children grow within that woman. Remember that, and know this wasn't my choice."

He stepped aside and Ristan, Zahruk, Asrian, Savlian, and Sevrin entered the dungeon, watching him. He bristled with power as he turned to stare at the sleeping form that was just becoming aware that they weren't alone anymore.

Nordic-blue eyes held his as she took notice of the room full of men, all ready to do what was needed to save her, even from him. Her hands reached for the covers over her body before she took note of her dress, and rose from the bed.

"What is going on?" she demanded, her tone tense and fear brightening her eyes.

"You're getting married," Ryder stated gently.

"But…no," she said shaking her head.

"You're out of time, and now you have other lives to consider. I won't chance the day changing one more time without protecting you and myself from what can happen if we don't fulfill it."

"But I'm pregnant," she argued, her tiny fingers

splayed protectively over her flat stomach. "I don't understand, there's still time."

"It's for the best," Sinjinn said softly. "You're better off with someone else. I can't do this. I was wrong, Icelyn. You're not mine, you are his wife."

Icelyn felt the floor falling out from beneath her. Her throat closed up with tears as they threatened to fall from her eyes. She stepped back as if he'd physically hit her with his words. She needed distance, needed to clear her head or shake him, one of the two. She opened her mouth to scream in denial at his words but the angry look he gave her silenced them. Derision dripped from his lips as he spoke.

"Congratulations, sweetheart," he hissed. "Welcome to the Horde, make sure you show my brother how welcoming that sweet flesh is."

"That's enough," Ryder warned, his eyes moving between them as his head shook.

He left the room with Ryder following close behind him, leaving Icelyn to watch him as he walked away. Once they were out of the room, and out of hearing distance he spun on him and trembled with anger.

"Tell him if he fucking hurts her, I'll kill him," he warned.

"You didn't need to push her away for this to happen."

"Yes, I did. She is mine, Ryder. She wouldn't have allowed this otherwise. If pushing her away means saving her, so be it. I took the hit, *I* took it. Not her, not Cailean. This is my fuck-up. I claimed his bride and mated my wolf to her. Now, lock me up because there's no way in hell I'm going to be able to handle their wedding."

CHAPTER
THIRTY-SIX

She was beyond numb; her hands were folded in her lap calmly. Synthia brushed her hair while Ristan's mate, Olivia, sat in front of her, talking about mundane things. Her belly was swollen, hugely so. She'd told her that due to the angelic nature of her heritage, and the demonic in Ristan's, that her pregnancy was past the six months that Fae pregnancies were known for. Olivia was in her eighth month, as big as a house, which meant Icelyn would be a palace when she was ready to birth hers.

"Icelyn, you can do this," Olivia said when Icelyn just continued to stare blankly at her. "I mean, it isn't the end of the world, right? Cailean is cute, and he's a gentleman beneath his rough exterior."

"This isn't going well," Synthia admitted. "You could tell us where the palace is, sift us to it, and we can take it from there," she offered hopefully.

"Not without an oath in place," she said softly. "Is this needed?"

They'd been dolling her up, preparing her for her own wedding, and to her, it felt more like a funeral. As if she was slowly preparing for final rites to be entered into eternal sleep within the mountain. But it wasn't, it was the beginning of the year and a day to her marriage. Yet all she wanted to do was crawl into a ball and forget the world.

Olivia finished with the lip gloss that could have easily been glamoured on as Synthia pronounced her hair was finished. Icelyn stood, mindful of the ball gown she wore. It was done with a shimmering blue skirt and an intricate, jeweled bodice that framed her small waist. Her hair had been piled above her head, the coffer a work of art. Her crown was tactful and simple; a single diamond sat in a platinum setting, marking her royal birth and mirroring the cold, lifelessness she felt.

"You look beautiful, considering you wish to be anywhere but here," Synthia pointed out, her violet eyes missing nothing.

"I want to go home," she replied honestly.

"Tell us where it is, then, and I'll keep Ryder from killing your family."

"You can put it in an oath," Icelyn replied icily.

"You and the oaths, look at the problem this one has created! You're pregnant with Sinjinn's children, walking down the aisle to marry his brother. Oaths create problems that we cannot foresee, so while I may promise to protect them, you won't get an oath from any of us. Accidents happen, bad things happen to good people. You can't predict the future, which is why I told Ryder this tithe business was going to backfire and it has, badly."

"My people would be the ones who got harmed, and I cannot live with that," she uttered.

Ryder entered the room and barely spared a second glance at Icelyn before he announced Cailean was ready. He held out his arm for Icelyn, and she stared at it, her heartbeat an endless drum that pounded in her ears. She accepted his arm after a moment of hesitation as they left the antechamber.

At the main hallway, Ryder nodded to Synthia, who moved into the room, her hips swaying as she made her way to the front pews. Deep breathing seemed to help Icelyn not hyperventilate as she allowed Ryder to walk her to where Cailean stood with his hair pulled back with a leather tie, his kilt, and high socks—strange wedding attire, but under the limited time, she could understand the need for it to be more traditional.

"You look beautiful as always, Icelyn," Cailean said smoothly, his voice a rather strange mix of uncertainty and something else she couldn't pinpoint.

"You look nice too," she said awkwardly.

The priest stood before them, his eyes filled with sadness and emotions that Icelyn couldn't understand. He didn't look like a priest per se, or a man of the cloth, and yet he nodded to Ryder and then Cailean.

"When you're ready, Alden," Ryder said before he stepped to the side, blocking any chance of escape off.

"You're here today to be given in handfasting to this man. Icelyn, Heir of Ice and Light, future Queen of the Winter Court, do you accept Cailean, Prince of the Horde and brother to the Horde King for a time of one year and one day?"

Icelyn's tongue grew heavy; her heart seemed

to be compressed as her stomach churned. Her eyes moved to hold Cailean's gentle blue ones. He nodded encouragement and then frowned when she began to nervously chew her bottom lip.

"Icelyn, you don't have any more choice in this than I do. You're carrying twins; their lives are yours to protect now. I'm here, standing in front of you to help you protect them. They're my brother's children, and you his mate. I promise it will be okay." Cailean leaned over, kissing her forehead in a chaste kiss meant to calm her.

"I do," she said as tears slipped from her eyes. It hurt, as if she was shattering in betrayal, and the bellow that shook the room was proof he'd felt it as such.

"Cailean, brother of the reigning Horde King, Prince to the throne of the Horde, do you take Icelyn, Heir of Light and Ice, to be yours for a time of one year and one day?"

"I do," he said without hesitation.

"This rope is a symbol of your vow to each other. It cannot be broken without both agreeing to unbind it. Should you both choose otherwise, then those who brought you together will be called forth to argue this marriages merits, in the eyes of the Gods, I pronounce you husband and wife."

She watched him using the gold cloth to tie their hands together. It felt as if each time around, her chest seemed to cave in a little more. The spot on her shoulder that Sinjinn had bitten her ached. It burned like the fiercest flames, searing her flesh.

"You will kiss your bride now, and I do believe arrangements have been made to finish the other part of this oath."

Cailean leaned against her, pulling her close as his lips brushed against hers. The room shook as a pain-filled scream tore through it. Tears fell unchecked as pain lanced her flesh, even as Cailean deepened the kiss.

It lacked fire. It lacked the connection she felt when Sinjinn's heated kiss quieted her fears and mind. He pulled back from her, offering her a wink as he held up his hand, and the entire assembly who soberly watched it unfold nodded.

There were no cheers, no applauding that occurred. Her family wasn't there to wish her well, in fact, she'd married with not one single person who knew her or cared about her here. She'd never felt more alone until now, standing in a room, married to a stranger, pregnant with his brother's babes in her belly.

"This way," Cailean ordered, directing his numb, unspeaking bride towards a back room that connected to the newly built church Synthia had asked Ryder to build for them.

Once they'd entered the room, he moved towards another door, pushing her into the darkness. She trembled, fearing what was to come next. His mouth touched her ear, and then the cold air told her he'd removed her clothing with magic.

She could do this. This would be the only time she had to do this, and for the babes growing within her body, she could withstand this just once. Her eyes squeezed shut as his body meshed against hers. She knew she was stiff; her hands were fisted at her sides, and her eyes were so tightly closed that she was afraid she may pass out before he even got it in. He entered her hard, stretching her full, her cry exploded from her lips, and then he withdrew from her. It was violent, and yet not.

"Did it work?" he demanded.

Icelyn opened her eyes and stared at where he should have been, but he wasn't there, and she was once again dressed. Sinjinn touched her face softly before he looked down at his brother, who was arranging himself into his kilt again.

Her eyes moved to what lay upon the table, bathed in soft candlelight. The oath shined, gold writing exploded over the surface, and the entire document turned to ashes. Her gaze swung from Cailean to Sinjinn, and then back to the oath.

"It's done?" she whimpered as her body trembled with fear, uncertain if they'd broken the oath and her last few moments were upon her.

"Did it work?" Ryder's thick voice whipped through the room as he entered it quietly, slipping in beside them.

"It disintegrated," Sinjinn replied as his thumb continued to stroke Icelyn's cheek comfortingly, as if he was afraid to stop touching her.

Ryder exhaled and stared at the three of them. "Welcome to the family, Icelyn. Betray us, and I will end you."

"Enjoy fucking my brother," Cailean chuckled. "I'm your husband for all events or anything that needs us to save face, but you are his. You will never share my bed or sleep with me. I give you permission as your husband to be with Sinjinn."

"You knew that this would work?" she asked hesitantly. "You knew this, and none of you told me beforehand?" she sputtered.

"No, but the oath was written to assure that vows would be exchanged, and the marriage would be consummated. It didn't state what or how far it would be consummated. I'm sure your father assumed any monster of the Horde would be unwilling to stop once they'd started."

"So you chose how you followed it? What if it meant fully... Well, you know what I mean," she stammered as she hesitated.

"Fully fucked? Consummated means you have acted in sexual penetration and the contract stated no contraception was used. You have fulfilled the oath that was stated, to the letter. When the oath is fulfilled, the contract turns to ashes and is archived in the library. And so it has been filed, and you're free to continue with Sinjinn if your husband consented. He has, but for all official engagements or purposes, you will be at his side to save face among the Horde, Icelyn. We will leave you now, and you can erase his scent from her as I can feel the beast within pacing with his need to do just that."

"Thank you," she muttered as she turned her tear-filled gaze to Sinjinn and waited for his rejection. He'd said horrible things to her, things that had made her want to rake her nails down his face, scarring him for life.

"Be gentle, he only sought to make it easier on you." With that, they were left alone to stare silently at each other.

CHAPTER THIRTY-SEVEN

Jcelyn stared at Sinjinn as if he was
her lifeline in the storm of emotions that pushed through
her. Her body ached, a reminder that Cailean had just
entered her flesh and stretched it, consummating their
marriage to soothe the oath and fulfill her end of it.
They'd done it, figuring out a way that nulled the threat
against them and her.

"You're okay, right?" he asked, turning to the door
that slowly closed behind Ryder and Cailean.

"I feel...dirty."

"Don't," he said softly. "You had to do it to break
the power your father held over you, over us. Cailean
had to do that, you understand that, right? He would
have gone further to protect you and the babes."

"I still don't feel pregnant," she argued.

What the hell had just happened? She'd married
Cailean, and he'd pushed into her body violently,
abruptly, and then just as quickly, he'd withdrawn. She
was his *wife!* Yet here she was, talking of babies with

Sinjinn, a man who knew her on a level no one else had, until tonight. Sure, in a twisted world it made sense, but shouldn't they have explained it to her first?

"You smell different." He shrugged. "I feel it, and I felt it when he'd finished, ensuring you carried our child. He fucked you for hours, emptying into your womb and then continued still. My wolf, he's never once done that or reacted to a bedmate, Icelyn. Then there's the mark on your shoulder, a mark the wolf only gives when he has chosen his mate. It's a once-in-a-lifetime thing."

"He should learn to ask first!" she hissed as her body trembled with hunger. It wasn't the reaction she'd expected, but even that slip of dick had her body reacting. "Why do I feel like this?" she demanded.

"Cailean is part incubus," he smirked, his hand reaching behind her neck to pull her closer to him. He sniffed as his lips curled into an angry snarl. "I can smell him on you, sweet girl," he warned as magic pushed through the room.

Cold air skimmed over her now-naked flesh and she gasped as his free hand found her flesh, pushing his long fingers through the wetness. He didn't stop, didn't care that she'd been nestled around his brother's cock as he flicked his finger against her clit, sending a moan slipping from her mouth.

"You're wet," he announced. "Cailean's magic really did affect you, didn't it?"

"I didn't feel it until now," she admitted as her mouth skimmed over his, letting his hot breath warm them. "I want you," she uttered as her teeth caught his lip, sucking it between her teeth.

"You smell like your husband," he growled low, the

sound reverberating from deep in his chest. He pushed her backwards, watching as she fell into the chair he'd materialized as her ass touched it.

"My husband..." she whispered on a whimper of sound.

"I can't believe I am saying this, but it's kind of hot that you belong to him and yet your sweet flesh weeps for me. I wish I could have seen you out there, the sweet tears that dropped knowing you didn't want him. I would have warned you of the plan, but we feared you knowing would somehow overwrite the willingness to fuck him or that the contract would sense it. You had to think you were fulfilling the agreement. But hearing you moan as he pushed into your body, I've never wanted to kill him more. But the salt of those tears stilled my need for revenge. It calmed the wolf to know that even though he wanted it, you didn't."

"He doesn't even know me!"

"He is incubus, Icelyn. He is the male equivalent to a sex God. His mother was succubus. He, therefore, is incubus and Fae; two breeds who fuck to feed. Any woman's flesh calls to him. They fall at his feet, begging to be used, and yet you cried through it. You would have done it, would have dried those tears and let him fuck what is mine because you were under oath. Now, now you're mine, and there's no one who can say otherwise. Do you understand me? For all royal decree, you are his and yet he will never taste the sweet pleasure that you hold. He sacrificed it for me, for you."

He pushed her legs apart and descended on her flesh as if he was starving. Her hands pushed through his hair, tugging it to her as his mouth sent pleasure rushing through her. Fingers pushed inside, bringing her orgasm to the edge as he held it just out of reach. She knew he did it on purpose, and for the briefest second, she wondered what it would feel like to know both men at once. To feel them as they pleasured her. Her eyes closed and in his place, Cailean was there, sucking her hood into his mouth as he smiled up at her with molten desire burning in his sea blue depths.

Sinjinn's mouth pulled away from her just as she'd started barreling towards the precipice. Green eyes the color of freshly bloomed leaves during spring stared up at her.

"You get this one time to imagine him fucking you. It's his magic calling to you, luring you to him. I'm about to erase his touch from you, and then when your flesh is being devoured, you will know it is me. If you close your eyes, I'll fuck you hard and fast and leave you needy for days."

"I don't know why that happened. I don't want him, I want you," she replied honestly with tears forming in her eyes.

He lifted to her, pulling her close as he kissed her tears away. It was a fucking mess, and yet this had been the only way to assure she was safe. It hadn't been ideal, far fucking from it. He'd felt it, her fear, her pain, her need to be saved, and Zahruk had held him back, fighting him off as he'd pushed forward; every instinct inside of him had demanded he go to her. He wanted to be the man waiting at the end of that aisle, the one who kissed her after she'd agreed to be his. It was supposed to be him, and yet there was no way around the oath. No way to skip past what had happened. Not with saving her and Ryder, and they'd come too far to lose it now.

He pushed into her body, picking her up as he buried his throbbing cock into her welcoming heat that enveloped him fully. Her hips rocked as he sat down, pulling her with him until she was riding him with abandonment in the chair he sat upon. Her hair was falling loose from her bridal updo, the crown catching the light with each lift and thrust of her body which sent him careening to the edge of release right with her own.

Her winter blue eyes never left his, and he swallowed past the thickness those beautiful eyes created in his chest. He had no idea how this would work between them, or if he could last an entire year without claiming her as his own, but for her, he'd move the fucking moon and catch every star. He'll right the wrongs of the past, and show her how beautiful and perfect she was through his eyes.

First, he had to find her father and murder the slimy bastard for telling this brazen beauty anything but the truth. Icelyn was magical, her body a work of art that he wanted to look at for the rest of his days, which both threw him and undid him at the same time. He had never wanted a woman as much as he craved her, and he knew he'd never get enough time with her.

Icelyn screamed as her body trembled violently, her flesh aching as he grew larger, filling her until she knew it would be hours before that cock softened to release her. She didn't care; instead, she leaned over and uttered hoarsely into his ear.

"Fuck me, wolf, I am yours," she purred.

"You're damn right you are," Sinjinn snapped as he traded her places, forcing her ass further into the corner of the chair as he pounded into her. His scent removed his brother's as the wolf bared its teeth and sank them into her shoulder, just deep enough to remind her who she belonged to and who had claimed her as their mate.

Ryder had feared his wolf's reaction; Sinjinn craved it. He felt the primal need to take her until she was nothing more than a screaming, sobbing pile of satisfied female. Her body gave as good as it got, pushing her own legs apart for him to move deeper, to fuck her without being interrupted. Heat burned against her, and her ice cooled it. It was a never-ending part of him that she could withstand, and he didn't have to fear harming her as the Djinn inside of him let his eyes burn with fire, his kiss scorching against hers. When his release exploded through him, he feared he would hurt her, even after assuming he couldn't.

Flames leapt from his hands as they turned black like burnt oak, and her ice exploded onto her flesh, protecting her from being burned by him. His mouth was too hot, scorching hers, yet frost formed over her mouth, turning his kiss into a tempting dance of ice and fire. His eyes captured hers, and she watched the flames dancing within their heated depths.

"My fire," she uttered as her body quivered and tightened around his. "You're mine."

"Say it again," he urged as he rocked his hips, already growing larger within her tight, needy flesh.

"You're mine, and I am yours."

"You terrify me," he laughed huskily.

"Why?" she asked as her hand slid between their bodies, finding her pleasure center to bring even more pleasure between them.

"Because I've never wanted anything as I do you," he admitted as he watched her. The need in her eyes softened, and a soft smile splayed across her mouth. She took his breath away, naked, wanton, and willing to play with his fire where no one else had ever before. They'd feared his flames, but this little wisp of a princess took his heat and fed him her frost.

"Don't get clingy," she laughed, and the smile brightened, and he exploded into her flesh without warning. His head rested against hers, his lips brushed her forehead as he cradled her into his arms without leaving her pussy.

"Too late, princess," he replied before he sifted them to his bedroom. "I'm unable to get enough of you."

CHAPTER
THIRTY-EIGHT

The next few days were an endless whirlwind of arguing the merit of the oath and protecting her people. The only lulls between it was when Eliran, who she learned was one of Sinjinn's brothers—and there seemed to be an endless number of them—examined her. He'd spent hours examining her, testing her for certain things, which seemed to end up with either his equipment melting or freezing and erring.

Today, though, she was laid on top of a medical bed, with a strange probe searching her flat stomach. He'd placed goop all over her, and then seemed to be pushing it against her stomach as he searched for the hearts of her babies. It seemed like a waste of time, but what the hell did she know?

Static was the only noise in the room, and her nerves were fried beyond her normal stress level as several people had crowded outside the room, waiting. Synthia stood to the side of her, holding her hand which, to Icelyn, felt strange and unwarranted, but she wasn't about to point that out to a Goddess.

The room exploded with a thumping noise and Icelyn jumped, her shoulders were pushed down by Sinjinn who had stood beside her, a smile lifting his lips as his eyes grew round with wonder.

"There's baby A," Eliran said, and Icelyn felt the blood leave her face as she stared up at Sinjinn's wide smile. Synthia squeezed her hand reassuringly as Eliran continued his search. Hollering sounded in the hallway as the men clapped each other on their backs and catcalled to Sinjinn about his skills to procreate. Like the Neanderthal needed encouragement?

More thumping started, and tears filled her eyes as she processed what it was. Babies. They had created life, and the proof was in the strong heartbeats that echoed through the room. Her eyes moved to the monitor, finding only a small little blurry spot that looked like a speck. Her throat tightened, and she closed her eyes against the stark reality that was playing out around her.

They were celebrating the lives she and Sinjinn had created, even her husband was. Life in Faery was so fragile, and every life mattered here. While the lesser courts had no issue creating female children, the High Fae struggled to conceive them. While the High Fae had trouble keeping their children alive or being accepted by the lands, the lowland Fae didn't. Her children would be a mix of both, and therein lay the problem she had to confront.

"What is the probability of them surviving birth?" her voice was so tiny against the celebrating men that only Synthia seemed to note her words.

"We are uncertain of it, but the Tree of Life is flowing

once more, and more and more, children survive," she said as she squeezed her hand together, smiling down at her.

"But you can't know if it will have enough magic to accept mine."

"There's no reason it shouldn't," Sinjinn pointed out.

"I am ready for whatever happens," Eliran said as he wiped the goo from her belly. "I have human equipment that we brought in, along with doctors who have studied pregnancy and what we assume created the disturbance in the land, and this isn't our first go at delivering babies, or multiple births."

"Rumor has it that the Goddess was cut open after death, and the babes were taken from her corpse. I'm sorry if I sound a little harsh, or fail to buy that you have a plan. No one can predict the Tree of Life, or if it will not accept a child, nor can you promise me they, and I, will survive the birthing process. Twins are rare, are they not?"

"Very, but once upon a time, they were expected."

"That was over five hundred years ago." Her eyes followed him as he nodded to confirm her fears. "Which means this is going to be a learning curve for you as well," she stated firmly, her eyes narrowing as his lifted to lock with hers.

"I will not let you or my brother's children die. I'm sick of bloodshed and losing. I will do everything in my power to keep you all alive."

She swallowed and nodded as her gaze moved to Sinjinn's, who watched her carefully. The pride in his gaze terrified her, making her stomach churn with the stark reality of just how fragile their situation was.

"I need fresh air," she whispered as she allowed him to help her sit up.

"I'll take you to the balcony."

"So I'm a prisoner still?" she seethed. Her emotions were going haywire, and the more she was constricted to the bedroom, the angrier she was becoming.

"You know you're not."

"No, but I'm not allowed outside. I am always watched, and even though I can't go home, I am forced to those rooms that you approve. I am your prisoner."

"You're free to go outside as long as you have guards watching you. We are at war, Icelyn. It isn't safe to be outside the gates."

"Fine, is there a garden?" she countered.

"Take her to my garden and allow her to catch her breath, Sinjinn. She's about to have a panic attack, and it isn't good for either her or the babes she carries. She's used to being able to come and go as she pleases, and while I agree it isn't safe that she do so, caging women can harm them more internally than externally. Just be careful since Erie disarmed the wards on her way out, and we have to replace them."

"Thank you," Icelyn stated as she jumped down from the table to stare at Sinjinn, who shook his head. "I'm not asking to be freed, I'm just asking for fresh air. I have been patient, but I am not used to being locked up in a castle. In mine, they preferred I was outside of it. I spent most of my time in the ice caves since no one else would dare enter them."

"You're not a prisoner, you're mine," he said gruffly.

"Technically...she is mine. I will take her out for

fresh air if you are busy," Cailean offered, his eyes sparkling with mirth.

"I'll fucking take her, asshole."

"I thought as much. Enjoy the fresh air, *wife*." Cailean winked and walked off, as if he'd only used their situation to piss Sinjinn off.

This entire situation was so weird that she wasn't even sure she understood it or wanted to. More than likely, she didn't. She allowed Sinjinn to offer her his arm for support, and with the brothers all smiling or patting his shoulder, they left the castle.

CHAPTER
THIRTY-NINE

Outside, the cold air soothed, calming the chaos that ravaged her soul with everything unfolding around her so rapidly. It was too much to process, and yet the idea of becoming a mother was settling over her with surprising ease after hearing their perfect heartbeats. Her gaze slowly descended over the brilliant splashes of dazzling colors that bathed the garden in every shade and hue with heady flowers that filled the air with their enticing scent. However, it wasn't just the flowers that soothed her emotions; Sinjinn and his overpowering presence eased the stress that threatened to consume her as well.

"You seem quiet," he whispered from directly behind her, forcing her to turn around to face him.

"I don't know what to say," she admitted, albeit begrudgingly. Her eyelashes were heavy with the tears that threatened to spill as she shook her head. "I married your brother. I'm pregnant with your children, and my kingdom is about to be laid to ruins. I don't know what to say, let alone how to feel about any of this."

"You married Cailean, but who cares? Fae take lovers all the time, it's as normal as breathing to us."

"Not to me! I don't take lovers, Sinjinn." Her eyes swung up to hold his with the anger she felt. That anger was driving her tears, and she hated that she hated the situation and not him. He was an oaf, yeah, but she had enjoyed being with said oaf. She didn't regret it, or how they'd ended up together, only everything else that they'd been forced into because they held no control over their own lives.

"You take me," he chuckled as he pulled her closer, pushing her wild hair away from her face as he pressed a kiss to her forehead. "You're going to have my babies."

Her arms wrapped around his waist as she placed her head against the warmth of his chest. The air was bitingly cold, something that normally didn't reach this far south into Faery, and yet she wasn't so sure that she wasn't the cause of it again. Her emotions were every which way and more, which sometimes could affect the weather.

"I can't believe you knocked me up," she whispered into the crisp, clean shirt he wore. Her hands bunched into it as she inhaled his unique scent of embers and spices.

"I can't believe you let me," he chuckled as she pulled back and made a fist to hit him with. He caught it, pulling her back against his chest as the first fluffy white snowflakes began to fall into Synthia's beloved garden. "You're making it snow," he acknowledged.

"I can't make snow this hard unless I'm upset," she admonished as her eyes lifted towards the skies and she narrowed her gaze as it seemed to intensify. "Only the king or current ruler of the court can make it come down like this."

"Maybe it's a winter miracle?" he uttered against her ear.

"It's a miracle that I don't break your neck for letting your brother do what he did without warning me."

"And if I'd warned you, you'd have fought it. It worked, didn't it? You've fulfilled the oath, and you're still mine. I didn't have to fight him for you, and make no mistake, Icelyn: I would have fought the Gods themselves to keep you."

The snow seemed to intensify as her mood grew angrier, her eyes wet with the unshed tears of uncertainty. She felt as if she was on a collision course that was set in motion before she'd ever realized she'd been set upon it. Her life had been a series of events that had pulled her in different directions until she wasn't sure which way she should be going, and yet he felt right.

This man who she'd shot with an arrow to scare off, the one whose kisses left her as hot as the fire that burned inside of him, he was *her* right. What had started out as something dark and deadly was now light and beautiful no matter how forbidden it had been. They'd fulfilled the oath, saving her and anyone else from paying the consequences of breaking it, from certain death. She pulled away from him and bent over to sniff a flower, turning back to him as words started to form in her throat, words she'd never thought she'd say in her lifetime.

"I…" Her words stopped, her eyes gazed into his as Sinjinn stared at her, his hand covering his chest as he coughed and stared down at his chest where an arrow protruded from it.

"Run," he uttered as blood exploded from his lips.

Her heartbeat exploded in her ears as she rushed towards him, pressing her hand against the spot that seemed to be expelling blood at an alarming rate from the gaping wound even though the arrow was still embedded in his chest.

Not now, not when everything was falling into place. Not as those words had been about to fall from her lips.

"Move!" she begged him as she started them towards the castle, only for a hand to rip against her hair, pulling her backwards, away from Sinjinn, who dropped to his knees without her support.

"Hello, darling daughter," the king whispered against her ear as he placed his other hand over her mouth with an obnoxious odor that made the world swim in her vision. "Bring him, he can be the entertainment."

Icelyn screamed silently for help. For anyone who could hear her screams and to appear and save them, but it was hopeless as the world went dark around her. Her body grew limp against her father's, and everything began to shut down as he continued to press the rag over her nose and mouth.

Sinjinn struggled through the pain as he watched her go limp against the Winter King's hold. She was handed off to one of his men, who stared down at the ripped bodice of her gown lecherously. He'd kill them all, one by one. He sent a message to his brothers, knowing they'd hear it and come for them, yet the time ticked by, and no one materialized inside the gardens. It would be moments before the guards passed by the gates to check on it because he'd asked them to allow them privacy. He wanted to kick his own ass as he stared out the open, unguarded gates.

"I bet you're thinking help will come before we leave here?" The king asked as he studied Sinjinn through ice-cold blue eyes. "The Mages have been very helpful lately, willing to do anything to remain hidden from you and your kind until they're ready to fight you. They are talented in blocking out communication and protective barriers." He shrugged as the white fur he wore around his shoulders shook with his laughter.

"You will die screaming."

"Probably, but not before you and that whore daughter of mine do," he said crudely, standing back up to his full height as he nodded in his direction. "Bring him, and place the scent blockers the Mages sent with us in the same wagon. I will not be denied watching him die this time, not after he's taken what is mine from me."

Sinjinn stared at Icelyn, her prone body cradled in the arms of the man who had been with her when she'd shot him. The one who had wanted to gain power, according to Ryder and what he had recanted about what had happened when she'd shot him. Bale, if he wasn't mistaken? He marked him for death, memorizing every minute detail of the man's face.

Pain ripped through him as men moved behind him, hefting him up as they started to withdraw from the garden. They didn't use the main door, which explained how they'd gotten in without him knowing it. Instead, they moved towards what looked to be a hidden entrance that he'd been unaware of until now, one used by the harem to obtain the fresh flowers would be his guess. Sinjinn struggled against the men, dripping blood everywhere in his weak struggle to escape their hold as droplets sprinkled the walkway.

The male behind them splashed a blue liquid that sizzled and offended his nose as it ate away at the concrete flooring. Sinjinn knew they'd used poisonous gas, one that would ruin any chance the Fae would have of tracking them, but what they failed to notice about the Horde was that they tracked through blood bonds, through something much deeper than scent, and the one thing they couldn't eradicate from them: bloodlines.

CHAPTER
FORTY

Icelyn awoke to something kicking her leg; her eyes were heavy as if someone had glued them closed. Her mouth tasted like she'd sucked on chemicals, and the more she licked her lips, the more she wanted to throw her guts up. Once she'd finally pried them open, it was to find her father staring down at her with hatred pouring from his gaze, and worse, lust.

"You shouldn't have trespassed against the court, Icelyn. Now no one can save you from me."

"I didn't have much of an option, now did I?" she groaned as she took in the damage he'd done.

Her leg throbbed from where he'd been kicking her for a while, apparent from the pain and bruises already forming on her lower calf. Icelyn's head pounded, but then he'd probably used chloroform or something similar to subdue her. Her hands were bound behind her back, making it impossible to sit up, but the worst part was Sinjinn's limp form that had been laid out beside her in the cart that was pulling them away from the

---

Horde, away from the people who could save him.

"You were always so willing to spread those legs for the simpletons of court, yet you refused to do as I bid and take a Horde Prince to your bed? Now you've damned the entire court, and they know who the blame lies with."

"The oath is sealed, and the Horde was appeased until you murdered their men!"

"No, Icelyn, until you sent my men out to fight them," he chuckled coldly. "Those who died were led astray by a perfect princess who convinced them to betray their king. They were dealt with, swiftly."

"You think they will believe that? The Horde knows who gave those orders. They know you killed their men. If you're trying to save face and live, you are a little late."

"I don't care what the Horde thinks, only what my people think."

"The ones you sent out to die? You are not the people's king, not the king by birth, and I know my mother is unaware of what you have done. She would never stand for this!"

"Oh, you've been gone haven't you? Your mother had a horrible accident, she's dead."

Icelyn stared up into Gerald's cold gaze. There was no emotion whatsoever in his icy blue depths. The hair on her nape raised in awareness at the changes in his eyes, the slithering insects that lay just beneath the irises. The flesh on his arms was off-color, a pale yellow color that seemingly pulsed with his slightest movement. As if he'd tried to steal brands, and yet failed.

Her heart pounded in her chest as a silent scream

curdled in her throat as she held it at bay. He'd killed her mother? He had been trying to kill Icelyn forever, but she'd been beyond his reach until now. Had he refocused his hatred towards her mother instead? Had her action led to her mother's death? Tears built in her eyes as she closed them against the hatred and victory she watched blooming in his eyes as the pain became too much.

"Open your eyes, girl," he demanded, and when she refused, his foot connected with her stomach and she wailed, her eyes opening wide as Sinjinn's growl sounded from in front of her. "I earned this; don't think you can take it from me."

"You bastard, how could you?" she demanded as she struggled against the ropes that held her. "She was your wife and my mother!"

"That whore begged him to fuck her in front of the entire court! I loved her, and she begged him to continue as I watched. So yes, she is no longer with us or part of this world, which is my world now. Mine, a world I have earned from the moment I was taught to take your mother's crown by force if need be!"

"You are only king because of her! You are nothing without her!" she hissed.

"I am nothing? I have her whore of a daughter at my mercy. The Horde King's brother at heel, and a few new allies who plan to help me rid this world of any who oppose my rule!"

"The entire world of Faery will fight your rule if you do this," she warned as she struggled against the rope that held her bound. Her eyes moved to Sinjinn's, his green glow telling her that he was fighting to get out of the restraints, but he was wounded.

Blood oozed from his wound, pooling around his body as he stared at her, trying to figure a way out of their current mess. Funny, since she'd shot him and he'd healed from it. Her eyes moved to the wound and the iron arrow her stepfather had left in it. Now that they weren't blocked by the magic the Mages had given them to use in the gardens, she could smell the magic attached to the arrow, and worse, poison.

It was stealing his strength, pushing more and more of the vile substance into his system. Her father still rambled on and yet she heard nothing over her increasing heartbeat as she stared across the small cart they'd been hidden within. It continued to hit bump after bump, telling her they were moving at an alarming rate away from the Horde, and any help that would have come for them.

"You think the Horde King will allow you to keep your throne if you kill him?" she tried, her mind racing with how to save Sinjinn before the poison was too deep into his system to be removed.

"I think you will never live long enough to know if he does or not. You see, I can't have you hanging around to ruin my plans. I will, however, let you live long enough to watch me kill your lover." He stood up, turning around to where Sinjinn lay prone, once more passed out from the arrow protruding from his chest. "They're vile creatures, and yet it's been said you screamed for him, begged him to fuck you just as your mother did for his father. Is it true? Did you beg him to fuck you?"

"You made this deal, you sent me to them!"

"To *be fucked*! You were never supposed to make it to their stronghold, let alone be with him, and yet that sweet little cunt of yours ruined everything!" His eyes glazed over with hatred as he pushed a blade through Sinjinn's chest.

Tears burned Icelyn's eyes as she bit down on her lip, preventing the scream that bubbled up in her chest as she watched her stepfather push the knife deeper as Sinjinn screamed in pain. His green eyes widened in pain as the iron blade was driven into his chest over and over again until it was a mess of mutilated flesh.

"How powerful are you now, asshole?" her father chuckled with a sickening reverberation that echoed in the cart. He withdrew the bloody blade and stared at the blood that bubbled and hissed on the iron blade.

"I will kill you," Sinjinn said, but it was lethargic, empty. His eyes lost focus and Icelyn closed her eyes, praying that her father didn't turn the blade on her and her unborn children. She wouldn't heal as Sinjinn could, and to die when she'd just discovered that she was irrevocably changed wasn't fair.

"Sire," Bale's deep voice filled the wagon as he entered it, uncaring that it moved at a breakneck pace. Hope flared into her heart as she took him in, only to be dashed away by the hatred she saw in his eyes as he looked down at her. The sound of hooves crunching over the ground met her ears as she studied him, watching her friend as he knelt down beside her, pushing her thick white-blonde hair away from her face. "We are almost to the tunnels," he confirmed as the king nodded.

"We've made perfect timing, and our friend in the tunnel, you think he will keep his word?" he asked, wiping the blood off the blade and onto his cloak before he moved towards the far end of the wagon, pausing.

"I think he will," Bale agreed as he stared down at Icelyn with something cold burning in his dull blue eyes. "And my promise, is she mine for now?" he asked.

"She is yours until we reach him, *Sir* Bale," he laughed coldly. "Why you would want to lie with a whore who willingly begged the Horde swine to fuck her is beyond me, but we made a deal, and I will honor it. Don't mess up her face, though, that needs to remain pretty until she is given to the monster, he wanted her as she is."

"Thank you, sire," Bale said with something cold in his words, sending a shiver racing through Icelyn as she continued to stare up at the boy she'd befriended as a child.

Once her father exited the wagon, she swallowed and watched him as he took in her disheveled appearance. His hand moved, grabbing her breast roughly as a groan expelled from her lip.

"Don't do this, Bale. You're my friend," she urged.

"You were never my friend. I only watch you for your father, and for his favor, you stupid bitch," he chuckled as he lowered his mouth, licking the side of her face as his hand gripped her breast painfully. He pulled back, staring down as his hands grabbed the front of her dress and ripped it apart, sending buttons scattering across the wagon floor. "I wanted to be your first introduction to pleasure, though, and yet you always refused me. I was only the poor wee lad who you pitied. You never cared how much I tried to catch your attention, or that I wanted to be the one who made you into a woman. I could have taught you so much before you were saddled with him, but then even he was unwilling to let me have you. I think he has a thing for you, something that's been festering for a long time. Now, now I get to fuck you until he decides to end your life or keep you, and then I get your sweet sister as my bride and finally get the recognition I deserve for having to watch you all these years."

"Bale, it was never like that between us, you were my friend. You knew that, and I didn't lead you on," she whimpered as she retreated from his touch as his mouth lowered to her exposed nipple. His tongue jutted out, tracing the puckered flesh as she shook her head, bile rising in her throat. "Please don't do this. If I ever meant anything to you at all, don't do this," she pleaded as hot tears of anger burned her eyes.

His free hand pushed against her sex, and he chuckled. "That's just it, Icelyn. You never did, you were a way to the throne, nothing more. I was going to be your husband if I could find a way to keep you in line and was willing to look the other way when he took you. I was going to fuck you and ruin you so that no one could argue that you were mine, and then everything would have fallen into place. Once I'd fucked you, rumors would have spread across the kingdom; your father would have forced you to agree to be mine for your failure to follow protocol."

"Who are you talking about? And my father is the one who gave me away!" she cried as he lifted the skirt of her ruined dress and stared down at her naked flesh.

"You don't get it, Icelyn. They would have never made it out of the Winter Court alive, but you ruined it. You showed them how to get free. I warned you not to go out hunting for him, and yet you ignored me. I begged you to stay with me while the princes made their way to the court, and yet you refused. I had it planned, and they'd never have taken you. You messed it all up! Instead of being my bride, you married a monster. Instead of giving me what I earned for years of dealing with your endless shit, he got you!" he stood up, turning to kick Sinjinn's unmoving body over and over again.

"Take me!" she screamed, her eyes swimming with tears as she stared at the man who had given her everything, who was now bleeding out and being abused, unable to recover from it with the iron poisoning him.

"Now you want me?" he laughed coldly as he worked his pants until he freed his flaccid cock. He moved with purpose, pushing apart her legs as he stroked it to no avail. Dangerous laughter bubbled in her throat as she watched him stroking his tiny cock as he stared at her cunt.

"Stage fright?" she laughed as she watched him with a deadly glare burning in her eyes.

He reached back and slapped her hard. She denied making a sound as he lowered his mouth, clamping it over her nipple as he continued to fondle the cock that refused to grow. He abandoned his cock and pushed his fingers into her flesh, clumsily using them as he roughly tried to coax her body to respond.

"Pray it rises because there are other things I can use to make this pussy come for me," he laughed coldly as he added another finger, and then another, until a whimper of pain expelled from her lips. "I bet you could fit my entire fist in here after fucking that monster. Shall

I cut his cock off and use it on you?" he snickered as he watched the fear that flared in her eyes as the words left his lips.

"You're enough." Even she heard the half-hearted lie in her voice as he pushed his hand against her opening, balling it into a fist as fear consumed her. "You're enough, Bale. But you're hurting me," she whimpered as he stared down at the flesh he was abusing.

It wasn't enough. He stared at her, punching her over and over again in the stomach as an ugly sneer covered his lips. She whimpered and cried as he hurt her, his cock responding as he punished her. He enjoyed hurting her, and she wondered how she'd never noticed the ugliness of him before now.

He pushed her legs apart, staring at her red flesh as he looked down to where his cock was now hard, ready to rape her. She closed her eyes as he settled between her legs and rubbed it against her opening as he moaned and hissed at the connection of flesh on flesh.

His cock began to push into her body, and then he howled with pain as he backed up, patting against his clothing that had burst into flames. Bale continued to slap at them until he gave up and began rolling on the cart's floor, unable to accomplish what he needed with the limited room. His cock was melting, and a silent laugh bubbled up from her throat as she watched him.

He rolled over her, searing her flesh as she watched him in amusement. Her eyes flickered to Sinjinn's, finding his hands black as the sweet scent of embers and cinnamon filled the wagon. Emerald eyes stared into hers, and she shook her head as the life began to fade from them.

Her chest ached as a scream of denial bubbled up from deep in her chest as he expelled a breath and silence met her ears. His heart stalled, his breathing stopped, and his lifeless eyes stared at her unseeingly. Everything inside of her exploded with denial as Bale continued to scream, his hand grabbing at his cock, which had been burned badly.

"You did this to me!" he accused as he kicked her over and over again, even though she didn't respond or acknowledge it. Her entire world was spiraling as she ignored the pain and struggled to comprehend what she was seeing. "You fucking whore!"

His foot kicked her in her stomach, and she hissed out a breath as she looked up at him, her hatred for him growing to an unbearable level. Ice thickened the air as she let the hopelessness and anger boil into her soul and explode around her. It wasn't an epic storm, but it was cold enough that Bale had to pause and break the ice that was beginning to encase him.

"I am the princess of the Winter Court, not fire!" she seethed. "*You* betrayed me! You were supposed to be my friend!" Ice clung to his skin, and as she watched him, Bale's body began to turn against him until there was no blood heating him from within; just ice that used every ounce of fluid in his body to compound and compress until he whimpered in pain. He swallowed, but his body was no longer his to control. She added power, unbridled power, until he shattered into a thousand tiny pieces and hit the floor as if he'd been composed of nothing but glass.

Her eyes moved to Sinjinn's, finding his vacant stare as she scooted towards him, pushing her magic into him as he lay unmoving. He couldn't leave her now, she wouldn't allow it. They had been through too much to get to where they were; they'd beaten an ironclad oath, and he wasn't getting away from her this easy.

"Stay with me, Sinjinn," she pleaded as her mouth brushed against his, coaxing life back into him. "Stay with us."

She pushed more magic into him, feeling nothing back from him. He'd overcome the arrow she'd shot at him, but that one hadn't been dipped in poison and she'd aimed it for organs she had known would easily recover from the wound. But she'd also known how much time she'd had to remove it before it could end his life permanently.

Closing her eyes, she sent a prayer to the Goddess, begging them to save him before it was too late. In her mind, she unlocked every puzzle for Synthia to reach them in the Winter Court, begging her to be there before they reached it through the tunnels, before Sinjinn died from the iron and magic poisoning him. She screamed Synthia's name over and over until her eyes grew heavy and wetness coated her thighs. Icelyn stared down at her exposed sex, watching as blood dripped down her thighs. Darkness welcomed her, and she no longer had the will to deny it, and with one last kiss against Sinjinn's unmoving lips, she let it take her.

CHAPTER FORTY-ONE

Rough hands picked her up, dragging her across the bloodied cart towards the opening. Her eyes gained focus and landed on Sinjinn, who was moving, albeit slowly as he fought against the people who dragged him behind her. She was handed down to men on the ground and then blinked as the ethereal Seelie Prince came into focus.

Her stepfather was going too far, making the wrong kind of allies for the Winter Court. This one, though, this one was going to bite him in the ass, hard. The Seelie were notorious for turning on everyone they'd ever helped, and if he thought they were going to let him off, he was wrong, dead wrong.

"And so my pretty has returned to me," he crooned as he waited just inside the tunnel, staring at her. His eyes dipped to her stomach, to the blood that ran down her thigh, and coldness entered his beautiful stare. His jaw clenched as he lifted those eyes to hers.

Blackish-blue hair turned into swirling strands as he

turned, eyeing Gerald with something akin to the hatred burning in them. Those iridescent eyes began to swirl with color as he smiled coldly to the king.

"Is she mine?" he asked, his voice a shrill of sound that made her need to cover her ears, to protect them.

"Eventually, if you hold up your end of the agreement, most of the women at the Winter Court will be yours to kill, except my daughter as we agreed. She will not be killed, but she is yours to play with for a while as was requested, but the court can be used as you wish. A buffet of pussy for the taking, all you can eat, Seelie Prince," Gerald agreed, his wintery gaze moving to hers as he smiled, showing his chipped teeth.

It was hard to believe she had once considered him handsome, even though he'd been trying to kill her at the time, but then she'd thought he was supposed to love her unconditionally too. She'd understood how her mother had once loved him, but more and more, his madness was revealed until it chipped away at the glamour he'd used to make them all see past his ugliness. To the true monster he'd always been.

The Seelie Prince moved, stepping outside the tunnel, and Icelyn whimpered as fear took hold of her. The endless possibility of what they could do once they'd been freed started to play out in her mind, and yet the moment he touched her arm, the pain abated, and he pulled her closer to his body, righting the dress that Bale had ripped apart.

"I can't have everyone seeing my Queen exposed, now can I?" he whispered against her ear as his magic slithered over her flesh.

She swallowed hard as he turned her around, his

eyes slowly moving to her stomach as if he could sense her delicate situation. His smile strained as he shook his head. Those colorful eyes seemed to look past her to where Sinjinn was now kneeling in iron chains.

"Oh, the web they weave for us," he smirked as he turned, eying the king. "And we should go, as I am hungry and you are about to be slaughtered by the Horde who is giving chase."

"They'll never discover the location of the Winter Court, not in a million years," Gerald snickered with confidence.

"You'd be surprised by what they can do," he said as he turned to Icelyn and winked at her. "Especially when they have those who want them to find it quickly," he said with a gentle shrug of his wide shoulders as his brands began to pulse over his naked chest. "Come, you can ride with me, Icelyn, I rather enjoy a pretty face over theirs."

"Lead the way, Seelie."

"Gerald, you know the way and being sneaky is beneath you, or is it your own daughter you wish to be beneath you? It's neither here nor there, really. Unless you want to bring up the rear and fight the Horde, I suggest you lead us, and I'll handle sealing the tunnels once it is needed."

Gerald glared at him before dropping his eyes to Icelyn and smiling victoriously. Those lecherous eyes lowered to her fixed dress and then went even lower to where her thighs were exposed.

"I'd like to watch you with her, at least once," he said as bile stung the back of Icelyn's throat.

"I fear I don't prefer an audience, or her father

289

watching me with her as I feed," he said as he folded his arms over his chest, staring down the king with absolutely no fear. "Not to mention it is a little twisted even for you, to want to watch your own daughter being fucked, is it not?"

"Oh, you see, she isn't mine. Her whore of a mother allowed herself to be raped by the Light King, and she tried to pass the little cunt off as my child. So fucking her isn't off the table for me. Not when I am not related to her in the slightest, so consider it, because I'm adding it into our deal. You will fuck her and allow me to watch as you take parts of her away from her. After all, that's how she will live beside me, mindless and willing to do anything I say."

"Interesting, so my little beauty is Light Fae? I'm intrigued."

"You have an order to fuck her until she bleeds, and then when she's begging for more, you will take away her mind and feed her back what I tell you to. That is the agreement we made, and you will uphold the deal."

"Is that so? You, the lesser being, think to give me orders? I agreed to help you because it intrigued me, but make no mistake, I am no longer weakened from the prison which held me, and you're not stronger than me. Tread carefully, King of Nothing, because that is what you will be should you think to give me new conditions or order me around."

Gerald turned a shade of mottled red, his anger visible as he stared down the Seelie, but where the prince had shown not an ounce of fear, Gerald stunk of it. Realization of who he had brokered a deal with was sinking in, and Icelyn knew he was forming a plan to trap his newest ally, and ice wasn't strong enough to accomplish it.

"You dare speak to me this way when I freed you? I brought you women to consume, to murder so that you were strong enough to leave these tunnels, and your word is bond, is it not?"

"It is, but I never agreed to be your fucking pet, Gerald. Remember that, because the moment you forget and treat me as such, your life ends." He smirked at Icelyn as he grabbed her arm, pulling her closer as horses were brought to them. "Up you go, my queen," he said as he sat her on the horse and jumped up behind her effortlessly.

His body dwarfed hers as she twisted to see where Sinjinn was placed, but the subtle tsking in her ear stalled her. "Do not let him see that you care or he will suffer ten times the amount he already has, princess."

"Why do you care if he suffers?" she asked softly, shivering as his arms wrapped around her as he grabbed the reins.

"Who said I cared?" he asked as his nose brushed against her ear. "You're in pain."

"How astute of an observation," she hissed as pain twisted her stomach.

"You're with child," he said.

"No," she word played as every instinct to protect her babes kicked in. There wasn't a child, there were two.

"Calm down, they're unaware of what you carry inside your womb. You will lose them if you don't get help soon. I can save them, but what it would require may be too much for you to endure."

"My firstborn son? No way," she whimpered.

His hand settled on her stomach and heat blossomed where he touched, the pain lessening as her eyes closed.

"This isn't some fairytale children's books, and I don't want a bairn. I meant, how I have to heal you isn't...proper, but my kind can heal with our mouths, among...other organs."

"You're lying," she hissed.

"I cannot lie, unfortunately. One of the less attractive abilities I inherited from my father; luckily I did get wings out of the match, which is more than my siblings got."

"How is it that you have wings and only the Horde King himself does?"

"Magic," he laughed huskily against her ear. "I'm my mother's son as well, and she was of sex and sin, and merciless. She hated us, those she created with him. Yet every time he came, she parted her flesh and let him fuck it to make more."

"How many of you are there left?" she asked, turning to stare at Sinjinn, who watched her with an intensity that punched her in the gut.

"Not as many as I'd like, but enough to set the world on fire in chaos and war, should we choose to," he admitted as he turned, staring at Sinjinn with a pained wince. "It's probably best they left that arrow in, for he won't like the way I save his young."

"I have not agreed yet. We also seem to have an audience, and unless you have a plan to rid us of them, it seems moot."

"Do you think I am not capable of making it so?" he asked, entirely too close against her neck as he inhaled her deeply.

"I am taken," she uttered.

"I'm aware." His lips brushed over her shoulder. "And impressed he finally placed a mark on you. I was beginning to think his kind weak since they have forgotten our ways. Tell me, does he make you scream? Beg to come until everything inside of you is ablaze with need? I miss fucking the most, hearing my partner beg me to allow them their release."

"If he didn't, do you think I'd want him to live?" she asked, straightening her spine as his erection pushed against her, letting its sheer size and length be known.

"Good, so he is worth saving," he chuckled.

"You can save us?"

"No, no, I am bound by word, which I gave. I will see this through until we reach the Winter Palace, and then I will make my way to the human world, where there seems to be an endless supply of wanton women just begging for real men who know how to make them come. This world is in chaos, and in a downward spiral. Should I stay, I'd have to fight my brethren for the throne, and I'm no longer sure I wish to sit upon it."

"You'll help me save the babes?"

"Ahh, so you are aware that two sweet babes have been planted and not just one," he uttered as his hand lifted from her stomach, hesitant as if he could feel her pain. "We need to do this soon, you're bleeding, and their cage is failing to keep them housed. You're about to miscarry."

"Okay, save them. I'll do whatever it takes," she whispered.

"And so the soon-to-be Winter Queen falls to the Prince of the Seelie," he whispered as he kissed her neck, sealing the deal.

CHAPTER
FORTY-TWO

They continued on for a little over an hour before Asher, as she had learned the Seelie's name was, called for them to halt. Gerald argued with him as Icelyn tried to remain on the stallion, hiding the pain that rocked through her body until sweat beaded against her brow. Her eyes moved to Sinjinn's as he sat on the horse, barely moving as his chest rose and fell, giving her some comfort that he was alive.

Those green eyes demanded she not do what she was about to, and even though it terrified her, she'd heard the rumors of the Seelie having healing power through sex or sexual contact. If it saved her unborn children, she'd sell her soul to the devil himself. Her gaze moved back to Asher who was walking back to where she waited.

"You will feed me, princess," he growled as he moved to assist her from the horse. "You, bring her boyfriend so he can watch the show."

The guards laughed as they pulled Sinjinn down from the horse, watching as he hit the ground hard, jolting the arrow that still had yet to be removed. His growl was the only sound that escaped, his eyes wild with hatred as he looked up at the guards and then to Asher.

He was picked up and forced to follow behind them as they walked towards the larger wagon that sat in the middle of the ground passing through the tunnels. Asher lifted her, pushing her into the privacy of the wagon as he turned, pulling up Sinjinn and then baring fangs at the guards.

"You're done here, get lost."

"If he gets free, he will kill you," one pointed out as his eyes narrowed on Asher.

"He has an iron arrow dipped in bane that is devouring him from the inside out. I'm also Seelie, his fucking match in strength and magic. So as I said, get lost. Three's already crowded, but Gerald wanted him to watch me fuck his girl."

"Make her scream so the rest of us can enjoy it." The third guard smiled coldly as he stared at Icelyn. "Stuck-up bitch never even noticed the dick around her, saved it for the Horde bastard, she did."

"It's my understanding that the lesser Fae preserve their innocence for their mates. Had she noticed your dick, she wouldn't have held her oath to the crown, now would she? I doubt that little thing in your pants is worth losing a crown over. Now go before I decide to include feeding from you to be included in my list of needs." Once they were gone, he turned, pushing his fingers through his hair as he knelt down in front of Sinjinn and eyed the wounds in his chest. "You're fucked, brother. That's iron dipped in bane, more aptly named in the lesser regions as Faebane. I can't heal you, not without them noticing it. I can save your babes, but I need you not to set me on fire. Do you understand me?"

"Touch her and you fucking die," he uttered barely above a whisper.

"That's the problem. I don't need to touch her per se; I need to lick her cunt to send my saliva into her womb, because in the next few moments, she will lose your children. I get it, you don't know me from dick, you don't trust me, and you damn well shouldn't because I'm not a nice guy. I've fucked women just to watch them lose their shit on my dick, but this one, this one is yours, and she is in danger of losing those babes she's been fighting to keep. She's been abused, almost raped based on the weak scent on her, and yet she's still fighting to keep them. So you're going to watch me eat that pussy and yeah, she's going to come for me because it's unavoidable. I'm damn good at fucking, but I'm the one who is going to save her and your unborn babes. Don't like it? Too fucking bad, brother. They're going to abuse her more, and your babes are strong, but they're not planted deeply enough yet to hold on through what she's going to endure before your people reach us. I know, because I'm about to block the only fucking path into the Winter Court."

"You can't think of any other fucking way than this?"

"It's my tongue or my dick, figured watching me fuck her would be a limit you'd rather not endure. I can't just spit on her cervix and make it better. I have to make her body respond so that it accepts what I offer, or beat that cervix up and color it pretty. Either way, those bastards are outside waiting to hear her scream for me, so you need to decide. Am I changing my mind and finding her lacking, or am I tongue-fucking that flesh?"

Sinjinn swallowed as anger and pain shot through him. His gaze moved to Icelyn, who was watching him with tears streaking down her cheeks as she pleaded with him silently. He wasn't sure what emotion to grasp onto, but the fact that she'd made a deal with this creature to save her babes, *their* babes, meant she wanted them. She wanted his kids to grow in her womb, to remain growing there.

"We are going to be okay," he said softly, knowing she knew what he was saying. "Help is coming."

"I don't need them to come and save us. He is leading me home, to where my power is the strongest. Once we are there, I'm going to kill every last one of them."

He stared at her, his heart sluggishly slow as the burning acid continued to push through his system. He didn't doubt she'd win against them on her own turf, but he wasn't sure he'd survive long enough to get there.

"When she comes, you feed and I won't," Asher said firmly. "Use it to hang on until they get to you. She's already shown the Goddess the position of the Winter Court, which I have no intention of being at when they enter it. So, yes or no?"

"Try not to enjoy it too much."

"I can't lie and tell you I won't; our father gave me your lame ass trait of being unable to lie. Unlike my brothers, I'm the only asshole inflicted with it," he shrugged. "You, pull up your skirt and get ready to go to heaven. There's going to be fingers involved, tongue, and a lot of fucking screaming. My name is Asher, not Sinjinn, don't confuse us, sweetheart."

"And what do I owe you for this?"

"You'll know it when the time comes, and it will, you will do it without hesitating. Understand?"

"I won't kill anyone for you or give you my children, ever. I won't compromise who I am or my integrity to help you. If what you need doesn't involve those, I accept."

"I won't take your babes, and I won't agree to the other things because visions change, and you may need to resort to murderous measures to do it."

"Does it involve killing or betraying anyone I know or care about?" she asked.

He pinched his nose and swung his iridescent gaze at Sinjinn. "Does she always ask so many questions?"

"No, she normally just swings first and asks you later."

"Someone you care about? No, someone you know? Maybe. Decide, because your father is outside pacing and my shield is about to drop which will allow him to hear everything happening in here."

"Agreed," she said as she slowly moved to do as he said, wincing as the cramps intensified with the slight movement. Her fingers trembled as she lifted her skirt and bared the abused flesh that was covered in fresh and dried blood, which stuck to her thighs. Sinjinn's sharp intake of breath made fresh tears form in her eyes as she turned away from him.

"It isn't your fault," Asher whispered as he waved his hand and her flesh was cleansed of the blood and proof that Bale had assaulted her. "You killed him; you blew him the fuck up. He has no control now. This, this is business, nothing more. Now pretend you don't want it, so that sick-as-shit father of yours enjoys it and gets his kicks off."

"Stepfather, thankfully," she muttered.

"Oh, sweetheart, your real father is twice as twisted." His eyes turned white as his flesh turned black, covering them with his wings as he blocked Sinjinn's view of them. A small kindness as his eyes dropped to her naked sex, and a sinful smirk covered his full lips. "You smell like peasant stock," he growled loudly, and she knew his shield had dropped.

His knuckles brushed her sex and pleasure ripped through her. It was a terrifying pleasure, the legendary sexual power of the Seelie in full force as he toyed with her, igniting the flame within. His fingers fondled softly, leisurely as he watched the heat blooming in her eyes as her will was removed and his replaced it.

Seelie were the closest Fae to being pure incubi. They could touch you and take away your will, or they could use it to gain any advantage they wanted merely by touch. Unseelie could make your body respond, but they needed you to want it first, to have the need to let them take it from you before their power could find a doorway into your mind. Seelie, they didn't need a door, they could touch you and gain entrance, and Asher had.

Asher's fingers pushed against her opening and then his tongue was there, lapping against the nub that was nestled in her platinum curls. Her moan exploded from her lips without warning as she rose to her elbows, staring down at him where he watched her with molten lava burning in his multihued depths. The stars had fallen from the skies, bathing both his flesh and his eyes in an endless cataclysmic event of beauty. He was everything deadly and beautiful in the world, and he wasn't Sinjinn. The pain in her chest ached, and he smiled as he started to move his fingers, bringing her closer to the edge without warning.

Her scream ripped from her lips without warning as he sucked her sweet flesh as his fingers brought her further and further over the edge until his fingers slipped out and his tongue moved to take their place. Her cries were endless as he touched her womb, pushing on it as he sucked and moved his tongue around until it started to grow, finding her sweet spot and teasing it before moving deeper.

She felt boneless, on the brink of shattering into tiny pieces that no one would ever be able to put back together, and then just as quickly as he started, he stopped. His wings tucked into his back as he slid from her, pushing his hand against Sinjinn's thigh, and power erupted into the small area.

Icelyn looked over at Sinjinn, finding him watching her with glowing green eyes that hungered to take her. Her hand extended and Asher pushed it down, shaking his head as he held his finger up to his lips.

"You taste good enough to torture, too bad you're unable to understand what just happened," he cackled evilly. His finger went up to his ear, and he twirled it around as he nodded towards the canopy.

She followed his stare to the silhouette of the man who stood outside, listening. Her legs dropped as Asher helped to fix her skirt, picking her up in his arms as he exited the wagon and placed her back onto the stallion.

"You didn't make her scream enough," Gerald complained.

"Out of practice, had her locked into mindless need before I even reached her tight cunt," he said crudely. "She did come for me, twice. Next time I'll fuck her in the ass, and you can hear her really scream for me, you sick fuck."

"She's not my blood."

"You raised her, which makes her yours."

"I tire of your shit, Seelie."

"Most people do, but then I'm not trying to make new friends. Leave the Unseelie in the cart, unless you plan to allow him to die before we reach your court?"

"He can stay there. We've wasted enough time letting you feed. Let's move," Gerald hissed as he moved towards his horse, fixing his pants as he looked back to glare at Icelyn. The smile he gave her made her blood curdle.

"He'd never live long enough to get to you with me here."

"You're different," she said offhandedly. "When I met you in the tunnel, you weren't like this. You wanted to eat me."

"I was starving and bound to that tunnel, princess. I couldn't feed unless someone removed the fucking spell from me."

"And he did?"

"No, the Mages did. They also tried to bind me and actually think they did."

"Bind you to what?" she asked.

"To your stepfather's will, and so he thinks I am his to rule even though he hates when I talk back to him."

"And are you?" she asked.

"To a certain point, but I'm not like other Fae. I'm what you would call an upgraded version. I am both Unseelie and Seelie mixed, and I read their minds and intention before they ever entered the cave. I also read their life's history through their thoughts. I know their hopes and their dreams, what they crave most and how they intend to reach it."

"You know how to bring them down, don't you?" she whispered through trembling lips.

"That I do, but you need to stop thinking that. I'm not helping them. No one fucking helped me. No one cared that we were starving to death slowly, or that time in our cells was endless and that we tore each other apart when the hunger became too much to bear. Everyone knew we were down there, and that we suffered, even those of us who had done no wrong. So don't think I'm a fucking hero, I'm the antihero in this world. I'm a selfish prick, one who could care less if this world kills itself."

"Even antiheroes need people, Asher. Everyone needs people. You're not the antihero in my world; you saved me from a loss that no mother should ever endure."

"I did it because I knew I needed you bound to me," he laughed coldly. "All it took was me acting nice, and you fell right into it. Don't look at me like that, you left me in that tunnel to rot, sweet princess. I don't need anyone, and I really don't care what you think of me. I'm not interested in making friends here. I'm more of a fuck it and kill it kind of guy. Pray I don't decide that I want to fuck you, because I'm the beast that lures its prey in and devours it slowly as it begs me to play with it. Sometimes, I play with my food just to hear it weep for me before I destroy them."

"I don't believe you," she whispered. "I think you are lonely and hate this world for forgetting you, and for that, I don't blame you. If you try to use me to do harm, though, I'll fucking destroy you. Maybe not today or tomorrow, but eventually, I will find you, and I will kill you."

"Careful, you're making my dick hard, and I'm hungry, princess. Talk like that is foreplay to me, and I like to play."

CHAPTER
FORTY-THREE

Their approach to the Winter Palace was silent as they crested the high mountain range that was bathed in the red hues of the sunset. Icelyn's eyes gazed down on the dome pillars that lined the palace, seven in all that appeared to the naked eye to be created of ice. Glowing wards hummed from the largest three, like a beacon that called to her soul as her own brands pulsed in sync with them. She was a part of this land, the deepest part of it was carved into her soul, and yet Gerald thought to take it from her.

It wasn't something the land would allow to happen. As far back as their history reached, a member of the blooded heir to the land had been sitting on the ice throne. They were the source of power that kept the land in check, kept it from becoming an arctic land of uninhabitable cold and brutal storms that pushed the living away from it. Without her bloodline here, no one would live long enough to call it home, and yet Gerald seemed to have forgotten that part of this wild, ice-covered land.

The horses moved slowly down the thin path through the mountains that led to the frozen lake below. Rocks crashed down the cliff as they pushed on, ignoring the precarious fall that awaited them should they step too close to the edge. The hooves of the horses crunched loudly against the frozen tundra surface as the group moved closer and closer, towards the silent palace below. Soberness settled deep in Icelyn as Asher wrapped her closer to his body protectively as her anxiety rocketed through her with what she'd discover once she reached the palace.

Even from their great distance from the palace, she could feel the hollowness of her people. The fear that consumed them with the darkness that was inside their court. As if a storm had settled above them, their breath held as they awaited their fate. Once they reached the frozen lake, the group paused and dismounted, knowing the only way across was to walk over it with their mounts behind them, carrying their belongings or abandoning both and pray they made it across.

"You've got to be fucking joking me," Asher growled irritably as his breath fanned against her ear, heating it.

"The lake should be fully frozen over by now, it should hold us," she assured him as she felt him dismounting behind her. Slowly, she followed him to the ground. She didn't wince with pain and looked back at Asher with suspicion.

He'd healed her with his touch and of course with his mouth, for which she was thankful. The bleeding had long ago stopped, and there'd been not a cramp since. Her hand skimmed over her stomach as she turned, staring at where the men had brought Sinjinn out of the cart that they would abandon here. Her eyes held his before his dropped to where her hand rested on her flat stomach. She let it fall to her side before she swallowed and turned to stare ahead, afraid that if she gazed upon him for too long, her stepfather would hurt him for fun or sport.

"Once we reach the other side, we're home free," Gerald snorted, his ice-blue eyes turning to pin her with his victory shining in the dull depths.

She swung her gaze to the landscape around them to ignore his lecherous stare. The trees were coated with ice, their leaves having long ago fallen from the branches to be replaced with ice crystals. The scent of wild berries and winter hung thickly in the air around them. The bitter cold chill of the breeze nipped at her flesh, in the tiny pink dress Asher had replaced the torn one with. At least it offered decorum of modesty, unlike the one Bale had torn in his haste to do harm.

Gerald started across the ice as it groaned in protest, sending a smile upon her lips as the land rebelled against him. He stepped back, clearing the frozen lake as he glanced down at it in anger. His scream tore through the frozen tundra as he reached for one of the men, pushing him onto the edge of the ice.

"It won't hold, sir!" he shouted as Icelyn watched him, knowing he was right.

It would never hold his heavy weight, not with it untied or fed power through the heir of her race, the land itself was rebelling and untying from the bond of their lineage. She watched him with a smile curving her lips as the king withdrew a sword and pushed it at the guard threateningly.

"Move! Or meet my blade," he sputtered angrily.

They watched in silence as the king raged and the soldier moved further onto the ice as it protested loudly. Scared eyes looked back at them from over his shoulder, judging which death would be more merciful. Her heart accelerated as the crack sounded, shooting directly for the man who had wanted Asher to hurt her in the cart. When the crack in the ice reached his position, it gave, sucking him into the icy cold grip of death that the frozen lake offered.

"You! Fix this, or he dies now!" Gerald snarled, pointing at Icelyn as he moved towards Sinjinn with malicious purpose.

Icelyn shook her head as she marched onto the ice without fear. She frowned at the man who held onto it for dear life. His green eyes held hers as he begged her to help him. Her feet slid on the ice gracefully as she slowly walked to where he held on, but remained just out of reach as he held his hand out of the water, towards her.

Once she was sure it wouldn't put her into the water alongside him, she knelt down and placed her palm against the ice. The connection was instant, the thrill of something much larger than her that grasped onto her as it shot through the world around her, sealing the ice back to the thickness which would allow them to cross it safely. The man screamed as she lifted her eyes, watching as the ice sealed violently, closing the weak spot as it severed him in half with a sick sound of flesh being severed by the glassy surface of the ice. Blood coated the ice as she turned and stared at her stepfather.

"This land is rejecting you," she uttered coldly, unable to hide the smirk she wore as the worlds leaked from her lips triumphantly.

"Is it? Or are you affecting it because you betrayed it and your people?" he shouted as he walked onto the ice. "You need a reminder of who is the king!" he said before he backhanded her, sending her head to the side.

Slowly, she brought it back and smiled at him as if she'd reached a breaking point of her sanity. "No, *it* wants *me*."

"Then maybe when he's finished with you, I'll let it have what is left!" His hand assaulted her again and again until she lost her footing, sliding onto the ice as Asher stepped towards her, blocking Gerald's assault from continuing.

"I did tell you not to touch her face, didn't I? I don't like broken things. You will keep your end of the deal as I have sealed the portals and barred any entrance through them into this world. Now can we move? I'm hungry for some pussy, and hers needs pounding."

Gerald snorted and watched her as she winced at his crude words. "Maybe she needs more than you can offer her, Seelie. She has been taking the cock of this monster, and according to the men, it's rather large. Maybe she needs more men to assuage her need? What says you, Icelyn? Are you the whore your mother was? Will you beg me to come?"

"I'd rather fuck your sword than you, Gerald," she hissed as she rose to her feet, knowing it wasn't time to attack him yet. She needed the land to replenish her power, to bond with her through the rite of the heir, which it had begun doing already.

"You may just get that wish, sweet daughter." His eyes glazed over as he continued to stare at her before he spoke once more. "I redecorated while you were out spreading your thighs for the ones who murdered my children. I do hope you like the new decor."

Asher's hand clasped hers tightly as he yanked her harshly to his side, tightening his grip even further in silent warning. She clenched her jaw as the reminder of who had sold her to the Horde danced on her tongue. She shook it off, staring down at the crystal-clear ice she stood upon and stifled a scream of horror as faces appeared beneath the icy surface on the lake's floor. He'd murdered the court? He'd gone madder than she'd assumed.

Asher winced as he stared down at the lifeless corpses that lined the lake bed. Her eyes lifted to the palace as they started closing the distance between them and it. Once they were close enough, Icelyn swayed on her feet as the bridge that they stepped onto swayed; covered on each pike of ice was a severed head of her mother's guard.

Once they reached the entrance of the palace, her eyes scanned the multitude of corpses that swung from the high walls. Her hand covered the scream that pushed from her lungs as her mother's beautiful face met hers, staring lifelessly into the sky. Her dress was mottled in blood, ripped open to expose her breasts with a sign pushed into them with icicles. The sign read in blood-red letters, *the whore queen who betrayed her king.*

Beside her were Lars, and countless others who had befriended Icelyn through the years. Tortured, and in pieces but placed onto the wall with ice to hold them together. He'd ripped them apart and then done this to make her see what he'd done while she'd been away.

"Don't react," Asher whispered harshly. "Don't even fucking blink at them."

Gerald turned around as she straightened her spine and glared at him. "I do prefer her like this, don't you? I'm finally able to know that she is not taking lovers to our bed anymore. Here, like this, she is faithful to her king."

"I'm going to rip you apart and enjoy every moment of it," she hissed as men exited the castle, moving towards them. She watched them as they lifted bows, aiming it directly at her. Her blood chilled as she took in the unfamiliar faces, and she screamed as volleys of arrows were let loose. Asher pushed her, moving at the last moment, but it was futile. They'd shot several at once, and he hit the ground, motionless, as she turned, staring at him and then the men who aimed the bows at him again, firing arrow after arrow until he was motionless.

"You didn't really think I'd let him feed on our people did, you? What kind of monster would I be then? Plus, you're not dying yet. I need you around until you can provide me with a suitable heir for the land to accept, Icelyn."

CHAPTER
FORTY-FOUR

Inside, the palace's courtyard was silent; not a single person spoke. She was pushed through the gates into the snow-covered courtyard, where once glorious statues had stood; they were now in pieces littered over the ground. Crimson blood stained the snow of the courtyard, proof of the king's crimes against his own court. Gerald pushed her to her knees, and she exhaled slowly, lifting her eyes to scan the crowd who cowered around them, watching her.

"Your princess has been found," he cried out over the hushed crowd. "Of course, her crimes will be dealt with, as is the law. I also give you her consort, Cailean, prince to the brother who helped slaughter my children, her consort and lover. As king of this court, I've chosen to be merciful to my late wife's love child, and take her as my consort for a time of my choosing."

Still, the crowd said nothing.

No one even flinched at his declaration.

Sinjinn's legs were kicked out from beneath him,

and he grunted as he hit the snow-covered earth with a hiss of pain. His wild green eyes settled on her as he slowly let them drift down her body to assure him that she was unharmed.

"You will never be his consort," Sinjinn said tightly.

"No, I won't," she agreed as she watched her father staring down the crowd.

Her eyes searched for her sister or brother in the masses, and yet they were absent. No matter how much she'd wanted to look away from the corpses displayed on the walls, she'd searched for them there too. Luckily, they hadn't been among those he'd slaughtered in his rage.

"Stand up," he ordered as he held his hand out for her, as if he was planning to help her up out of kindness.

Icelyn slowly lifted to her feet as she stood rooted to the cold, unforgiving snow she'd knelt on. When she failed to move fast enough, he closed the distance between then and gripped her by her hair, ripping it from her scalp as a scream tore from her lips.

"When I say you move, you fucking move," he snarled.

"You simply said to stand, *father*," she reminded him through a strangled tone as rage pushed through her.

"Don't play word games with me, bitch," he chuckled as he pushed her back to her knees as the crowd watched in silence. As if he was trying to show dominance where he had none.

Stepping beside her, he pulled on the arrow, eliciting a groan of pain from Sinjinn as he manipulated the iron of the shaft through the crusted blood. Fresh, red blood covered his chest as Icelyn bit her lip to keep the scream from reaching her lungs. Her stomach somersaulted as bile built at the back of her throat, threatening to come up. Her hand covered her mouth as Gerald moved the arrow closer to the surface and then suddenly pushed it in deeper. The cry of pain that erupted from him was too much, too raw.

"Who is in charge now, Horde swine?" he chuckled coldly, his eyes filling with maddening ire as he watched him tremble from the poison and iron that ravaged his system. "I also took down a Seelie Prince; now, who in our line can boast of such an accomplishment?" he continued, and this time the crowd responded with horror as Asher was dragged in and dropped by a group of men Icelyn had never seen before.

Mages.

Her blood chilled as it turned into ice within her veins as she locked eyes with Sinjinn, knowing he sensed the same thing she had. Sweat dripped from his dark head, pooling at his temples before it slipped down his face. Fire burned in his eyes, but the pain was crushing him, of that she was certain. New blood ran in rivulets down his ruined chest, and her eyes burned to let the tears fall freely for the pain he must feel.

"I asked you who in our line has ever accomplished such a feat?" the king shattered the shock and silence as his deep voice echoed through the large courtyard.

"No one, because no one would have raised the ire of the Seelie to take down one of the royal princes," Icelyn answered breathlessly as her eyes remained on Asher's sightless eyes. "No one in my *family* would have been foolish enough to assume that the bond the prince shares with his brethren wouldn't have been awoken when one fell, Gerald. When you harm one, they all descend upon whoever was reckless enough to incite their wrath as one *force* of vengeance. That was why they were, instead, locked away where they were unable to attack those of the lesser courts. Not until *you* released him, and by doing so, you've released them all. They will come for you, for us, for anyone who helped to bring the prince of their race to his knees—you have doomed us all."

"No one will fall for that old legend told to keep their children in line," he laughed silently as he stared at her. "No one believed the legends of the Seelie, not then and not now. You think I didn't know about the legends; I assure you, I did. Even if it is true, this court is hidden from all, protected from the likes of the men you've been fucking. Why don't you share with this court which of them has been between your thighs? Oh, that's right, both of them have tasted of our sweet winter princess, haven't they, Icelyn?"

"Because you *gave* me to both of them, yes, they've both tasted what you will never taste, stepfather," she hissed.

His assault was so quick and unexpected that she didn't have time to brace against it. His fist balled up and smashed into her nose, splattering blood against the soft, white snow as pain tore through her. It was jarring, debilitating. Icelyn lifted her eyes to hold his as blood dripped from her nose, covering her pink dress until crimson covered her chest. Her face pulsed with pain, and yet she refused to cower before this murderer. Her arm lifted as she wiped the blood away with the back of her arm and smiled coldly at him.

"You're no better than your mother, lying down to spread her legs with whoever was willing to fuck her. She, too, gave no fight against the king when he took her, and yet you, on the other hand, welcomed both of these men to lay down with you. You will be punished as is the law for betraying this court. Take her and her lovers to the dungeon and be sure they can see her cell. I want them to watch what happens when one of our own takes something as vile as them as their lover in this court."

Icelyn was lifted harshly by the Mages, barely able to bring her feet beneath her to walk as they moved swiftly towards the palace. Her face burned from the pain and yet she wouldn't let them see her flinch, not even when she tripped and barely got her hands out in front of her before the ground slammed against her head.

"Get up," the Mage said icily as he didn't wait to see if she would, and instead, pulled her up by her hair.

Pain assaulted her as her eyes watered from it. A little more power and she'd bring down this palace upon their heads with the rage that was boiling beneath the surface. They made it down the winding staircase with ease as she was pushed into a cell that slammed closed the moment her guards exited it.

"We need food," she said, knowing she needed to feed the babes nestled in her belly to gather some sense of strength since she wouldn't be able to pull from either male now that both were wounded badly.

"You can starve to death for all we care," one of the guards said as he stepped from the shadows and watched her. "You are a pretty one, aren't you? And these are the type of things you enjoy fucking?" he laughed as if he'd found it despicable. His eyes glowed as he watched her, his own hunger igniting as his turquoise eyes slid down her body. "What a waste."

"You're a Changeling," she uttered as she watched him, noting the wolf markings that lined his arms in thick tribal bands. "You're a shifter, right? You should run while you still can. The Horde is coming, among other things."

"Abandon my post? And die the death of a traitor? No, I think not, princess. You made a choice to fulfill an oath, but not all of us are given choices in life, now are we?" he said as he touched the bars and stared into the prison cell, watching her closely. His turquoise eyes dipped to where her hands shielded her belly, and he frowned. "I wish you luck, princess, because eventually, he will realize your delicate condition, and hell hath no fury like a king denied his heir."

"You could help me," she whispered as the other men moved around the outside cells, securing the other two prisoners.

"I could, could I? And meet my death to save you? A Fae who left me in the human realm to be abused? No, no, I wouldn't risk my life for yours. Your kind has never lifted a finger to help me, so why should I help you?"

"Because it isn't about the past," she uttered as tears slid from her eyes. "You and your kind think we have had it any easier? Did you ever stop to think that maybe you were spared a worse fate by being taken out of this world? I watched the Horde King cook my brother and sister and feed them to my parents. Now I am prisoner of my stepfather, who plans to rape me. My mother is hanging from the walls outside the palace, along with everyone I have ever cared for or about. So you think you have had it rough? Gerald gave me to the Horde to pay his tithe and now blames me for upholding that oath. An oath he made, not me. My entire life has been given to my court, dictated by others, and now it's to be taken away because of a man who is crazy enough to think his madness will make him king. No, no you are probably the lucky one who escaped such a brutal fate in this world. Yet here you are, bitching because your mother probably tried to save you the only way she knew how to."

"You should rest. He won't be waiting very long to start his new line of heirs with you," he offered as he nodded towards the bed. "Sleep and gather your strength, for if you're right, and the Horde is on its way, we will be facing a battle and he has no intention of losing, neither do we."

She narrowed her eyes on him as a grunt sounded from across the cells. Asher was being chained to the ceiling by long, iron chains that kept him suspended in the air. The poisonous arrows had been left in his body to weaken him, yet his eyes opened from across the space, finding hers and holding them. He was alive, and he was pissed. Her heart sank as his eyes continued to stare at her, anything but normal as they glowed hauntingly. They were iridescent and glowing, hunger banked in their depths mixing with murder.

Her heart sank with what he was, and what that look meant. Icelyn backed away from the bars until her back touched the cold ice of the wall, knowing exactly what

Asher was doing. He was calling the Seelie to him, and it didn't matter if they liked one another, it meant he was bringing hell down upon the Winter Court, whether he meant to or not. Hell was coming, and no one would survive it, no one.

CHAPTER
FORTY-FIVE

Icelyn awoke to the smell of food nearby. Her eyes popped open, and she sat up slowly, staring at the guard from the night before as he placed the tray on a table. Her mouth watered as her stomach let loose a growl of need. She stood from the bed, stretching as she stared at his stiff back.

"You need to eat it quickly."

"What's your name?" she asked barely above a whispered breath as she turned and found Sinjinn and Asher watching her carefully. Both watched her like she was their last meal, and it terrified her. Other than them, the entire prison looked emptied out.

"Sebastian, my name is Sebastian, but you won't be calling me by my name, princess. Now eat, because you have moments to shove it into your mouth before the others return."

Icelyn moved from the bed, descending on the mutton and bread with vigor as she dipped it into it, and shoved an un-ladylike piece into her mouth. Her moan echoed through the prison, and three males groaned, which brought heat to her cheeks. She eyed Sebastian beside her as she continued shoving smaller amounts of food into her mouth, savoring it as it heated her belly.

"Is this your food?" she asked when he continued to watch her hungrily.

"Doesn't matter," he acknowledged.

"Here," she said, offering him part of the bread she'd been about to shove into her mouth.

"You're starving, and Gerald has yet to mention anything about feeding you, so fucking eat."

"He has never cared for the hungry or the hurt before, why should he start now?" she challenged.

"And you do? Save it for someone who will buy your bullshit," he muttered before he grabbed the tray. Icelyn reached for the cup, downing it in a single gulp before she wiped her mouth off with the back of her hand.

"I fed the poor every day since I was old enough to hunt wild boars. Someone had to feed the starving people. My brother, he has helped me as well. He is still helping the people here, the ones not high enough up for my father to worry about."

"Lane is dead, princess," he said gently as he watched her. "He fought your father when he announced what he would do to your mother. No one is feeding the poor anymore because they now lay in the icy drink outside the palace walls."

Icelyn swayed on her feet as she shook her head as tears filled her eyes. The food she'd eaten came up violently as her body wracked with sobs. How could he have killed his own son? Lane was his, his flesh and blood, and yet he'd murdered him?

"Frostine?" she whispered as she wiped her mouth off again, staring at him through the tears that blurred her vision.

"No one knows where she is," he replied. "She disappeared before this started, as if she'd known it was coming. Gerald either murdered her, or she somehow got away. I have to go," he said as he scratched his neck, staring at her uncomfortably. "I'm sorry about your brother."

Icelyn watched Sebastian slip from the cell before she sat on the bed numbly, listening as the door closed and sealed behind him. Everything she'd fought for was gone, gone by the hand of a murderous bastard who had gone mad. If she hadn't fought to protect them, hadn't argued the oath to Ryder, they might still be alive.

She curled into a ball and wrapped her hands around her middle as sob after sob exploded from her to echo through the dungeon. She could hear Sinjinn gurgling as he tried to speak to her, Asher's heavy breathing as he worked to dispel the poison from his system, and heavy footsteps as the guards returned to their post.

The guards laughed and made jokes about her fear, the reason they thought those tears fell so freely now. The pain threatened to consume her, to rip her apart as everything crashed down on her. How could he have done this? How could he think killing his own son was a good idea? Lane had been gentle, loving, and he'd been kind to the court no matter their stature within it. This world was unforgiving, and any sign of kindness was construed as weakness.

"That's enough, assholes," Sebastian said as he

pushed one, and grabbed the other who stood outside her cell, snickering. "Return to your stations and knock that shit off. Gerald wants no one interacting with these monsters until he's ready to deal with them."

She lifted her tear-filled gaze to his and watched him as he bowed his tawny head and shook it. He seemed conflicted on what he wanted to do, but deep inside, she knew he wouldn't betray his cause. Not with what would happen to him if he did hanging over his head. How many of the other Mages were like him? How many of them had been left in the human world and managed to hold some sense of humanity within them.

A hissing noise sounded from across the cells, and she watched as Asher lifted his head, staring at her. His flesh was bronzed once more, filled with pulsing brands that were a silvery, iridescent color, glowing along with his eyes.

Icelyn moved her gaze to Sinjinn, finding his green emerald orbs glowing as he watched her as well. His dark hair was matted with blood, and yet the look in his eyes was sheer determination. Sitting up, she moved closer to him and settled on the floor, wishing she could be in his arms, using his comfort to shield her from the pain she felt from her loss.

An apple rolled across the floor and Icelyn watched it as it stopped just outside of her cell. Her eyes lifted, drifting over to where she assumed Sebastian would be, but it wasn't him who stood in the shadows. Her heart raced as her eyes widened with sheer terror as she took in her delicate, gentle sister who was trapped in this endless shit show with her. She'd prayed she had escaped, but this? This was bad.

Frostine's whitish-blonde hair pulsed with a hue of blue made darker by the dungeons dimmed lights. Her outfit was as black as night, leather pants and a tight top to match it covered every inch of her flesh. Her finger came up to her lips as she signaled for her to remain silent.

Icelyn's heart kicked into overdrive as she stared at her beloved sister, who slipped back into the hidden passageway without a word. Fear ripped through her as the new predicament hit her. Frostine was alive and hiding in the palace still, which would only keep her safe until it moved, which would be soon. It was already failing, the ice weakening as it began to thaw around them.

"Icelyn," Sinjinn's deep voice pulled her from her shock.

"Sinjinn," she whispered as she turned to take him in. Unlike Asher, he wasn't healing. He was worsening with the poison still ravishing his system. Icelyn sent her magic searching for him, closing the distance between them as it reassured him that she was there. "You can't die on me, do you hear me?"

He snorted as a small smile settled on his lips. What she couldn't put into words shined through her eyes; that he couldn't die because he was going to be a daddy. He couldn't die because he was the one person in this world she'd given herself to; all of who she wanted to be was because of him, and he didn't get to die now and take it from her. A single tear slipped from her eye, and she wiped it away as she shook her head.

The world was so cruel, to give her a taste of love and then rip it away from her. She'd never believed in love, never bought into the idea of it. Her entire life was about duty, and who she would become one day, and there had been no place for love in that world until him.

She wasn't going to lose him now. Her eyes closed and she sent a silent prayer to the Gods and Goddesses, or whoever may be listening. In her mind's eyes, she showed them the Mages, the lake which would remain frozen only a few more hours before it would weaken and become impassable. Her vision changed to include Sinjinn and the poison that was killing him slowly, to the Seelie Prince who watched her even now, his gaze heavy as his smirk lifted his sinful lips. She showed her Frostine, hiding in the walls, and Sebastian who had offered comfort, even though it could have cost him his life.

With her prayers sent, she moved back to the bed, curling into the fetal position as she begged the land to give her strength to endure, to persevere against the monster that had raised her, and she begged Freya for strength and courage against the insurmountable odds she faced.

"Hold on, Icelyn. We're almost there," Synthia's voice entered her head as a wave of comfort settled over her. The whispered words shook her, and hope briefly flared in her chest as Synthia's voice vanished again.

"I'm afraid you'll be too late to save us," she replied to the empty cell as her heavy lids closed.

CHAPTER
FORTY-SIX

The cell door opened and Icelyn turned, staring into the darkness of the room. The scent of berries mixed with fresh snow as she sat up. Frostine stood beside the bed, kneeling down as she stared at Icelyn.

"What are you doing? You need to hide now," she uttered thickly as she stared up at her sister.

"Mom, Lane, everyone who wasn't worth keeping alive, he killed them all. Where were you, Icelyn? We needed you, I needed you! You are the only one who can confront him and you were gone. I had to hide in the walls because I knew he would kill me too. I knew it as deep as I know that he will kill you once he has sired a bastard heir upon you."

"Frost, you shouldn't be here. You need to hide," she whispered urgently.

"Here," she said, pushing something cold and metal into Icelyn's hand. "Tomorrow morning he comes to kill the Horde Prince. The court is failing; it's weakening rapidly without mother's essence feeding it, and the bond will never reach deeply enough before it starts to come down. It's now or never, because if the court falls, it will not be able to feed you enough power to kill him, and you have to. You're the only one who can do it."

"I love you, I'm sorry I wasn't here. I tried to hurt the prince, to make him leave. I thought if I hurt him, he'd leave us alone. Instead, I was stupid. I messed up and now everyone is paying the price because of me. Gerald is insane."

"He has lusted after you for many years, Icelyn. Mother saw the sickness in him and refused to believe it at first. She shielded us from it, from the truth of how cruel and sick he was because she didn't want us to hurt over it. Lane, too, they tried to protect us, and now they're both gone because we didn't fix it before his madness consumed him. Don't you see it, Icelyn? He took out everyone who could argue that he couldn't have you as his consort. He's become obsessed over it, and once I figured it out, there wasn't a day that went by where he wasn't always watching you. Gerald has made it appear as though he never wanted you, but since there is no heir who has not trespassed against the kingdom, he's being forced to accept you against his wishes for the good of the kingdom. He's set the entire thing up because he thinks it will end with him having you without anyone being able to challenge him or his rule as king. He never believed you were his because there was never a bond, and so his anger turned into hatred as he hunted you down. The last few years his anger twisted into something much darker. The attacks against you lessened. The assassins failed on purpose, allowing you to escape. He let everyone think what they wanted to, including you. Even you cannot disagree that each attempt became clumsier and more unskilled than the one before it. Do you remember when we were in the meadows, and the men tried to take you, not kill you? They aimed to kidnap you, and who do you think they would have delivered you to?"

"That is insane," she uttered as bile roiled in her belly. "I was his daughter, maybe not by blood, but by right, I was his. How could he think this is right?"

"How could he think killing his own son was right? I watched him rip Lane apart with his own hands from inside the walls," she uttered thickly as her throat tightened against the words. Footsteps started down the stairway, and she moved, rushing towards the open cell door. Her eyes were wild as she turned and looked back at her sister. "Lock it, now," she ordered and disappeared into the shadows.

Icelyn rose and crossed the distance, closing the cell and locking it before she moved back to the bed, pushing the key to the cell beneath the mattress. She curled onto it, turning to stare at Sebastian, who moved towards her with long strides. The men behind him cracked jokes, snorting as they moved as a group towards Sinjinn's cage.

"Time's up, boy," one laughed as he waited for Sebastian to open the cell. Those turquoise eyes turned, staring at her as he clicked the key in, opening the cell before the other two moved into it, punching Sinjinn in the stomach as they abused him.

"You too, princess," he said as he stepped closer as she slipped from the bed. "The king wishes to speak to you before he prepares the day's entertainment."

"Which is?" she asked softly, watching his face as it tightened and he flinched.

"Cutting the prince up to send him back to his brother piece by piece. It is to be done over the entire day, with his death being drawn out until midnight as the palace will be moving shortly after that, and all of us with it."

"Why are you telling the bitch anything, it's not like she gets to watch anything happen. The king just wants her to know her lover is going to die as he fucks her." One of the men said, his dull grey eyes diluted with drugs that oozed from his pores. Opium, they'd been indulging in the king's opium, which meant the king, too, would be high.

"Because I don't answer to the fucking king, do you, Joffrey? Or do you still answer to the one true king?"

"I follow our king, you know that," Joffrey hissed.

"Good, then you know why I don't care what the fuck this one said to do or not to do. I hate these assholes and bow before no Fae King in any realm. I'm here because we were ordered here to secure this place for his welcome into this world, and that means no one here will survive anyway, so what does it matter if she knows her fate?"

"What if she tells the king?" he retorted.

"The king isn't interested in anything she says, nor will he believe her. He wants what lies between her legs."

"I can't say I blame him for that, she's pretty. I bet she's never had a real man between those silk thighs of hers. Maybe we should show her what real men are like, yeah?"

"Joffrey, if you want to fuck some fairies, go fuck the whores upstairs who are spreading their thighs for us willingly. She's off-limits until the king finishes with her; afterwards, he may toss her to us."

"Maybe I want her because he does," he scoffed as his hand reached across the space, grabbing Icelyn's breast.

Ice formed over his fingers, burning as it attacked the deep tissue of his hand and moved up his arm. Her eyes watched it with pride as it pushed through him, aiming for his internal organs.

"Fucking bitch!" he snarled, and Sebastian's hand settled on her back.

"Enough."

Icelyn turned her eyes to Sebastian's, watching as he silently warned her to stop. She pushed the other man's offending appendage away, watching as it cracked from being frozen by her touch. The ice began to melt as Sebastian watched it. Her eyes lifted to find Sinjinn staring at her with a silent plea in them.

"I love you," she whispered as she held his stare. "I don't know when I fell for you, but I did. Know that you were loved by me. Hold on as long as you can, please. Just hold on for me."

"You're going to survive this, and you're going to live for me. Do you hear me? Live, no matter what the cost is, you live," Sinjinn uttered hoarsely.

"Isn't that sweet," Joffrey laughed as he punched Sinjinn, making him double over with pain.

"Why don't you take this arrow out and fight me like a man, boy?" Sinjinn hissed.

"Because I'm not suicidal, duh," he laughed coldly.

"Kiss me," Icelyn whispered to Joffrey as she pulled his lips to hers and kissed him without warning.

He inhaled sharply as his lips turned blue. Ice moved through him until his entire body was solid with it, and his pain-filled scream was stuck on his face. Icelyn pushed him, watching as he fell to the floor, shattering as if he was crafted of the most beautiful red glass instead of organs.

"Anyone else desire to touch him?" she uttered as she lifted her eyes to the one male who had been kind to her. His turquoise eyes watched her carefully, ready for her to attack. Her chest heaved with anger and loathing, but worse, warning.

It hurt to see his mistrust, but she was done with this shit. The abuse was enough; the pain they inflicted for fun was enough. This entire situation was ending tonight. Her gaze skimmed over Sebastian before it settled on Asher, who smiled and nodded his head, as if he read her thoughts.

"Let's go, now," Sebastian growled.

"What about Joffrey?" The other guard shrieked. "The bitch needs to pay for what she did!"

"She will, by the king. Joffrey was an asshole. He was told to stop, and if the others had been here, they'd have murdered him anyway for fucking anything Fae that had a slit he could fit his tiny cock into. Rules are made to be followed, are they not?"

"I hope the king fucking rips you apart, bitch," he hissed.

"You wish he had the power to do so, but he doesn't."

"You have no power here anymore! None of you, not even the king; you're all dead men walking! When the others get here, we will execute every last one of you," he hissed.

Icelyn swallowed as she stared him down, hating that her stepfather had been so foolish to trust creatures who wanted to destroy them so badly. She dismissed him as they started forward, her fingers brushing against Sinjinn's as she fed him some of the power she'd collected in the limited time they'd been here. He could hold on, he had to. Synthia had said they were almost here, but would they reach them in time?

Before the Mages did?

They were separated at the top of the stairs, Sinjinn being led into the great hall as she was taken to the king. Once alone, Sebastian paused and turned to look at her. His bright eyes took her in as he reached for her hand, pushing it against his palm.

"You have to get out of here tonight. Tomorrow the Mages will be here, and no one will survive. They want this kingdom because it can withstand the Horde King and remain hidden from him and his kind. Because it alone moves to remain hidden, and they will be safe here while being closer to him. I will be down tonight to open your cell, and you will join your sister in the walls until I can get you both out of here safely."

"You should hide, because I won't. This is my home, Bastion."

"Why did you call me that?" he asked. "My name is Sebastian."

"Because I can, now take me to the king. I need to know his plans."

He escorted her the rest of the way there in silence. She didn't ask him how he knew her sister was in the walls, because she'd caught her staring at him as he'd come into the dungeon. It had been a familiar stare, as if she knew him, and while it was unsettling, it wasn't of consequence right now.

At the door, the guards watched her until they opened it, leading her into where the king sat staring at himself in the mirror. His ice-blue eyes lifted to hers as he held them in the reflection.

"Leave us," he ordered, waiting for them to exit before he spoke again. "I'm going to rip your lover apart unless you beg me not to do it. If you agree to my terms, I'll spare them both for a time, but only if you play the part of my whore, Icelyn," he said huskily.

"Do you think I care what you do to them? Remember, stepfather, you sent me to one and gave me as a gift to the other. I am unattached to either. I am Icelyn, Heir to the Winter Court, the heartless ice princess who thaws for no man."

"Your mother begged me to kill her, just as she did for him as he fucked her over and over again."

"My mother wanted death, of that I am certain. She wanted to never feel anything again after she was forced to eat her own children. Besides, let's just be honest here, your dick wasn't the same as the Horde King's, he was High Fae, and you are just…less."

He moved faster than she expected, knocking her backwards with blow after blow until she hit the floor. He loomed over her, staring down with malice and lust as she pulled her legs beneath her and rose back to her slight height to face him.

"Daddy, you hit like a bitch," she laughed through the blood that dripped from her nose into her mouth.

He slapped her again, and she laughed as his anger

built. He continued, uncaring that she no longer laughed as he hit her continually until she was crumpled to the floor. Following her down, he pushed up her skirt and hissed musty breath into her mouth as he forced his kiss onto her unmoving mouth.

"You'll scream for me, even if I have to add enough inches of ice to achieve it! You are nothing! Nothing but a used-up whore that allowed monsters to fuck her! You were supposed to remain pure, untouched or tainted until I killed your whore of a mother and took you! You were never supposed to end up with him, and yet you didn't obey me! You ruined everything and Lane paid the price for it, my own son thought to stand against me!" He pushed her legs apart and she laughed at him as bile churned in her stomach.

"You are insane," she whispered as she pushed her ice claws through his neck, letting the blood splatter over her face as it bathed her. "You were supposed to protect me. To shelter me from the monsters, and yet you were the monster who preyed on me." She pushed him over, staring down at him as he gasped for air. Her fingers trailed over his stomach, opening it up.

One by one, she removed his useless organs, watching the pain it inflicted on his face until her icy claws skimmed over his heart.

"Oh, you do have one, don't you?" she crooned. "I was sure you'd misplaced it."

He screamed, alerting the guards, and she laughed as she twisted her hand, removing his heart as she stood up, materializing twin ice blades. If her kingdom was going to fall, it would be because she brought it down. It wouldn't be because the Mages took it over; this was her home, her legacy, and they'd fucked with the wrong princess.

"All hail the king," she uttered as she faced his guards.

CHAPTER
FORTY-SEVEN

Icelyn dragged her father's lifeless corpse through the empty hallways and down the stairs that led to Asher's cell. Outside of it, she dropped it and moved into her own, grabbing the hidden key. One dark brow lifted as a sinful smile spread over his mouth.

"I do prefer my meals to have a pulse, Icelyn," he laughed as she opened the cell and stepped into the cage that kept him prisoner. "I'm surprised you remembered me, considering they're torturing your lover above."

"I have an issue," she said as she nodded to the corpse that was already healing. "He isn't normal, he's regenerating. He can't be left alone until we can figure out how to kill him. Call in your debt, Seelie," she uttered as she ripped one of the many arrows embedded in him, out.

"It's not time," he shrugged as the chains clanked with his slight movements.

"You will die here, you understand that, right? This palace is about to move and anything attached to it won't be the same when it reappears again. I know you've called for your kind to come find you, but they won't make it in time."

"Oh, my sweet girl, they're already here," he smirked as he lifted his gaze to stare over her shoulder. "Any moment now and the screaming will begin."

"Asher, I need your word that if I let you go, you won't eat my entire court on your way out."

"I'm starving, Icelyn," he murmured as his eyes turned iridescent as he stared down at her. "And you're fucking delicious."

"I'm not on the menu, Seelie Prince. Now give me your word that you won't fuck your way through my court and destroy it on your way out," she argued barely above a whispered breath.

"I won't fuck you, or kill you either, Ice Queen," he said huskily. "I saved your children, so I have no intention of unseating them within your womb no matter how tempting that sweetness between your soft thighs is. Trust me, my cock wouldn't just abuse that sweet flesh, it would wreck it. Besides that, I have a use for you still, one that doesn't include what you can give me."

"Your word, Asher, now!" she demanded as she ripped another arrow out without warning, watching as he flinched. Her face was heated from his words, but her anger and the ice pulsing inside of her was growing out of control with the need to find Sinjinn and protect him.

"I won't fuck my way out of your court, but I will feed to gather strength, Icelyn. I won't go back to being weakened from lack of feeding. Not to mention, there's a fucking war party right outside this palace, three in fact. All wanting to murder your people," he said with a grimace as she pulled another one out, and then the last one, slowly as she stared up at him. Her hands reached for the iron chains, burning the palms of each hand as she ripped them down, freeing him. "You shouldn't trust me."

"No, but for some reason, I do," she muttered as she stepped back, watching as he stretched his neck and smiled at her. "And you gave me your word," she finished with a tight-lipped smile.

"I never promised that I wouldn't kiss you," he chuckled before he pulled her mouth against his and slid his tongue over her bottom lip. "I could be the biggest asshole right now and make you beg me to fuck you."

"You won't, because we're running out of time. Now come help me save the man I love," she urged as she reached down and grabbed the body of her father, which had begun to regenerate. "Guess he's got some secrets of his own," she mused.

"He's been altered genetically," Asher said as he bent down and studied the organs which were rapidly growing. "Interesting, yet unexpected. Fun, though, I guess he made a deal with those assholes that locked us up?"

"I don't know, but he has to have been working with them for a while if he's changed genetically. I'm still trying to compartmentalize how he achieved this deal with so many eyes on him. He's the king, the king goes nowhere without his personal guard."

"But he had them with him, and they seem to not like you very much. Especially after you used the ice to cut one in half on our way into this hellish frozen palace," he laughed as he ripped out Gerald's spleen and held it up to his eyes for a closer examination.

"What is it?" she asked.

"Trouble," he snorted as he tossed it aside and started towards the staircase. "I'll drag Daddy, Icelyn. You should save what little strength you have left for what comes after you save your lover."

Icelyn followed him closely, her strength regenerating by the land which fed her endlessly as the ice strengthened beyond the palace. It would continue until the world around them was stable enough for the court to exit the palace and travel across the lake in time for it to move. Yet time was running out, and three armies marched towards them.

~Sinjinn~

The burning in his arms was debilitating, but the poison that rushed to his organs as it deteriorated them slowly was proving to be fatal. He knew he wouldn't make it out of this alive, but she had to. Icelyn had to survive to keep his children alive. She deserved more than this, than the madness of some madman who lusted after his own daughter.

He'd seen it, seen the wild eyes that watched her every move as he pretended to hate her. Sinjinn had seen it all before, knew the madness that blossomed in those ice-blue eyes like he knew the flesh on the back of his hand. He'd seen it take hold of his own sire, watched him rip people apart to assuage the monster within; that never-ending need for more, to take more, to become more. It was why they'd ended his reign, why they'd killed him to be able to continue on without having to fall to his vile, evil plan for them all.

The whip sliced against his back once more and his knees threatened to give out. His back was ripped open, sliced by the bite of the whip as the Mage wielded it skillfully. The entire court had been forced here to watch him die, all but Icelyn, who was somewhere in this palace with the king, which they had made sure he'd known about in vivid detail before they'd tied him to the posts.

She was strong, stronger than they knew. Icelyn had been silently feeding him power and strength to keep him alive from the poison. She was everything he'd never known he wanted, and everything he'd thought he didn't deserve. Yet she was his, and she'd told him that she loved him.

Pain burned across his back as the cattail sliced through the already oozing wound as a mass of power erupted through the crowd. His legs gave out as he lifted his eyes to search for the disturbance. A hooded figure stood in the middle of the room, a familiar one with sapphire eyes that stared him down with a wicked smile as blades were produced from thin air.

"That's my brother," Zahruk hissed as he sent the blade sailing end over end until it stuck in the eye socket of the Mage who had been wielding the whip. Sinjinn stared down at the poor bastard before he lifted his dark head and smiled. "And this is going to be fun."

The entire room erupted into chaos as the Horde sifted inside the castle, and blood splashed over Sinjinn as Synthia appeared before him, ending the life of a Mage who had rushed towards him with a large blade. Her hair was splattered with blood as she bent down before him, untying his legs.

"What the fuck took you guys so long?" he hissed.

"It wasn't easy to find, even with her help. The entire fucking world is *white*!"

"Find Icelyn, Synthia. It's too late to save me," he growled.

"I'm a Goddess, Sinjinn, remember?" She scoffed as her hands lit up and she placed them on his cheeks.

He felt a violent pull as she turned a glowing hue of gold as she removed the poison from his system as Adam worked to remove the ropes holding his arms. He stared into the Dark Prince's eyes and frowned as he realized why he would be with the others. The wounds sealed, and yet he still felt fucking weak as a babe.

"She's mine," he warned.

"Calm yourself," Adam muttered as he freed his hands and held him up. "The worst that will happen is I fuck her, and she gives me an heir, and that will end it. Ryder's unsure if the prophecy is still even in fucking play, so let's worry about getting you the fuck out of here first, okay?" he snapped as he locked eyes with Synthia.

"We're not done discussing the fucking zombie in the closet, Adam," she growled.

"Yes, we are," he countered.

"Can we find my pregnant mate and worry about who shoved the zombie up whose ass later?" Sinjinn growled as a head crashed against his chest. "Zahruk, kill them gentler or some shit."

Zahruk's eyebrows hiked to his hairline as he frowned and shook his head, staring at Sinjinn as if he wasn't sure who the hell he was. "What the fuck did you just say?" he sputtered as his foot lifted, kicking one assailant as he sent his blade sailing towards another's neck, severing it as he maintained eye contact with his brother.

"Where is she?" Sinjinn snarled as he stood, using the help Adam offered as he stared across the room to where Icelyn stood with Asher, her father's corpse beside them on the floor. He swallowed hard as he took in the Seelie beside her, the struggling body she picked up and began to drag with her, and the blood that coated her hands and arms. Fuck, she was fierce, and her eyes found his over the fighting as a sexy-as-shit smirk lifted her lips.

She started forward through the fighting, uncaring that the Horde swung wild blades that could end her life and he couldn't move. His mouth opened as she dropped Gerald and turned to look down at him as a blade sliced towards her stomach. Gerald had picked up a discarded sword and swung it towards her with purpose.

"You are mine!" Gerald shouted crazily, blood bubbling from his mouth as the blade sliced towards Icelyn's midsection.

The entire room paused, watching as Icelyn held up her hand to deflect the blow. She'd never stop it before it reached her. A dark obsidian wing stuck through the Winter King's chest and lifted him into the air. Sinjinn dropped to his knees, staring at Ryder, who held the king with his wing. Icelyn stared up at his brother and nodded as twin ice swords formed in her hand. Her movements were precise, elegant as a dancer who had practiced the step a million times and perfected it. One slice and his arms both fell from his torso, and then his legs. The blades dropped, shattering on the floor as blood pooled around them. Her lips moved, but he couldn't make out what she said from his distance.

"Take me to her," he growled at Adam.

"This is her fight, Sinjinn. This is her battle, and she doesn't need you to save her. She's handling it," Synthia muttered. He turned, moving towards her as Synthia grabbed his arm and held him back.

"Let me go, you have no idea what I've had to watch her endure!" he snapped harshly.

"I do, but you can't end this for her. This is her fight, her demons to slay, and only she can save herself from them."

He turned, watching as she slapped her stepfather over and over, her ice-sharp claws shredding his face as she screamed until the palace trembled around her. Synthia was right, but he'd failed her. He'd failed to protect her and didn't deserve her.

"I am the Queen of this Court and you, you are nothing!" she hissed as she severed his neck from his head as Ryder lifted his wing, sending the king's body into the air before his wing severed that, too, in half.

Icelyn dropped to her knees in the pool of blood, sitting there as the fighting began anew. Synthia helped him while Adam joined in, taking him to stand behind the Queen of the Winter Court, whose shoulders shook as tears dropped to the floor in ice form, shattering.

He knelt behind her, pulling her into the warmth of his body before she spun around, knocking him backwards as she kissed his face in the midst of the chaos. His hands cupped her cheeks as he stared into her brilliant blue gaze and uttered the last words he'd ever thought to say in this lifetime.

"Forgive me for failing you," he uttered. "I love you, Icelyn. I love you too," he muttered as her mouth crushed against his as bodies slammed against the floor around them.

She lifted her head and shook it as her hair fell around them. "There's nothing to forgive you for," she uttered through another round of kisses. "I love you too, Sinjinn." He smiled against her lips as she rested her forehead against his. "The High King of the Mages is coming," she whispered as she lifted her head to stare at the people who watched her. Horrified that she would kiss the son of the monster who has started this fight several centuries before, she was sure.

"What did you just say?" Synthia asked.

"The Mages are coming," Icelyn whispered as she found one of the Fae heading towards Sebastian. "Not him! No," she rose, rushing towards the Mage who had helped her. "Not him, he helped me. You will spare him."

"Move, he's a fucking Mage," Savlian growled.

"I said not him," she growled back, her arms crossing as she stared him down. "He helped me, and if it weren't for him, Sinjinn would be dead. So you will stand down," she challenged as she stared into the deadly brother's eyes.

"Woman, I've had it to my nut-sack with females demanding shit lately. This isn't how these things work. Men tell you how to do it, you do it, end of fucking discussion!"

"Excuse me?" five feminine voices all said at once.

"Oh, you're so fucked now," Asrian chuckled as he

lifted his hands, staring at Savlian. Lilith was at his side with a pointed look that said exactly how screwed his brother was.

"It's how it fucking works!" he argued.

"Not your smartest move, Sav," Ryder grumbled.

"All balls and no brains, or big balls for thinking you could say that and live through the repercussions. I mean, have you met these women?" Adam asked. "They're not normal, bro."

"I'd run," Synthia offered.

"I don't fucking run," he hissed.

"Enough, we need to focus," Ryder demanded, and all eyes turned to him, where he stood covered in blood.

CHAPTER FORTY-EIGHT

Icelyn watched in silence as Ryder stared down Asher. They stood nose-to-nose as they all waited to see what happened. Asher didn't back down, didn't cower in the face of the one being who could end his long existence as the entire assembly held their breath.

"You're one of us," Ryder said after a few tense moments. "You helped them? Or did you just tell my brother that so you could..." He paused, turning to look at Icelyn who narrowed her eyes on him. "Do what you did for selfish reasons?" he amended, and when she nodded, he shook his head, but not before tossing Synthia a look of utter annoyance.

"I'm a selfish prick, of that you can be sure, Horde King. She was miscarrying, and unless I had acted quickly, she would have. Not to mention it washed away the guilt and self-blame of what happened before she reached me."

"And that would be?" he asked, eyeing Icelyn and

Sinjinn, who both stared back at him, mute on the subject. "Throw me a fucking bone," he demanded.

"Icelyn was abused at the hands of someone she thought was her friend," Sinjinn replied carefully.

"The one who thought he loved you, or the one who wanted to gain from you?" Ryder asked as he lifted a dark brow as his golden eyes sparkled. At Icelyn's irritated stare, he continued. "And did he pay for his trespass against a woman who obviously didn't want it?"

"She turned the water and blood inside of him into ice, and he exploded," Sinjinn shrugged, as if it wasn't a big deal.

"After you lit his dick on fire, of course," she reminded.

"And how did Asher help you?" he asked, lowering his tone.

"Let's not talk about that," Sinjinn warned.

"He spit on my cervix," she replied with a shrug, and when Sinjinn glared over at her, she frowned. "What, he did."

"I did a little more than that," Asher smirked as his glowing eyes held hers.

"And you don't want him to die for it?" Ryder asked carefully, his golden-hued gaze slid to the black of the beast that waited for her permission to end the Seelie Prince's life.

"He saved my children."

"At a cost," he argued.

"How much would you give to save the lives of your children, Ryder? Because I'd sell my soul to the devil himself to protect them," she uttered thickly.

"You did," he snapped harshly.

"No, I made a deal with a Seelie Prince who is cursed to the same shit you and your kind are. His word is bond, and if he breaks it, I can take his fucking soul. I know my way around your kind because I've studied them to bring you and your kingdom down since the moment your father did what he did. I know the rules you play by because I knew a day would come when I'd need to use them to fight back against you. I'm glad it wasn't with you, really, I am. I am not as weak as you think I am; I am the Queen of this Court, which may mean nothing now that the Mages are coming, but I am still the Queen of a people who need help, and I'm asking you for it now. I'm asking *you*, who *was* here the day that your father destroyed my world, to help me save it now."

"You don't have to ask for help, Icelyn. You're family, and while we are on the subject of the Mages, I need to know why you forced Savlian to stay his sword and not remove Sebastian's head."

"Had he not helped me at the cost of his own life, we would have lost Sinjinn. He snuck me food, Ryder. I'm not like you and your caste fully, not yet. I had to feed to be strong enough to give Sinjinn enough emotion to stay with me. He also stopped the guards from hurting me, and while it may not sound like much, it was huge at the time. He's also been leaving food at the hidden panels for my little sister for weeks. Sebastian's kept her alive, and that to me is everything."

"Fine, but he stays in chains. He can't be trusted," he muttered as his eyes watched the shifter, staring him down with a silent warning before he spoke again. "If you think to run back and tell the Mages anything, I won't blink as I take your life. I am the King of the Horde, the one you guys think to bring down. It won't happen. Ever," he snarled.

Synthia clapped her hands, drawing her husband's eyes in her direction. "We have more pressing issues at the moment. The Mages are on their way, this palace is failing, and there are too many people to sift to a secure location. That means we have to get them out of here. If what they say is true, Ryder, half of the Mage army is on their way to this palace to wipe out the Winter Court. That means other courts may need us as well, now. They have to go through the Summer Court to reach Winter, and the Spring Court. They may inflict enough damage that those courts crumble, and we need to be ready if they need us. We need to prepare to send those courts help immediately, or check on them ourselves as we make our way home."

"There's also the Seelie who are on their way here as well," Asher offered even though he hadn't had to. "I can't make them stop. They were alerted to my distress when I was a pincushion."

"Pincushion?" Synthia asked as she stared at him, letting her gaze drift down his naked chest that was pulsing with those eerie brands.

"The Mages decided to see how I looked decked out in arrows," he grumbled with a shrug. "When the Seelie Princes or Princesses are in distress, we're unable to ignore the call of retribution to whoever trespassed against one of our own. My guess is that they're outside waiting to see who emerges."

"Fucking great," Ryder growled. "And how many

of them did my father sire?"

"Enough of them that we lost count," Asher shrugged and winced as the wounds in his stomach began bleeding.

"I don't dare assume that they'll think twice about attacking when they find the Horde here?" he asked with something cold in his tone.

"I think that they've been starved long enough that they won't be picky on who they eat."

"So we should prepare to fight them as well?" Synthia asked as Asher turned, staring down the length of her and back up with heat burning in his iridescent eyes.

"Beautiful, but not Fae," he uttered as he rubbed his thumb over his bottom lip.

"She's my fucking wife, and if you even think about it, I'll rip your spine out before you are aware it's even been removed. You don't touch what is mine without paying for it in blood."

"She might be worth it," Asher uttered and then turned, staring at Icelyn, who frowned at him. "Don't be jealous, Ice, what we had was a onetime thing. Plus, your man is hungry, and he cannot stand the sight of me after watching us together. Go feed him, he's held on for you," he said gently as he smiled weakly. "I will feed from the women who fed the Mages so willingly, if I am allowed to do so?"

"Make it hurt," she said as she turned, staring at Sinjinn, who still remained beside the dark-haired stranger who assisted him. "By your leave, your highnesses," she muttered absently. "I need to be sure my king is strong enough to travel."

"Time is of the essence, Icelyn. There's also someone you need to meet before you assist Sinjinn," Synthia said carefully. "You were bound by oath to marry Cailean, but you also were chosen by the land to inherit the Light Heir brands. Adam is the Dark Prince; his destiny is to take the Light Heir long enough to secure an heir who can heal the land."

"I'm a little pregnant right now," she uttered as her throat tightened. "I'm also in love with Sinjinn, so asking that of me is... I'm done being touched by anyone else. I've been almost raped by someone I cared greatly for. I've had to make a sacrifice to save my children that was rather awkward, and Cailean had to stick his thingy into me so that the oath was fulfilled, and I think it is enough dicks for now."

"Oh, I'd agree, but the land needs you to take one more for the team." Synthia shrugged when Icelyn just continued to stare at her angrily.

"It's neither here nor there, and right now you're not going to worry about it. You've been through enough shit," Ryder said gently, his golden eyes locking with hers as he frowned. "Go to your king, and Icelyn, I give you the power to annul the marriage at any time you choose to. There's one condition: that you take someone from the Horde as your husband for a year and one day, or longer and more permanent, should you choose to."

"Okay," she said as she chewed her bottom lip. "I'll stay married to Cailean until someone else offers me more."

"Go, we're running out of time," Synthia urged.

Icelyn turned towards Sinjinn, rushing into his arms as he opened them and pulled her mouth against his.

His kiss was searching, as if he wasn't sure she'd accept him. His eyes were banked in fire; his touch scorched the flesh on her arms as her ice rose to protect it.

"I don't know what I did to deserve you, Icelyn," he uttered. "But I hate that I couldn't protect you from this. It's my job as your mate to keep you safe, and I failed the first time it was put into question."

"I was coming to save you," she whispered.

"The princess isn't supposed to save the prince," he muttered awkwardly.

"Who says so? Men? Women are just as capable of saving the day, Sinjinn. Had your brothers not arrived when they had, I'd have saved you and that's okay. Sometimes it's not the prince who saves the day. Sometimes the princess saves him, and they ride off on a dragon into the sunset." She shrugged as she pulled him with her towards the hallway.

"Icelyn, you've been through too much for me to expect you to feed me."

"That's just it," she uttered. "I need you to erase the feel of them from my flesh. To write your name on it so that it is the only thing I feel," her words trailed off as he pulled her closer, accepting the support she gave him as they made their way to her room.

"That I'm game to do, my fierce little princess."

CHAPTER
FORTY-NINE

Her bedroom was exactly how she'd left it on the day she set out to capture the Prince of the Horde. The ice-blue bedspread was smoothed out perfectly, and yet she knew it wouldn't stay as such once they'd finished on it. There was nothing inside this room she couldn't live without; nothing except the man who had changed her world and turned everything upside down.

This male had made her see things through newly opened eyes. He'd taught her love; true love was something that was so deep that the thought of losing it was visceral and an earth-shattering pain that consumed you from within.

Icelyn had hidden it, she'd been afraid to even feel it for fear her stepfather would murder the man she loved before she could save him. It had felt wrong to ignore him, to ignore the pain he was in, and had she shown anything towards him, he'd have been used against her.

"I'm sorry I seemed so cold out there, when you

were hurt and needed me," she whispered thickly as her chest tightened and tears filled her eyes.

"You were protecting me," he said, surprising her as he wiped the tears away with his thumbs as his forehead pressed against hers. His breath fanned her lips, and she lifted on her tiptoes, kissing him as his magic wrapped around her, singeing the pink dress she still wore until it drifted to the floor as nothing more than ashes. He lifted her body, cradling her as he walked them towards the bed, not wasting a moment of the stolen time they were using to make him strong enough to protect her.

Once there, he gently lowered her and stared down at her perfect body. She had nicks and scars from training or other swordplay. Her slim hips were tiny, and yet he knew how she used them to rock his perfectly balanced world off its axis. She'd shot him, dragged his ass into a cave, and then she'd pleased him with her untried body until they were both breathless. This was his fucking mate, the one his wolf had claimed. This was his perfect. She was flawed so perfectly that she shined from within brighter than any other woman who'd caught his eye, however briefly.

"Watching you with Asher..."

"You enjoyed it," she laughed softly. "I felt you here with me during it," her hand touched her chest. "I felt the need you had to join us."

"I'm not going to lie," he uttered as he removed his shirt, revealing a wall of muscle that was already mending. "I got hard, and the noises you made? No matter how much you tried to stop me from hearing them... I was turned on watching your face as you found pleasure from his mouth. Maybe I'm a bastard for thinking it, but you were so hot as his mouth fucked your sweet flesh. And you fed me still; you didn't do it just to save the babes. You did it to save me, to feed me. Still plan to kick his ass for touching my girl, but I don't hold it against you. I need you to know that."

"I knew if I came, you'd feed," she admitted. "He was good, but you're better. Plus, there was no connection from him, and that is something I crave more than the pleasure of the flesh," she admitted. "In the garden, I wanted to tell you I was falling for you, but when I almost lost you, I knew this was something I wanted more than I could put into words. I knew I loved you then, and I still love you now."

His thumb looped down through the buckles of his pants as he pushed them down, stepping out of them to reveal his cock that throbbed with the need to be nestled in her sweet cunt. His hands touched her lightly, skimming her thighs as they dropped open and her legs parted with invitation.

"I'm afraid to hurt you," he admitted.

"You won't," she said huskily as she lifted herself onto her elbows and stared at him. "Erase the feel of them from my flesh. I've won, Sinjinn. Those who tried to hurt me are gone from this world because I made it so. I took their power to control my fear and my future away from them, and now I'm just asking you to make me feel you. Make me feel what it is like to be loved, to be cherished. I won't give them control over me anymore. I need you."

Her plea sliced through his chest as his mouth lowered to the sensitive flesh on the inside of her knee. His lips kissed every inch of it before moving to the next one as he settled between her legs. Sinjinn lifted her leg, kissing her calf all the way to her ankle as he made sure every single inch of her knew his kiss, knew it was cherished. Once he'd finished with her legs, he pushed his tongue through the wetness of her cunt, lapping at it until she was thrashing against the bed, her fist gripping the blankets as the first orgasm rushed through her blindingly.

He began slowly kissing her hips, nipping at the bones that defined her well-muscled body. His mouth hovered over her navel, and he uttered gentle words to the little babes that grew within before he continued his slow, leisure travel up her body, sucking each nipple between his teeth before her sweet noises had him pushing his cock against the slick wetness that begged to be fucked.

His entrance was slower than he'd ever been before, feeding her inch after inch of his cock until he was buried in her warmth. He'd melted a cock to keep it out of her, because this part of her? This was his and his alone. He'd watched his bedmates take lovers, and while it had never bothered him before, the thought of anyone else entering her cunt made the wolf within rise up and growl in warning. Hell, it hadn't approved of Asher with her, but it had watched them, and it hadn't reacted, which was strange. Yet his mind wandered to this sweetness she gave him, and they both saw red. There was no way Adam was fucking her, period.

He lifted her body, settling her legs around his hips as he used his hands on hers to slide her to the very tip of his cock before she slid down it, crying out his name as the impending orgasm began to grow in her belly.

She was beautiful. She was his mate in every way that would ever matter to him. They'd been through hell, and yet she had come out stronger, more determined to win, and even better, somehow she'd fallen in love with him, as much as he'd fallen for her.

Her mouth found his as her hands cradled his jaw, holding him to her with a moan as he increased his speed, hitting her sweet spot over and over until her kiss was frenzied and the only thing that she could coherently say was "fuck," as he held her in the throes of her orgasm for long enough that it turned punishing. Her eyes opened, and she cried out as her teeth found his lip, nipping against it as her growl reverberated through her chest, exploding from her lips with his name on the curse.

He pushed her down onto her back against the softness of the bed, grabbing her arms as he held them above her head, nipping the mating mark on her shoulder as her body quivered around his. His teeth slid over the flesh, never puncturing it as his tongue searched the scar, enjoying the way it sent sparks through their bond. His own orgasm took him by surprise as her body clenched down, sucking against his as her orgasm milked his cock until he released his need into her warmth.

"I love you," he uttered. "I don't know how or why it happened, but I think you shooting me turned into the best thing to ever happen to me."

"I hunted you down and claimed you," she laughed huskily as heat flushed through her cheeks. "I think I fell in love with you when I said 'I do' to your brother, and the beast howled in pain. I wanted to soothe it, to promise it that we'd be okay and yet I didn't know if I could, or even if we would be okay. That's when I knew that I wanted you and that nothing else mattered."

"I'd never felt more torn apart when you said it," he admitted as he kissed her neck and nipped at her ear as he settled beside her. "It was like a part of me had been ripped out through my chest, and I think that part of me was you. Then when I watched him trying to not touch you to finish the oath, I wanted to murder him. I wanted to rip him apart, but the tears that rolled down your cheeks, that told me everything. It stopped me from hurting him, and then you were mine. We made babies, Icelyn."

"Two," she said as she turned to look at him. "I never even thought about being a mother or having children. I just thought what would be, would be. That I'd marry whoever my parents decided on, and then it was you. I mean, I shot you to get out of this," she laughed as her hand skimmed over his chest, following his brands.

His hand settled over hers as he kissed her cheek. "It's time," he uttered as he dressed them both with his magic, pulling her against him as he rose from the bed.

"They're here?" she whispered.

"They're close enough that we can hear their war drums. I'm guessing someone escaped to tell them that we were here or they wouldn't be pounding those drums," he grumbled as he pulled her mouth to his and kissed her until her toes curled and need pooled in her nether regions once more.

"We have to get the court out before it's too late."

"Let's go save our people, shall we?" he offered as he stood up and held his hand out for her. She placed her much smaller one into his large hand, watching as his fingers folded over hers.

"Our people," she uttered as they headed towards the hallway together, to save the people they would fight to protect, together.

"Our people, Icelyn."

CHAPTER FIFTY

The chaos of moving an entire court of people, including the people outside the palace, was maddening and stressful, and yet they had gathered everyone they could into the mountains that surrounded the Winter Palace. They'd taken what little time they could to secure her mother and Lane's remains down in the magical crypt that would reappear with the magic of the palace. It was the one thing that would remain the same no matter what happened with the palace when it reappeared.

"That's not an entire army," Ryder grumbled.

"No, but they came in expecting a fight with their incessant war drums announcing them. I'm guessing that the rest are hiding somewhere else. They'd have to think they actually stood a chance against us to bring in their king," Zahruk agreed. "Still, there's only one type of Mage I like."

"And what type is that?" Sinjinn asked.

"A dead one," Zahruk smirked as he cracked his

neck, looking like he wanted to be down there meeting them blade to blade instead of hiding in the mountain range.

Icelyn watched as the Mages crossed the ice. They started their way towards the palace as the Fae and Asher began using magic to lock them into their icy grave. Her own magic pulsed, creating mythical ice creatures that rose from the snow flurries into dragons, phoenixes, and other large flying animals that sent the hair of those closest whooshing into the air around her. Her brands glowed, sending more and more magic into the creatures that was both ice and light, which seemed to intensify the beings.

With one soft issued order, they took to the skies and started towards the monsters who thought to claim her home as their own. They'd thought them too weak to withstand their assault, and maybe they had been with Gerald on the throne, but she was not. Hail started to assault them as the creatures reached the first of them, ripping them apart with shards of ice teeth that was sharper than any blade they wielded. Fire exploded beside her, and she watched as Sinjinn became fire, the Ifrit within exploding into blue and red flames that rushed towards the ice, burning the Mages until they moved together, weakening the ice.

No one spoke, and yet everyone worked together to herd the Mages into a tight circle that would weigh too much for the weakening ice to hold. Ryder's magic exploded beside her, momentarily forcing her to lose focus as she turned, watching the Horde King where his brands pulsed, slithering over his flesh as black eyes stared out of the beast. They focused where the Mages who had wronged him now gathered together, to die. His hands moved, fingers drawing an intricate pattern that seemed to turn the ice to no more but ice cubes at the edge of the great lake that stretched for miles around the palace.

Synthia smirked as she held Icelyn's eyes, and then her hand smashed against the ground, and it split, tearing through the ground in front of them and the mountain as it rushed down towards the palace. The men on the ice began to scream as it gave out, sending them to the watery depths of the freezing lake. One by one, they broke through the ice into the drink of the lake, which would keep them frozen until the land returned them to nothing but bones.

"The Seelie are here," Icelyn uttered as she turned around feeling an overwhelming power, staring into the eerie eyes of seven Seelie Princes and one Princess, who watched them as they murdered the Mages. They didn't move, didn't make a motion that would be perceived as threatening. Instead, they stood there silently, watching, enjoying the chaos below with a cold detachment that sent a shiver of warning up her spine.

Asher stepped from the Horde and smirked at them as he moved to stand closer to them. His hand pointed to the Mages who were still fighting to remain above the surface. "It is done, it is finished," he said.

"And you found those of our blood," one said as his rainbow-hued eyes took in Ryder, judging him the most threatening. "And our father's heir, Asher? You've been busy, especially since we judged you to be too busy fucking to do otherwise."

"I did, yes," he admitted.

"And we are welcomed?" another prince asked carefully.

"That has yet to be established, but then I didn't intend to stick around," he informed them.

"They're at war, are they not? I like war." The prince shrugged.

"If they have enemies we can feed from, that would be welcomed," the princess said as she stared down at the men dying below. "I need to find someone to fuck, and fighting is the same thing, right? I have cobwebs growing between my legs, and you guys are boring and not something I wish to fuck, no offense."

"Elysian, your cobwebs are your own issue," another prince said.

"Where is the army?" Asher asked.

"Feeding on the rest of those assholes," the prince said.

"Emric, inform them that we may have a need for them, but to not overindulge as they gather their strength."

"As you wish, King Asher," he snorted.

"All hail the king," another one of them said with a mischievous grin on his lips.

"Oryn, I'm glad to see you survived, brother. This is Ryder, you're a lot like him but being as we're all brethren, it makes sense. Ryder, these are the strongest of those your father created with my mother. They'd like to join your war, but I'm sure you're not interested. I'm guessing they voted me king in my absence, since I was the only one who didn't want it. So tell them no, and we'll be on our way."

"Yes," Ryder said, and Asher shook his head and

turned it, staring at him.

"What?" Asher hissed as his eyes widened. "I don't think I heard you correctly."

"The last time any of the Fae denied another caste from joining their court, we ended up with creatures trying to destroy us. Such as the assholes drowning down there right now. You're my brother, and while I don't have to like it, I'm not going to say no just because of what you are. We're the Horde, after all; we accept all unwanted caste, and that's what you were until now. So welcome to the fucking family, if you betray me, I'll hang your corpse from my walls. You won't find any love for our father if that was what you are thinking, and we have new rules we play by. I'll tell you them as we start towards the stronghold."

"You assholes think this is a good idea? Kaius, Elysian, Emric, Oryn, Rys, Ragnar? Anyone think this *isn't* a good idea? I wanted to head to the human world and feed, not go to fucking war. I mean, I'm down to play with the skulls of our enemies, but this? It's not our fight. Those fuckers are not *our* enemies."

"Asher, all of Faery is at war and is trying to save it right now. Besides, the human realm is currently dancing with the devil, literally," Synthia scoffed. "That is, of course, unless you're afraid to fight?"

Asher snorted as he cracked his neck and looked at Icelyn. "Well, little Ice Queen, it looks like you were right. I want a war drum, though, and swords. I wanted fucking blades that can sever flesh like the silk cloth being sheered by the scissors of the Fates themselves."

"You're right, he is related," Zahruk smirked, his sapphire eyes alight with joy. "Have you been trained for war, or just fucking?"

"I was born to go to war; though I do prefer to go to war with a female in a warm bed, my blade has never missed an enemy's neck yet. I am skilled for battle, because what else did we get to do in our cell?" Asher growled as he frowned at his siblings who closed rank behind him. "I can't believe you assholes made me king when I wasn't there to argue it."

"Stop whining, you're the only one who didn't want it. You kept us from ripping each other apart for the entire time we were locked up down there. You were the only one who could keep us together and acting as one for the day we escaped, Asher. You were my first choice as king," Elysian said softly as she patted him on the back. "There's also the fact that you'll need a queen and none of the others wanted to deal with that shit."

"Oh my God," Synthia snorted as she started to laugh. "They're like you guys, but brighter."

"They're not brighter than us," Ryder growled as he narrowed his gaze on them. "Maybe a little more so," he begrudgingly admitted.

Icelyn stared down at the men who now floated over the surface of the lake as the palace started to crumble around them. Frostine slipped her fingers through hers as they watched it crumble to nothing as it sank into the lake below it. It would be a long time before it came back, which meant her court was homeless and would roam until they found it again.

"It will be at least twenty years before it will appear again," Frostine whispered. "What will we do, where will we go now?" she asked.

"We'll go home," Sinjinn uttered on her other side.

"You'll come with us. The others will go to the Hidden Realm, where they will be safe from the war that is coming. Icelyn will remain with me, where she will be protected as my queen, in our home."

"You'd let us all come with you?" Frostine asked as the entire mountainside went silent. The court listened as they spoke, knowing their fate was what was at stake here.

"I will protect this court with my life. I will protect your queen with my dying breath and you with her. I vow to be a kind king and a good mate to your queen. I will discuss the details further with you all soon, but first there's something I need to do," he uttered as he pulled Icelyn aside and stared down at her. "Marry me; divorce my brother and marry me. I love you, and I want to spend my life with you, however long it may be. I want you by my side for it. I want this, and I want our children to know that they were created from a union of love. This may have started out as something dark, but you're my light; the ice to my fire, Icelyn. Let me love you forever."

"You want me to divorce Cailean?" she laughed as her heart hammered against her chest. "I mean, we haven't even really given our marriage a go yet. I was planning to see if maybe it worked out with him. Plus, I may end up actually liking him better." She shrugged as his mouth curved into a frown.

"You want to stay married to him?" he asked carefully.

"No, but I couldn't make it easy on you, could I?" she laughed as he pulled her closer, staring into her eyes. "Yes, yes, a thousand times, yes! I'll marry you,

Sinjinn."

"Right now, right here, before your people and mine?" he asked, and when she nodded his eyes burst into flames as he smiled, revealing twin dimples she'd never seen before.

"Yes," she uttered breathlessly as she kissed him hard, uncaring that everyone was watching.

Twenty minutes later, after Ryder had agreed to marry them with her palace floating upon the moonlit surface of the lake, and the bodies of their enemies among the debris, she was made Sinjinn's wife before her people and his. Of course, it wasn't actually official until they had destroyed the oath, but it had been enough to put her people at ease to make this journey to the new home easier. The moment she said I do, he had her in his arms, kissing her until her insides burst into flames as her ice banked the heat he fed her. The crowd cheered, which felt strange since the last wedding had been so different, and this one was so right.

"I can't believe you said yes," he chuckled as they started their trek across the land she'd called home, leaving to head to his until the palace called her home again.

"How else was I going to make you suffer for the rest of my life?" she laughed.

"This shit is getting old," Zahruk huffed as he turned, tossing them an irritating look over his shoulder.

"Your time is coming, brother."

"I'd rather swallow swords."

"Not swords, but I think you need to fulfill the oath that you signed long ago soon. The moment this war ends, you're up, Zahruk."

"Ryder, don't press your fucking luck. I'm hoping I get lucky and end up dead before this shit ends. It would be a kindness to that mushy shit happening lately."

Icelyn stared back at the strange assortment of men and women who followed them into the unknown. Her hand settled on her stomach, cradling her unborn children as she surveyed those who followed them through the Winter Court. The Seelie, who were the worst of the Fae, laughed among each other as they spoke like family. Frostine helped one of the families as she hefted a child onto her hip, cradling it as they moved forward.

She wasn't sure what would become of them all, but she knew whatever they faced, they'd face it together. Family was everything; even though it wasn't always the one you were born into, it was those you adopted along the way. Those who came and stood beside you, and said I'm here and I'm not leaving you. She'd allowed her palace to fall to protect it, to sink into the lake without trying to save it at all. She'd wanted to see who jumped over the proverbial side of the ship, and who would abandon her in their darkest hour of need: No one had. They'd all remained beside her, knowing that whatever came at them, they could handle it together.

These were her people now.

Her family.

The ones she'd least expected to save her had done just that. Asher smiled at her, as if he read her thoughts again, and he nodded as his smile dropped and he looked forward. He definitely was one she least expected to stick around, but he was here; he'd stayed with her. To her, that made him family. Even if he was an evil, twisted fuck, he could stay as long as he behaved. She ignored the hoot of laughter that sounded from him as she settled her head against Sinjinn's arm and allowed his arm to slip around her shoulder.

"What set him off?" he asked as he tossed a look over his shoulder at the Seelie King.

"Family," she whispered.

"Whose family?" he asked.

"Yours, mine, ours," she smiled softly as she whispered. "This is us."

"This is us, my Queen."

~ The End *~*

About the Author

Amelia lives in the great Pacific Northwest with her family. When not writing, she can be found on her author page, hanging out with fans, or dreaming up new twisting plots. She's an avid reader of everything paranormal romance.

Stalker links!

Facebook: https://www.facebook.com/authorameliahutchins

Website: http://amelia-hutchins.com/

Amazon: http://www.amazon.com/Amelia-Hutchins/e/B00D5OASEG

Goodreads: https://www.goodreads.com/author/show/7092218.Amelia_Hutchins

Twitter: https://twitter.com/ameliaauthor

Pinterest: http://www.pinterest.com/ameliahutchins

Instagram: https://www.instagram.com/author.amelia.hutchins/

Facebook Author Group: https://goo.gl/BqpCVK

Made in the USA
Middletown, DE
13 December 2023

45379835R00215